We'll Quit When We're Dead

We'll Quit When We're Dead

A Kori Briggs Novel

A.P. Rawls

We'll Quit When We're Dead

A Kori Briggs Novel

A.P. Rawls

FIRST PRINTING

ISBN: 978-1-7372613-2-2
eBook ISBN: 978-1-7372613-3-9
Large Print Edition: 978-1-7372613-5-3

Library of Congress Control Number: 2021918856

UWS
Upper West Side Press, LLC

This is a work of fiction. Names, characters, places, and incidents either are the product of the author's imagination, or are used fictitiously. Any resemblance to actual persons, living or dead, businesses, companies, events, or locales is entirely coincidental.

ALSO BY A.P. RAWLS:

The Dark Tetrad:
A Kori Briggs Novel

PRAISE FOR *THE DARK TETRAD*:

"Fans of spy actioners will revel in this swift-moving adventure and its delightful heroine… a refreshingly modern feminine take on James Bond."
—BookLife

"A bracing tale with a gutsy hero for fans of secret agent thrillers…Rawls' thriller begins with 'unsettling news' and rarely flags. Kori Briggs is a capable hero who is not unnecessarily complicated by a formulaic, psyche-scarred backstory… She's got intuition, grit, and gumption; the confidence invested in her is justified. The book is well paced…old-school fun."
—**Kirkus Reviews**

CHAPTER 1

Dane Reinhart walked briskly along the Embarcadero. He had his hands dug deep into his jacket pockets, his right one gripping the letter he'd been slipped at the coffee shop at the entrance of Pier 1, just next to the Ferry Building and adjacent to the Golden Gate ferry terminal. His plan was to guard the letter with his life.

Reinhart turned up Clay Street and began the trek toward the Fairmont Hotel. He knew it would take about a half hour, but he liked the walk, even though he also knew it would continue to get steeper and steeper. Such is the character of San Francisco's streets. Reinhart hated taxicabs, so unless the weather prevented it, he always preferred to walk. Tonight, the weather cooperated. It was chilly but clear with only a light breeze. The walk felt good and he was invigorated, not only by the trek, but by the nature of the business he had been investigating.

Besides, the walk back to the hotel could have been ten times as long and it wouldn't have fazed Agent Dane Reinhart. He was in top physical shape, as were all the agents of Rampart, a US intelligence agency so secretive that its existence was unknown even to the CIA. Rampart had been established during the Cold War as part of the executive branch of the US government. It had been a time of double agents and compromised loyalties. A higher grade of agents had become necessary, a kind of super-group, but a small, tight-knit one. There were never more than eighteen or twenty members of Rampart at any given time. This eliminated the levels of bureaucracy that plagued other intelligence agencies. Rampart was nimble, its agents ready at a moment's notice to deploy anywhere in the world.

The Cold War had long since ended, but Rampart remained in operation. If anything, the world had only become more dangerous. And now, Rampart was operating even more freely. It had recently become unencumbered from the supervision of the executive branch, a separation made possible by the president himself. So long as Rampart was beholden to any governmental entity, its overall directive could be betrayed by politics. The president had seen it happen with other agencies whose agendas had become skewed to fit the power structure of the moment. Skewing Rampart's agenda was unthinkable. That agenda was simple and it needed to stay that way: keep the US—and the world—safe. The president loved Rampart. In his estimation, it was the only politically untainted organization left, and it was this that caused him to release it from the management of his own office.

At Kearny Street, as the grade started to rise, Chinese restaurant and shop signs began to appear as Reinhart was now walking through Chinatown. He turned at Grant and began heading toward Sacramento Street. The grade flattened out in this direction and the sidewalk was bustling with people walking under red lanterns strung across the street, past Chinese restaurants, jewelry stores, gift shops, and massage parlors. The scent of incense and roast duck wafted in the air. Reinhart knew that most of the pedestrians were tourists. A little-known fact was that more people visited Chinatown each year than the Golden Gate Bridge.

Reinhart would have loved to have slowed down and enjoyed the sights and sounds, but time did not permit. In fact, he picked up his pace. In his room at the Fairmont was a briefcase, and in that briefcase was a secure, triple-encrypted imager. Transmitting a photograph of the letter by way of, say, a smartphone, was inconceivable. Far too risky. Reinhart knew that if the letter were to somehow find its way into the public sphere, the end result might be nothing less than war. **It might come to that anyway**, Reinhart thought, **but at least we have a chance to stop it**. Sending the letter via the imager would make it impossible to trace and impossible to hack, the safest means of transmission known to technology. The only eyes upon the letter would be the eyes of Rampart Director Richard Eaglethorpe in Washington, DC.

At Sacramento, the people thinned out. Reinhart turned and now began walking up the steep grade toward Nob Hill where the stately Fairmont had rested since its opening in 1907. The street lighting was diminished now, and long shadows were cast by the street lamps across the sidewalk. A block from the hotel, the street empty of people now,

Reinhart passed a narrow passageway that ran between two buildings. Steel bars and a gate spanned the three-foot-wide corridor. He glanced down the dark strip out of habit, but Reinhart was not especially worried about any sort of surprise assault. Nobody knew Reinhart's business in San Francisco and it would hardly have been possible for someone to have followed him this far from the pier. He was a Rampart agent. He would have sensed it.

And that's why the shadowy figure lurking in the corridor took him aback, leaving him too little time to react. It was just a silhouette for the nanosecond that Reinhart had to process what he was seeing in the figure's hand between the steel bars. In daylight, he would have recognized it instantly as a Taurus nine-millimeter Luger, complete with an Omega silencer.

Nobody heard the shot. Nobody saw the body of Rampart Agent Dane Reinhart drop to the ground. And nobody saw the shadowy figure come out from behind the gate, rifle through Reinhart's pockets, seize hold of an envelope, and disappear into the San Francisco night.

CHAPTER 2

In an outdoor café a block from the Neckar River in Heidelberg, Germany, a woman, toned and athletic, with long, straight, dark hair was sitting at a small table, drinking a copper-colored, full-bodied, bock-style beer made from a brewery just up the street.

"Do you really have to leave, Kori?" the strapping young man across from her asked. US Air Force Captain Shane Scott had wavy blond hair, a square jaw, and crystal blue eyes that the woman couldn't seem to look away from.

"I'm afraid so. I feel as if I've been away too long as it is. Oh, not that I'm not enjoying my time with you." Kori Briggs reached across the table and took Shane Scott's hand. "You know that, right, babe? This has been the absolute best time."

"Sure, I know. We've talked about it. You're married to your work. And I'm married to mine. What a pair we are, huh?"

Kori smiled. "We'll see each other again. Soon, I'm sure." Truthfully, she **wasn't** sure. In fact, if she had to bet, she'd bet against it. But then it was always like this. She would find herself with strong feelings for someone, someone like Shane, but those feelings only advanced so far. Love? She supposed she'd felt it before. Maybe she even felt it for Shane. There was no denying the chemistry. A week of lovemaking had proven that. But did she feel the kind of love where you just want to drop everything that was important to you before and allow yourself to be swept away? The life-changing kind of love? The kind of romantic love of books and movies?

And could she drop everything else even if she wanted to? Maybe that was the real question.

"I hope you're right, darling," said Shane. "This

has been wonderful. Or should I say **wunderbar?** You're special, you know. You really are."

Kori smiled. "So are you."

"So what's next? Another big assignment? More world-saving?"

Kori chuckled. "Nothing so grand, I'm sure. Actually, I guess I'm awaiting word. Haven't heard anything yet."

"As if you'd tell me anyway. I still don't even know who you work for."

"Well, the thing is, I could tell you and you still wouldn't know."

"You're a woman of true mystery, Kori. To be honest, I have to admit that that's part of your appeal."

"I see. So I suppose I should remain so, eh?"

"And therein lies the classic catch-22. I want to know more about you, but that would lessen the intrigue."

"Yes, I can see that I must be quite a conundrum."

"Indeed."

"And you? What's next for you? Back to Ramstein Air Base?"

"Yep. Back to Ramstein Air Base."

"Hmm…flying fighter jets around for a living. Captain, no less. Soon to be Major. Good work if you can get it. I think I'm jealous."

"I seriously doubt that. But, no, I won't complain about my work."

They smiled at each other and Shane brought Kori's hand to his lips and gently kissed it. "Listen," he said, "I hate to say it, but it's getting late. Frankfurt airport is an hour from here. If you're going to catch your plane, I suppose we ought to get moving. Reluctantly, I might add."

"Reluctantly," Kori agreed.

The goodbyes at the airport were heartfelt but awkward, as goodbyes between lovers are, especially the kind where both parties know it's probably final but nobody wants to say so. You want to smile, you want to convey something positive. You speak lightly, even flirtatiously. You speak as if you're going away for a couple of days instead of the rest of your life. Inside, you both know the reality of the situation but neither wants to say it aloud. Your heartache becomes a solitary thing, the one thing you cannot share with the other.

At the gate, Kori Briggs settled into a chair and checked her first-class boarding pass. Window seat. Perfect. Aisle seats always left more room for interaction with others, the last thing she wanted on a long flight home. Nestled up to a window with a scotch was all she was in the mood for.

Her phone rang. She thought about letting it go to voicemail, but something told her it might be important and she answered.

"Agent Briggs?" came the voice of Kori's boss, Rampart Director Richard Eaglethorpe.

"Chief?"

"Where are you, Kori?"

"Frankfurt airport. I'm heading back to DC. In fact, we're just about ready to board."

"Well don't. You're not going to DC, Kori."

"I'm not?"

"Afraid not. Glad I caught you in time. Listen, turn your ticket in and get yourself on the next plane to San Francisco. We have a situation on our hands."

"San Francisco?"

Eaglethorpe paused for a moment before continuing. "Yes. We've lost an agent, Kori," he said, his businesslike voice softening. "Reinhart."

"Oh, no," said Kori, knowing by the tone of Eaglethorpe's voice what "lost" meant. "Dane? I didn't really know him, but he was a good man, Chief. And a damn fine agent."

"Indeed he was."

"What happened? And what was he doing in San Francisco?"

"Frankly, we have more questions than answers at this point. Dane was shot last night. His body was found about a block from his hotel. He'd called me earlier in the day. Regrettably, I couldn't spend a lot of time on the phone with him, but he said he had something for me, something to show me. He said he was going to send me an encrypted document or a letter or something. Evidently, he was working on a case."

"What case, Chief?"

"Well, that's just it. We don't know. He'd apparently discovered something and was investigating it on his own. He mentioned it to me for the first time yesterday on our phone call. He couldn't get into all the details, but promised he would explain once I'd received whatever it was he was going to send. I had the impression he didn't have it at the time of the call, but that he was going to go get it. From where or whom, I have no idea. Needless to say, I never received anything. That phone call was the last I heard from Dane."

"Any idea what he was talking about?"

"No. But it sounded as if he was going to send me proof of something. Evidence, perhaps, of whatever it was he was looking into. He mentioned a 'smoking gun.'"

"Do you think his murder was related to it?"

"It has to be. Whatever he discovered, it must be pretty serious."

"So it would seem."

"And now, Agent Briggs, you know everything that I know. We need answers, Kori. I want you to fly out there and see what you can learn. I'll text you the contact information of the San Francisco police detective who's investigating the murder. That would be a good place to start. Also, search Reinhart's room. His last security check-in had him at the Fairmont, room 512."

"Right, Chief. And don't worry. I'll find the bastard or bastards who killed Dane."

"Be careful, Kori," said Eaglethorpe, slipping into his fatherly persona. "Whoever it is, I think we can assume they're dangerous. Maybe desperate. Watch your step. And keep me informed at all times, okay?"

"I will, Chief."

Kori hung up and walked to the counter to

inquire about flights to San Francisco. The next one was one leaving in two hours. It would have to do. Kori ambled into the concourse bar and ordered the scotch she had assumed she'd be having on the flight to DC. She thought about Dane Reinhart and wondered about the case he'd been working on. It was serious enough to get him killed. What had he stumbled upon? What could it possibly have been that he was going to transmit to Eaglethorpe?

Eventually, vaguely, she realized that thoughts of Shane Scott had taken a back seat. There was business that needed tending to. Or, as Sherlock Holmes might have said in one of the Conan Doyle books Kori read as a teenager, **the game was afoot**.

CHAPTER 3

"Your boss said you're with a national intelligence agency." Detective Mack Walton, stocky, with short, steel gray hair, probably about fifty, and wearing an off-the-rack suit, was standing at the spot where Dane Reinhart's body was found. "What, like the CIA?"

"Yes, something like that," Kori replied. It was a cool, clear morning and the black coffee Kori was sipping was bringing her to life again. She'd landed in San Francisco the previous night, but it was morning as far as her body clock was concerned.

She'd checked into the InterContinental Mark Hopkins hotel across from the Fairmont but couldn't sleep a wink. She tossed and turned and finally, at around 5 a.m., dropped off into a deep slumber, only to be awakened by her phone's alarm just a couple of hours later. She dragged herself out of bed, took a quick shower, dressed, and grabbed a cup of coffee for the prearranged meeting with Detective Walton.

"Well, this must be something serious," said Walton. "I didn't know what to make of your boss's phone call, but then it was followed up by an order from **my** boss, who had apparently received it directly from the White House, of all places. Just who are you people?"

Rampart might not have been under the supervision of the president anymore, but it remained a sort of at-large piece of the executive branch, thus providing the agency with resources it would not otherwise have access to, like phone calls to other law enforcement agencies requesting—even demanding—cooperation. Rampart would always stay in the loop, receiving intelligence and delivering it.

"We're just a group of patriotic Americans, Detective, trying to make the world a safer place," Kori replied. "That's about all I can say."

"Uh-huh." The detective looked skeptical. "Well, I have to say, I'm not in the habit of sharing my casework with mysterious strangers. This is a local police matter, it seems to me."

"I don't know what to tell you, Detective, other than that by its very nature, it goes beyond local jurisdiction. You see, this is no ordinary murder case. Dane Reinhart had information that concerns the national security of the United States."

"Oh? And what information is that exactly?"

"That's what I need to find out. That's why I'm here."

"Okay. But how do you know he had any information at all?"

"Because it was his job to have that kind of information. That's what we do, Detective. Now, what can you tell me about the murder?"

Walton shook his head and decided not to fight his natural inclination to be obstinate. Hell, maybe this woman, whoever she was, could actually make his job easier. Might as well let her. "Well, he was hit by a nine-millimeter slug coming from that direction." Walton pointed toward the narrow corridor that ran back from the sidewalk. "We looked all around the area for footprints. Couldn't find a thing."

"What was the time of death?"

"We figure it was around midnight."

"Who discovered the body?"

"A cabbie. He drove up the street and his headlights caught sight of your man. He thought maybe it was just some drunk passed out, but there was something about the body's positioning, sort of splayed out, that made him pull over and get a better look. That's when he saw the blood and called 911."

"How did you identify the body?"

"His wallet and ID. That's what's strange. Nothing seemed to be missing. This was no robbery or mugging gone bad. My guess is that the murderer knew the victim."

"Nobody in the vicinity saw anything?"

"Nope. We canvassed this whole area. Nobody heard a shot or witnessed a struggle or saw a thing. I don't know who you're looking for, Ms. Briggs, but I can tell you that you've got a professional on your hands."

"So it would seem."

"Now, look, Ms. Briggs, you can provide a lot of assistance to me, and yourself, if you can tell me whatever you can about Reinhart and his work. By all rights, I ought to be the one interviewing you, not the other way around. You're the only one here who knew the deceased. I could take you down to the station and make you give me a statement, you know. Ask about your whereabouts at the time of the murder, for instance."

"Look, Detective, I'm sure the White House explained to your boss the situation and how this needs to be handled."

"Yeah, yeah, I was told all about the protocol. But put yourself in my shoes. I'm sitting here with a dead body and no clues. Now you must be able to tell me something. Anything would help. Now, when I'm starting a case with no clear evidence, I have to start looking for a possible motive and work it from there. So maybe you can at least tell me this much: who would want to kill your man?"

"Well, it's hard to narrow down, Detective."

"Try."

"If they knew who he really was? At least seventeen foreign governments and probably a dozen domestic terrorist organizations."

"What, seriously?"

"I'm afraid so. Did you bring his phone?"

"Yes, just like your boss asked. Here." Walton pulled a smartphone out of his pocket and handed it over to Kori. "Won't help you much, I'm afraid. No contact list, no list of recent calls, nothing. It's almost like it was wiped clean."

"Thanks," said Kori. "I appreciate your time, Detective. I'll be in touch." Then she turned and began walking back toward the InterContinental, leaving Detective Mack Walton wondering just who, or what, his investigation was getting him involved with.

Kori sat by the window of her twelfth-floor room at the InterContinental, looking out toward San Francisco Bay. The hotel had been constructed in 1926 on the site where Mark Hopkins, one of the founders of the Central Pacific Railroad, had built a mansion for his wife in 1878. The mansion initially survived the great 1906 San Francisco earthquake, but fell victim to the fire that followed. The affluent founders of the railroad, which formed the western part of the First Transcontinental Railroad in the 1860s, all built opulent mansions on what was then called California Hill. Leland Stanford, founder of Stanford University, was among them. These early citizens of San Francisco were known, a little pejoratively, as nabobs—conspicuously wealthy people, another way of saying "fat cats" or "big-wigs." Nabobs was eventually shortened to Nobs and today, the California Hill section of the city is officially known as Nob Hill.

Other rich and famous people built mansions in the area, and whenever Kori was in San Francisco, she liked to imagine the scene back in the late 1800s—stately Victorian homes, women with parasols, men in top hats, the clip clop of horses pulling carriages up California Street. Of course, she could never picture herself in one of those Victorian dresses, complete with bloomers, corset, petticoat, and whatever else made up the female costume of the day. She preferred her black, one-button Burberry blazer overtop a white silk blouse, with straight pants and her black leather Gianvito Rossi ankle boots. Simple. Practical. But that didn't pre-clude her from feeling at least a wisp of appreciation for the romance of that bygone era. It might have been fun to dress up and climb into one of those carriages and be whisked away to a formal gala somewhere, maybe down in the ballroom of the very hotel in which she was staying, waltzing into the wee hours and drinking the finest of champagne.

On this particular morning, Kori had waltzed into the hotel's breakfast bar and grabbed a bacon, cheddar, and egg croissant to go, along with another cup of coffee. Now sitting by her window, she had just finished using her tablet to upload the encrypted data from the chip of Dane Reinhart's phone and was talking to Director Eaglethorpe.

"Did you get it?" she asked.

"Got it," said Eaglethorpe. "I've relayed the data to Cooper. He'll unlock it and we'll see if we can find a clue from maybe the phone number of someone Reinhart might have called recently. Or a text message, or something."

"Let's hope there's something there, Chief. Of course, the detective thought the phone was wiped clean."

"Good. We put a lot of man hours into this technology. I'm glad to know it works. Was the detective of any help?"

"Not really. I mean, he seems competent enough, but if anything, he only confirmed that it was a professional job. The scene of the crime was spotless. This might be a tough one to solve, Chief."

"Well, get yourself on over to the Fairmont and check out Agent Reinhart's room. Maybe there's a clue there someplace. I'll contact you after Cooper has combed through the phone."

"Roger, Chief."

Kori hung up and went back to the pressing task at hand: finishing the croissant. Then she called her mother. Joan Briggs, sixty-four, lived in Alexandria, Virginia, with her Jack Russell terrier, Baxter. Kori was an only child and she and her mother were close. It had been just the two of them while Kori was growing up. Her father had left when Kori was three and had never come back. The one regret Kori had about her work was that she could never, under any circumstances, reveal it to Joan. Rampart agents were sworn to secrecy. Even spouses were left in the dark. It was for the protection of the agency, but also for the protection of friends and family members. Joan believed that Kori worked as vice president of sales for a company in DC called Gladstone Conveyor. And that's what it said on the door of Rampart's headquarters on a secure floor in an office building on L Street.

"Kori!" her mother exclaimed when she answered the phone. "Are you still in Heidelberg? I thought you were coming home yesterday."

"I was, Mom, but I got rerouted. I'm in San Francisco."

"San Francisco? What on earth for?"

"My boss sent me here. He needs me to make a sales pitch to a company that's opening a huge distribution facility close by. It's a pretty big deal. Could mean a bonus."

"Well, I certainly hope so. My lord, that company just works you to death, Kori. I've got a few choice words for that boss of yours. So how long do have to be there? Did you have a good time in Germany, dear?"

"Just a few days, Mom. And Germany was wonderful. It was a nice vacation. As soon as I get home, we'll have dinner together and I'll tell you all about it."

"That sounds lovely. How about Sunday?"

"Well, let's play it by ear, Mom. I'll have to let you know."

"Of course. I understand."

"So how's everything there? How's Baxter?"

Kori made a habit of turning the conversation back toward Joan in order not to have to answer too many questions about her work. It wasn't hard to do. Joan didn't really have anyone to talk to and she always relished the chance to chat with Kori about her life. Kori let her chat, which is what Joan did pretty much nonstop for the ensuing fifteen minutes.

"Well, listen, Mom, I better get going," Kori finally interjected. "I need to prepare my notes for the pitch. I want to be prepared, you know. Give Baxter a scratch for me. I'll call you soon. Love you, Mom."

Kori hung up the phone and then grabbed what was left of her coffee and headed out, entering the Fairmont Hotel next door just a few minutes later and getting past the electronic door lock of room 512 with her universal swipe card. The card had been Agent James Foster's invention. He and Darren Cooper were Rampart's top technical geeks. Their knowledge of digital technology, or pretty much any technology, for that matter, was remarkable to Kori. She liked to think she kept up pretty well with the latest advancements in her field, but Cooper and Foster always seemed to be ahead of her. And ahead of the rest of the intelligence community too, for that matter.

The view of San Francisco Bay from Reinhart's room was adequate, but Kori much preferred the views from the higher rooms in the taller Inter-Continental. Nevertheless, the room was luxurious and tastefully appointed. Obviously, Reinhart had shared Kori's predilection for posh, historic hotels. Detective Walton had no idea Reinhart had been staying at the Fairmont because Rampart agents never checked into hotels under their own names. And it was a good thing, because the room had been left untouched, the "Do Not Disturb" placard still hanging off the doorknob. If there was any kind of clue to Reinhart's murder, maybe Kori could find it here.

Kori sifted through Reinhart's suitcase, feeling a twinge of guilt in going through the personal belongings of her deceased colleague, but knowing there was no other choice. She came across the imager that Reinhart had planned on using to send his letter to Eaglethorpe and powered it up, hoping that maybe something in the imager's memory could shed some light. She entered the restricted code and then scrolled through the list of sent items, but there had been nothing transmitted within the previous month.

She looked through Reinhart's shaving kit and then through the pockets of the clothes hanging in the room's closet. **Good taste**, she thought, shuffling through the shirts and slacks, but she came up empty. Finally, she searched the desk. In the top drawer was a small hotel notepad, and scrawled across the top page was a single line: **Pier 1 – coffee shop**. It wasn't much, but at least it was a place to start.

CHAPTER 4

Along with nice hotels, Kori and Reinhart also shared a penchant for long walks, but on this jetlagged morning, Kori decided to take an Uber to Pier 1. The curved northeast edge of San Francisco is lined with long piers jutting out into San Francisco Bay, even-numbered ones running south from the Ferry Building, from where commuters take ferries to Oakland or Berkeley, and odd-numbered ones running north and west to famed Fisherman's Wharf. Kori had the driver drop her off in front of the Ferry Building where she spotted the coffee shop a couple of hundred feet up the waterfront at Pier 1. She strolled up the sidewalk and entered the shop, breathing in the rich coffee aroma and wishing she hadn't reached her caffeine limit for the morning.

It was a longshot, but her only choice, really, was to simply question the employees. "Have you seen this man?" she asked the baristas behind the counter, showing them a picture of Dane Reinhart on her phone. Surprisingly, one of them had.

"He was here the other night," piped up a young woman with pastel pink hair and black lipstick and eye shadow.

"Are you sure?" asked Kori. "I mean, a lot of people must come in here every day."

"I remember everybody," the young woman smiled. "It's a gift."

"Indeed."

"Plus, he wasn't too hard to look at. Tall, fit. Sure, I remember him. Is he in some kind of trouble?"

"You could say that. Was he with anyone?"

"Yeah, another tall, fit guy. He wasn't too hard to look at, either. They sat right out there," the young woman said, pointing toward one of the outdoor tables. "I was working that night. They both had cappuccinos. I always remember drink orders, too."

"Can you remember anything about the other guy? Apart from the fact that he was tall and fit and ordered a cappuccino?"

"Well, he had dark hair. Clean shaven. He was probably around forty, I would guess. Maybe a little younger. I can tell you that I'd never seen either one in here before."

"Where can I find the footage from those outside security cameras?"

"In the back office. Are you some kind of cop?"

Kori reached into her purse and pulled out her leather ID holder, opening it up to reveal a badge on one side and a picture ID card on the other that read: **National Bureau of Criminal Investigations**. Nowhere did it say Rampart.

"Wow," the girl said. "So what did these guys do?"

"That's what I'm trying to figure out. Can I see the footage?"

"Sure."

In the back office, the video from the security cameras that night showed that an envelope had been passed from the other man to Dane, the envelope that presumably had gotten Dane killed. But the angle was bad and the resolution was low. Kori couldn't see much more of the mystery man than what the girl with the pastel pink hair had already described to her.

"You've been a big help," Kori said to the girl as she left the shop. "Thanks."

"You're welcome. Let us know if you need anything more."

Kori hesitated at the door and said, "Well, there is one more thing. Why don't you grab me a couple of those madeleines to go?"

Out on the street, the day had shaped itself into a warm, pleasant one. Kori walked along the waterfront nibbling on the madeleines with no particular destination in mind. A tall, fit guy with dark hair was her only clue. Who was he? Was he Reinhart's killer? A friend? A colleague? An informant? And why were they together in the coffee shop in the first place?

She ambled along until she got to Pier 7, a long, skinny, wooden pier lined with benches and light posts and meant for strolling and scenic viewing. She walked it to its end, waves lapping against the pilings with a cool breeze coming in off the bay. The San Francisco–Oakland Bridge was visible to her right. She turned and looked back toward shore, the tall Transamerica Building in view. Just then her phone rang.

"Briggs," she answered.

"Eaglethorpe here, Agent Briggs."

"Hi, Chief. What's up? Cooper find anything on Dane's phone?"

"Well, there's a solitary number that we haven't been able to identify. Everything else is accounted for and nothing seems out of the ordinary. Just this one number. It's got a Canadian area code, British Columbia to be precise. But we can't trace it to anyone. It's as though it doesn't exist. We've called it, and there's never an answer. No voicemail or anything. It just keeps ringing. But Reinhart called that number several times over the past week and received an equal amount of calls from it. Including the day of his murder."

"We have to figure out who belongs to that number, Chief. And I think I might know."

"Oh yeah? Talk to me."

"Well, there was a note in Reinhart's hotel room about a coffee shop. I just left there. One of the barista's identified Dane's picture. Said he was in a couple of nights before with another guy. They sat outside and drank cappuccinos. Security video shows the other guy passing Dane an envelope. That's about all it shows, but I'll bet you a hundred bucks that phone number belongs to that guy."

"I wonder what he was doing in San Francisco."

"For that matter, what was Dane doing in San Francisco? He makes his home in Denver. Why did they meet here?"

"We figure that out, Briggs, and we figure out the murder."

"Yup. Or at least take a big step in that direction."

"All right, sit tight Agent Briggs. We'll see what we can do on this end about tracking down the owner of that phone number and I'll be in touch."

"Roger that, Chief."

Kori hung up and looked around the pier, noticing some of the other people—tourists taking pictures with their cell phones and locals dangling fishing lines into the water. An old Otis Redding song started playing in her head. Then she noticed a person who instinctually stood out to her. A brawny man with a heavy black beard and cream-colored jacket was loitering along the edge of the pier, trying, it seemed to Kori, just a little too hard to look casual. Kori took out her phone and held it up in the direction of the Transamerica Building as if she were taking a picture, but out of the corner of her eye she was looking at the bearded man. He was looking at her. She snapped a photo and then slid the phone into her purse and began walking back toward the sidewalk. Behind her, she sensed the man following.

At the sidewalk, Kori turned and continued walking along the waterfront. Then she crossed the Embarcadero at Broadway and began walking back toward the Ferry Building from the other side of the street, essentially pulling a U-turn. She took out her phone as she walked and reversed the camera to see behind her. The man was still there, still following.

At Washington Street, she took a right and walked to Montgomery. At Montgomery, she took a left. In both instances, the man did the same. At California, a crowded cable car made a stop and Kori hopped on and slid between the other passengers toward the far end. Ordinarily, she would have enjoyed a ride on one of San Francisco's legendary cable cars, the only mobile member on the National Register of Historic Places. But this was no time for tourism and sightseeing. She glanced behind her and the man had hopped aboard the cable car too. There could be no doubt now. With the cable car still in motion and a half a block to go before the Grant Avenue stop, Kori leaped off and ran down Quincy Street, ducking between two buildings. There she waited. She didn't have to wait long. Sure enough, she heard the rapid footsteps of the man who had been pursuing her.

She pressed her back against the wall of the building toward the man and as he went by, she sprang out from between the buildings. In one fluid motion, she grabbed the man's wrist and brought it behind his back, shoving it upward and causing the man to scream out in pain and fall to his knees. She pushed him down on his stomach and pressed his head against the pavement.

"Okay, who are you!?" she demanded.

The man remained silent.

"Tell me!" she yelled. Then she twisted his hand further up his back. "Don't make me ask again!"

The man moaned in obvious discomfort but said nothing.

"I've got all day, Sporty," said Kori. "We'll just sit like this for as long as you like. I'm comfortable here and I've got no place to go. How about you?" She had her knee firmly planted in his back now and was grinding his head into the sidewalk. Still he refused to talk.

Kori searched through his jacket pockets and brought out a nine-millimeter Luger with a silencer. "Interesting choice of weapon," she said. "Something tells me it's not just for self-defense."

Meanwhile, a small crowd had begun to gather at the commotion and someone had flagged down a passing police car.

"Ma'am!" Kori heard someone saying, "I'm going to have to ask you to release that man."

Kori looked up and saw a uniformed officer coming through the crowd of onlookers with his hand reaching for the gun on his hip, ready to draw it out. The crowd, sensing a violent altercation, scattered, but everyone hung around close enough to watch whatever it was that was about to unfold.

"Relax, officer," Kori said. "I was just defending myself."

"That may be, ma'am, but it looks to me as if the threat is over," said the cop, a muscular young man with a long nose and a pointed chin. "Now stand up, leave that gun on the ground, and back away slowly. No sudden moves."

Kori did as the officer ordered, leaving the Luger on the ground, but sliding it out of the reach of the bearded man. "Look, officer, I'm an agent with the US government. I think you'll find that this man is involved in a murder that took place here two nights ago. Call Detective Mack Walton from homicide."

"I'll need to see some ID first, ma'am."

Kori reached slowly into her purse and pulled out her **National Bureau of Criminal Investigations** ID and badge. Since the organization was a cover and didn't actually exist, the officer hadn't ever heard of the National Bureau of Criminal Investigations. Nevertheless, the woman certainly seemed official and her mention of Detective Walton gave her enough credence in his mind to take his hand off his gun and pull out his handcuffs instead, using them on the prostrate man on the sidewalk.

That man, safe from the reaches of Kori Briggs for the moment, decided to start protesting to the officer. "She attacked **me**, officer," he pleaded. "She came out of nowhere and threw me down. I was just walking along, minding my own business. That's not my gun, it's hers. Am I under arrest? I want a lawyer. I haven't done anything. She's crazy, I tell you. She was trying to kill me!"

"Okay, okay, just relax," said the cop. "I'm calling Detective Walton down here and we're going to get this all straightened out." The cop pulled the bearded man up and sat him down against the wall of the building and searched his pockets. "Sir, don't you have any identification?"

"I uh…I left my wallet in my other pants."

"Uh-huh." Then he radioed for Walton who was soon en route. While they waited, he turned to Kori. "You know, I'm going to need to search you, too."

"I understand, of course," said Kori. "Have at it,

Officer." She pulled her purse from around her shoulder and laid it on the ground. "You'll find my own gun in there. A Glock G43 nine-millimeter. I have a permit for it, of course."

"Fine," said the officer, as he took the purse and sifted through it, pulling out the gun plus the ID holder, looking at the ID a little closer now. "So what exactly is this National Bureau of Criminal Investigations?"

"It's a US government intelligence service, Officer."

"Really? How come I've never heard of it."

"We like to keep a low profile."

"I see. Card says you're based in Washington, DC."

"Yep."

"So what are you doing here?"

"Investigating a murder."

"So you said. What murder?"

"Nob Hill. Detective Walton has all the details." Then, pointing toward the handcuffed man sitting with his back against the wall, Kori added, "My guess is that this lunkhead here is involved in it. More than a guess, in fact. I'm sure of it. Do you need to frisk me, or is the purse sufficient?"

The officer looked Kori's firm body over and, against a few base instincts, decided that perhaps discretion would be the better part of valor. "I don't think that will be necessary, ma'am."

A few minutes later, Detective Mack Walton pulled up to the scene.

"Agent Briggs," he said, stepping out of his car. "Somehow I knew I hadn't seen the last of you." Then he turned to the uniformed officer. "So what do we have here?"

"I'll tell you what we have," Kori interrupted. "I've made a break on the case of Dane Reinhart's killing."

"Oh, yeah?"

"Take that gun with the silencer to ballistics. I'll bet you a dozen jelly-filled donuts that it'll match the slug from Reinhart."

Walton glanced over at the bearded man sitting with his back against the building. "And I take it that the gun belongs to this unfortunate guy?"

"You bet."

"It's not true!" cried the man. "I'm telling you, that's her gun! She attacked me, Detective. Out of nowhere. If anybody ought to be arrested, it's her."

Walton turned to the officer. "Okay, so what exactly did you see?"

"Well, when I got here, this woman had the guy face down, her knee into his back and holding his right wrist, basically threatening to break his arm.''

"Is that right Ms. Briggs?"

"You're damn right it is. Good thing for him that the officer came along. This guy has been following me all morning. He's the killer of Reinhart, I'm certain of it. And he was about to be my killer. Why do you think his gun has a silencer?"

"Don't listen to her!" said the bearded man. "She's crazy. I'm telling you, she attacked **me!** That's **her** gun!"

Walton strolled over to the man, gestured toward Kori, and said, "Do you mean to tell me this young woman, probably half your size, just randomly picked you out on the street and decided to attack you for no reason?"

"Oh, I'm sure she had a reason."

"Like what?"

"How would I know? She's a lunatic."

Walton was silent and the man, sensing a lost cause, finally said, "I want a lawyer," and then shut up.

"Okay, Ms. Briggs," said Walton. "We'll check out the gun and see if there's a match. In the meantime, we'll hold this guy on suspicion. I'll question him at the station."

"I want a lawyer," the bearded man cried again.

"Why don't you let me question him, Detective?" said Kori. "I was doing fine until your man got here. Give me five minutes."

Walton chuckled. "I have no doubt you'd get more out of him than we probably will, but I'm afraid I can't do that."

Kori briefly contemplated taking the man into custody herself. She knew that with a single phone call, she could override the detective's jurisdiction. But she also knew that she needed the police department's cooperation. For the time being, it was probably better to play ball.

"Okay, Detective. He's all yours."

"We'll take good care of him, Ms. Briggs, don't you worry. Now, if you want to give me a statement about what happened here this morning, I'll take it and then let you go on your way. I'll be happy to call you later this afternoon. I should have the ballistics report back by then, and maybe some more information about our suspect here, if we want to call him that. Fair enough, Agent Briggs?"

"Fair enough, Detective Walton."

CHAPTER 5

The best thing about the InterContinental was the Top of the Mark, the hotel's iconic nineteenth-floor lounge, boasting a 360-degree panorama of the city. Kori sat at window table with a view of the Bay Bridge, working on something called a Golden Gate—vodka, coconut rum, peach schnapps, and orange juice. The bartender had recommended it and Kori didn't feel as if she could turn it down. She was also working on an appetizer—the Giant Pretzel, which was exactly what it sounded like, with a choice of honey Dijon mustard or beer cheese dip.

She'd ordered both. Earlier, she'd eaten lunch in Chinatown to kill some time and was now enjoying cocktail hour while waiting for Detective Walton to call. But when the phone rang, it was Eaglethorpe.

"Agent Briggs, what have you learned?"

"That Dijon mustard goes better with a Golden Gate cocktail than beer cheese does."

"Huh?"

"Sorry, Chief, just thinking out loud. Truthfully, I don't have any news since we spoke this afternoon. Still waiting on Walton's call to learn about our suspect and the gun. How about you guys? Anything?"

"Not really. We've gotten nowhere on this phone number. It doesn't make any sense. We've pulled the records from every phone company—landline and cell—in British Columbia and the number simply doesn't exist."

"And nobody answers when you call it?"

"No, and I don't think they will. I mean, think about it. If you go to this much trouble to conceal your number from the public, you sure as hell aren't going to start picking up calls from numbers that you don't recognize."

"Sure, that makes sense. Well, then I guess—wait a minute!"

"What, Briggs?"

42

"What you just said. Of course the other person won't pick up from a strange number. But I have Reinhart's cell phone, Chief. Who's ever on the other end of that phone will recognize it."

"Of course! Okay, I'll text you the number. Call it from Reinhart's phone, Kori. See if someone answers and try to find out who they are. Let's get to the bottom of this."

"Roger, Chief. Will do."

Kori took another chunk of the pretzel, dipped it in the mustard and then washed it down with a swig of her cocktail. She pulled Reinhart's phone out of her purse and thought about what to say, deciding that she'd wing it based on the response that she'd get. Eaglethorpe's text came in with the number and she dialed it. It picked up before the second ring.

"Dane?" came a man's voice from the other end.

"No. I'm an associate of Dane's," said Kori. "My name is Briggs. And you are...?"

There was a silence of several seconds. And then, "How do I know you're an associate of Dane's?"

"You don't. And there's really no way you will. Such is the secretive nature of our work. I'm going to have to ask you to take it on faith."

"That's a lot to ask."

43

"Maybe. But the fact is, I don't know who you are, either."

Another long pause. Finally, the man said, "My name is Evan Banks. I'm with the Canadian Security Intelligence Service."

Kori sensed the man was legitimate. Nevertheless, it wouldn't hurt to test him. "Canadian Security Intelligence Service, huh? Then you must know Kenneth O'Brien."

"Of course. He's the assistant director."

"Indeed he is. Tell him Kori Briggs says hello. We worked with him on a case in Montreal a few years back. The Lockwood extortion case."

"Yes, I remember hearing about that case." The voice softened. "Okay, I'll believe you're who you say you are. But I don't understand. Where's Dane? Why do you have his phone?"

"I'm afraid Dane was murdered two nights ago."

"What?!"

"Yes, I'm sorry. Were you close?"

"We worked together. We often traded information. And, yes, he was my friend."

"Well, we're all kind of reeling a bit. When we lose an agent, it's never easy."

"No. It's not." The line went quiet for a few moments and then Banks spoke again. "Well, what else can you tell me? He was killed two nights ago, you say? I had coffee with him that night."

"Yes, cappuccinos."

"How do you know?"

"I found an address for the coffee shop in Dane's personal belongings. Talked to one of the baristas there. What time did you meet him?"

"Ten o'clock."

"Dane was killed not long afterward. A block from his hotel, as a matter of fact."

"My God. Was anything found on his person? A letter perhaps?"

"No, but he told our director that day that he was going to send something. Did that letter come from you?"

"Yes."

"What was in it, Mr. Banks?"

"I can't tell you over the phone."

"I understand. Let's meet somewhere. Are you still in San Francisco?"

"Unfortunately, no. I flew home after that meeting. I'm in Vancouver. Ms…Briggs, is it?"

"Yes."

"Ms. Briggs, I can tell you this much. That letter was credible proof of a pending terrorist attack on your country."

"Really?"

"Really. But I can't say any more without sitting down with you face-to-face."

"Based on recent events, I'd say that sitting down with you is a rather risky proposition, Mr. Banks."

"Come to Vancouver. You'll be safe here. I promise."

"Why didn't Dane meet you there?"

"San Francisco was his idea. He chose it more or less randomly. I came from Vancouver; he came from Denver. Why would anyone suspect we'd both turn up in San Francisco?"

"Well, apparently somebody did. And he's being held in custody right now, charged with Dane's murder."

"You found his killer? Who is it?"

"I'm waiting to find that out. I'm expecting a call from the investigating detective any moment now."

"Listen, Ms. Briggs, how soon can you get here?"

"How serious is the threat of this attack?"

"Your associate, and my friend, was killed because of it. I'd say it's pretty serious, Ms. Briggs."

"Point noted, Mr. Banks. I'll be there tonight."

Kori was down in her room packing up her things and getting ready to call Eaglethorpe when Detective Mack Walton called.

"Your man's name is Johnny Gardner," Walton said. "But he didn't volunteer that information. We had to run his fingerprints through the system. He's from Grand Rapids, Michigan. Thirty-three years old, divorced. Sells forklifts for a living. For the most part, he's been a law-abiding citizen. Ex-Navy SEAL, as a matter of fact. That's why his fingerprints are in the system. No arrest record. Just a few traffic tickets. And believe it or not, that's about all we know about him."

"What about the slug?"

"Fits the weapon, just as you said. It would seem as if he's our murderer. Or at least the leading candidate. The problem is, we don't have a motive and he's not saying a thing. But I have a sense that you know his motive, Agent Briggs. Maybe you can share it with me so that I can properly kick this thing along to the DA."

"I wish I could, Detective, but I'm not sure myself. Not exactly. In the meantime, certainly you have enough to hold him, what with the ballistics report."

"Of course, but you could make my job easier, Agent Briggs. Tell me what you know. We're on the same side, after all."

"Sorry, Detective, you know as much as I do."

"You know, White House or not, if you're withholding information I could have you arrested for obstruction of justice."

"Based on what? Your hunch that I know more than what I'm telling you? That seems pretty thin to me."

"Maybe it is, but it doesn't make it any less true." Then Walton decided that good old-fashioned pleading might work better. "C'mon, Agent Briggs, work with me. Be a good citizen. Help me out, huh?"

"Listen, Detective, as soon as I know more, I'll let you know. Believe me when I tell you that you'll get everything you need on Johnny Gardner. I'll make it my mission to see that Gardner never sees the outside of a prison cell again. Now, if you'll excuse me, Detective."

Kori hung up the phone and placed a call to Eaglethorpe.

"Chief, what do we know about a Canadian Intelligence officer named Evan Banks?"

"Banks? I don't know. Why?"

"He's the guy who belongs to the phone number. And the guy that Reinhart had coffee with."

"You talked to him?"

"Yep."

"Nice work, Kori."

"Yeah, but he wouldn't tell me anything. Not in person, anyway. He's in Vancouver and I'm heading to the airport now to meet with him. It would be nice to know I'm not walking into something dangerous."

"Right. Hang on a second, Kori." Kori could hear Eaglethorpe in the background talking to Cooper. Then he came back to the line. "Okay, Cooper is checking the system for Evan Banks. What was your sense?"

"I think he's for real, Chief. He knew the assistant director's name, he even knew about the Lockwood case. And he answered the phone asking for Reinhart by his first name, so he obviously had a working relationship with him. And frankly, he seemed kind of broken up by the news of Dane's death. He called him a friend."

"Canadian Intelligence, huh? Well, that would explain the cloaked phone number. Just like ours. Did he say anything at all about what he and Reinhart were working on?"

"A terrorist threat to the US. That's what the letter was about, the document that Dane said he was going to transmit to you. But that's all he'd tell me over the phone."

"Okay. Hang on, here's Cooper."

Darren Cooper picked up the line. "Kori, Evan Banks checks out. He's been with Canadian Intelligence for about fifteen years. Pretty highly decorated, too. In fact, I recall Reinhart mentioning a Canadian contact from time to time."

"Banks said that they traded information."

"Well, that's him then. He sounds like a valuable contact. You should go meet him."

"One step ahead of you, Coop. I'm heading to the airport now. Put the Chief back on, will you?"

"Sure thing."

"And thanks, Coop."

"No problem, Kori. That's what I'm here for. Stand by for the chief."

"Chief, I've got another name for you," said Kori when Eaglethorpe regained the line. "Johnny Gardner. That's the guy who tailed me this morning. And the guy who killed Dane. Ballistics matched the gun that Gardner was carrying. But get this. He appears to be just an ordinary guy. He's a forklift salesman from Grand Rapids, Michigan with no criminal record."

"Hmm…odd."

"Yes. And apparently he's not talking."

"What would an ordinary guy from Michigan be doing in San Francisco gunning down a Rampart agent?"

"Your guess is as good as mine, Chief. Want me to fly to Grand Rapids and nose around after my stop in Vancouver? I'd be happy to. As it happens, I'm only 300 miles away from a free roundtrip flight to anywhere in the world."

Eaglethorpe chuckled. "Don't worry about it, Agent Briggs. I'll send Vasquez there. You just get yourself to Vancouver and find out what Banks knows."

"Roger, Chief."

"Oh, and Kori?"

"Yes, Chief?"

"Just out of curiosity, where would you go if you had a free trip to anywhere in the world?"

"Anywhere, Chief?"

"Anywhere."

"Home, Chief. I'd go home."

CHAPTER 6

After Kori packed, she headed over to the Fairmont and packed up Reinhart's things. She folded the clothes carefully, almost reverently. She would make certain that his personal items would be sent to his next of kin. There would no doubt be the inevitable questions asked by family members. Answering these was Eaglethorpe's job. Kori was glad it wasn't hers. Eaglethorpe would come clean, telling the family of the heroic exploits of their loved one, making them understand the importance of his work. He'd talk about the intelligence agency Dane worked for, but the name Rampart would never be mentioned. His family would most likely assume CIA.

From the Fairmont, Kori took a cab to the airport, boarded the first plane to Vancouver, and landed at Vancouver International after midnight. Waiting for her in the concourse after she made her way through customs was a tall, fit man holding a sign that read: "Edwards."

"Hello," Kori said, approaching the man. "I'm Julie Edwards. Are you my driver?"

"Hello," the man replied. "Yes, I'm Bob Russell. Welcome to Vancouver. First time in our city?"

"Oh, no, I've been here a few times before. It's quite lovely."

"Can I help you with your things, Ms. Edwards?"

"Thank you, yes."

The two moved in relative silence through the concourse, down the escalator, and into the short-term parking garage, making only routine small talk now and again. The man took Kori's bags and deposited them into the trunk of his car and then opened the passenger door. Kori nodded politely and slid into the front passenger seat. Only when they'd left the airport and had accessed the highway, did they speak more openly.

"Nice to meet you, Agent Briggs," the man smiled.

"My pleasure, Agent Banks." Indeed it was. Evan Banks had thick black hair, a chiseled face with sharp cheekbones, and dimples when he smiled, Kori's certain weakness. **Not too hard to look at**, the girl with the pastel pink hair at the coffee shop had said. She wasn't kidding.

"You'll stay at my place for the night," Banks said. "It's safe. It's about twenty minutes from here and I have a guest room that I think you'll find comfortable."

"Thank you, that sounds just fine."

"When we get there, I'll tell you everything I know, although I have to warn you that afterward you'll probably have more questions than answers. Of course, I was very sorry to hear about Dane. He was a good man."

"Yes, he was. And a top-notch agent. You'll be glad to know we've identified his killer."

"Really? Who is it?"

"Well, that's just it. A nobody. A guy named Johnny Gardner who sells forklifts in Michigan. A man who seemingly would never be involved in the murder of an intelligence agent."

"How strange."

WE'LL QUIT WHEN WE'RE DEAD

"By the way, did Dane tell you about us? About our organization?"

"Not much. And after a while, I stopped asking. At first I thought he was CIA. But he wasn't. Neither are you, are you, Agent Briggs?"

"Please call me Kori. No. I'm with…another agency. And I'm afraid that's about all I can say."

"I understand. Dane said the same. And I ask for no further explanation. I dealt with Dane enough to know you're on the side of the good guys. That's enough for me. I imagine all governments have secret organizations, mine included. Tell me something though, if you don't mind. Do you ever become concerned that by operating in the shadows, without public oversight, that your organization can go rogue?"

"How do you mean?"

"Well, I'm sure you're all good, upstanding people, but a super-secret organization, out of the spotlight of any kind of serious scrutiny, can pretty much do what it wants, right? In the hands of the unscrupulous, that would be very dangerous, it seems to me."

"Yes, I see what you mean. Well, I can tell you that we're very careful about who comes aboard. Every agent is meticulously screened and chosen.

We're all pretty much apolitical and our agency's agenda is purposely limited. We're interested only in defense, and only in direct physical threats, at that. Our goals are simple and streamlined. Our allegiance is to our nation's safety and security and we never venture beyond that. And believe me, that keeps us busy enough. Especially these days."

"Yes, I imagine so. Certainly, I can see the appeal from an agent's perspective. I am constantly having to answer to people who do not understand the often sensitive nature of our work."

"I imagine it can be a real pain."

Banks lived on the fifth floor of a building on Beach Avenue in the West End section of the city, overlooking English Bay. When they got there, they took the elevator up to his condo and Kori watched as Banks accessed the door with a key code. Once inside, he closed the heavy steel door and punched a number of buttons on an alarm system keypad hanging on the foyer wall right next to a small monitor that showed the hallway outside.

"Get a lot of door-to-door salespeople around here, do you?" asked Kori.

Banks smiled. "I told you you'd be safe."

He showed Kori to the guest bedroom where Kori dropped her things and then the two went out to the living room where Banks offered Kori a drink.

"Is there a good bottle of scotch in the house?" she asked.

"Johnny Walker?"

"Sure, that'll work."

"Ice?"

"Under normal circumstances, but don't bother. Neat is just fine."

Banks poured two glasses of scotch and handed one to Kori. "Please," he said, "have a seat."

Kori sat on the sofa as Banks walked over to a small desk in the corner. Kori gazed about the room. The lighting was low. The furniture was classic dark leather. A heavy, burgundy Oriental rug spread out below her. Built-in bookshelves comprised an entire wall. The curtains were drawn, but Kori knew the windows faced the bay and imagined a delightful view. The place was neat. It was tasteful, and definitely masculine. She liked being there.

Banks punched another keypad at his desk and opened a drawer from which he pulled an envelope.

"I think I trust you, Kori," he said. "But I needed to see you here in person first. I hope you understand." Then he handed the envelope to Kori and sat down in the chair adjacent to her.

Kori slid a letter out of the envelope and looked it over. "I don't understand," she said. "This appears to be a letter from the Iranian consulate in Istanbul, Turkey."

"Exactly."

"I'm afraid my Persian is a little rusty. What does it say?"

"It's from a high-level official on the consulate staff. Consul general, in fact. It's an order for the implementation of a plan to attack, by some means, which I do not know, the United States on its own soil."

"Good God. Really?"

"Yes. This is the original. I made a copy of it and it's that copy that I delivered to Dane Reinhart at the coffee shop in San Francisco."

"It doesn't appear to be addressed to anyone."

"Exactly. We have no idea who this order is meant for. I presume the addressee was left off purposely."

"And it's from the consul general? How high up does this directive go then?"

"Who can say? I'd like to think that it originated at his level, but we know that a lot of communication goes through the consulate in Istanbul, more than what goes through the Iranian embassy in Ankara,

Turkey's capital. It's kind of a hotbed of chatter between Iranian government leaders in Tehran and Iranian foreign agents in the Middle East. If this letter came from higher up, from the president or even the supreme leader of Iran—"

"It would be an act of war," Kori said, finishing the thought.

"Indeed it would."

"How did you come by this?"

"I have a contact in Istanbul. An informant who works at the consulate. He intercepted it and handed it to a man we have on the ground there. That man personally couriered it here to me. I called Dane at once and set up our meeting."

"Why didn't your informant just take it to the American consulate in Istanbul? Cut out the middleman, so to speak? Why take it to your guy on the ground, a Canadian Intelligence officer?"

"Good question. The informant is a man named Hajar. I met him years ago when I was stationed in Toronto. Hajar was a student at the university, majoring in political science. Our agency would put on seminars from time to time and I was frequently tasked with speaking to the students about what we did, in general terms, of course. Nothing specific. Anyway, when Hajar graduated, he went back to

Iran. He'd been a young boy during the '79 Iranian revolution and had always been a loyal subject of the regime. After his education here, he worked his way into the Iranian government and ended up at the Turkish consul general's office.

"But a few years ago, he began having second thoughts about the Iranian leadership—the human rights abuses, the lack of any form of democratic participation by the people. He was able to get more news in Turkey about his government than he ever got in Iran. It opened his eyes. I think the final straw was Iran's foray into nuclear weapons. He worried about it. He feared for his people.

"Well, somehow he remembered me, tracked me down, and called one day out of the blue. He wanted to work with us, he said. I barely remembered him, but of course I encouraged his openness. Before long, he was passing information along to me from whatever scraps of intelligence he could glean from his work at the consulate, some of which I'd pass along to Dane. Truth be told, most of it was useless. There wasn't much he could give us that we didn't already know. But this last scrap, well, this was something else. Why didn't he take it to the Americans you ask? First, he and I had built a good working relationship over the past few years. He was comfortable with me. He trusted me. Second, I think he was afraid."

"Of what?"

"I'm not sure, but the last time I talked to him he mentioned something about being concerned that he would be found out. Apparently, several at the consulate were suddenly questioning him quite often, asking him to account for his whereabouts at all times. There was even a visit from the embassy in Ankara. Hajar felt a rising level of suspicion. Now, maybe it was his imagination, but nevertheless, he didn't dare make a trip to the American consulate or even think about being seen with an American. And so I put him in touch with our guy in Istanbul, who nobody at the Iranian consulate knows, and they met secretly. That's when Hajar handed over the letter he'd stumbled upon."

"I see."

"And then our guy brought it here to me personally, knowing I had a trusted contact in Dane. Maybe it's overkill, but we decided that this letter needed to be handed off in person. If we just passed the threat along verbally, it would seem like all the other intelligence chatter that constantly spews forth. We get threats every day. But one like this? On government letterhead? This is real and your people need to see it. This is no run-of-the mill terrorist organization blowing hot air. This is a sovereign nation planning an attack."

"Of course."

"So, anyway, after I got it, I called my favorite American intelligence agent. You know the rest." Banks looked down and was quiet for a moment. "I'm afraid, Agent Briggs, that I've gotten your man killed."

"Nonsense," said Kori, reaching out and touching Banks's arm. "You did the right thing. Dane was the guy to call. You can't take responsibility for what happened after that."

"Thanks for saying so. Still, it's kind of hard, considering the chain of events."

"Did you know Dane well? You mentioned that you considered him a friend." Kori sat back and took a sip of her drink.

"Yes. I met him on a case that brought him here to Vancouver a few years back. My agency was following up on those bomb threats made by that psycho who had come here from Portland."

"Yes, I remember the case."

"Dane came up, and together we were able to nab the guy and send him back to the States. Dane and I enjoyed each other's company. A few months after that, he came on vacation with his girlfriend. I think they broke up since, though."

One less loved one to have to explain things to, thought Kori.

"Anyway," Banks continued, "we visited Gastown and went out on a whale-watching boat and ate at some nice restaurants. It was just an all-around good time. I liked Dane. I'm very sorry I put him in harm's way."

"Hey, we all know the risks. It's part of the job. Dane wasn't a civilian that inadvertently got caught in the crossfire. He was a soldier, like you and me."

"Yes," said Banks. "Yes, I suppose so." Banks looked up into Kori's eyes and forced a smile, but Kori could sense melancholy. "Do you ever wonder if we're making a difference?" he said at last. "As 'soldiers'?"

"I know we are. Sure, sometimes we have setbacks and sometimes it seems like the best we're doing is treading water, but I like to believe that, in the long run, we're getting somewhere. We're winning. In fact, I'm sure of it."

"I wish I could believe that, Kori. But surely you can see that this is not a war that can be won. We terminate one threat, another threat pops up somewhere else. Things seemed peaceful and on track just a week ago. And then this came up. I'm afraid that there will always be something like this. The world is such a dangerous, dangerous place. We will always be chasing something. Are you familiar with the myth of Sisyphus, Kori?"

"Sure, the guy in Greek mythology who was sentenced by Zeus to roll a boulder up a hill for eternity."

"Yes. Don't you ever feel as if that's all we're doing? Rolling boulders up hills endlessly?"

"Maybe," Kori said, thoughtfully. "But that's the nature of life itself, isn't it? Do we ever really get anywhere or solve anything? And does it matter? Remember what Camus said: 'One must imagine Sisyphus happy.' The struggle itself is enough to fill the heart."

"Hmm…isn't it pretty to think so?"

"Listen, there is no finish line, Evan, if you're looking for one. Not until we're dead, that is. We'll have to keep fighting; it's what we do. Even more, it's who we are. We'll quit eventually. We'll quit when we're dead."

Evan smiled and placed his hand over Kori's. The smile was broader now and the dimples more pronounced. "Thanks, Kori. I guess I needed to hear that. Sometimes the state of the world depresses me."

"Of course. We all feel it sometimes. No one's immune to the emotional downswings this line of work comes with. But that's when you have to fight back the hardest." She squeezed his hand and they leaned closer to each other, holding each other's gazes. Each felt the pull of the other. Both wanted it. But both also understood the necessity of keeping relationships of their sort pure and uncomplicated. They were two intelligence professionals, sworn to duty and to the completion of the task at hand. Romance, if it were to be in the cards, would have to wait. And that was fine by Kori. As alluring as this man sitting next to her was, she couldn't see making the jump from Shane Scott to anybody—no matter how alluring—just yet. She needed time. And she needed to keep her focus on the job. Rampart Agent Dane Reinhart was dead and there was a real and active threat to US security.

Simultaneously, each released the other's hand and both leaned back again. Kori broke the awkward silence. "So…what's a girl have to do to get a refill?" she said, waving her empty glass in the air.

"Oh, pardon me," Banks chuckled. "What kind of host am I?" He grabbed the bottle of scotch and poured two more glasses.

Kori picked up the letter again. "It's a bit of a mystery, isn't it?"

"The nature of the threat?"

"Well, yes, that, but I was also thinking about the death of Dane. What's the connection? How does a forklift salesman in Grand Rapids get involved in an Iranian consulate plot in Istanbul to attack the US?"

"Assuming he was involved in the plot."

"He must have been. It's too much of a coincidence. You hand an incriminating letter to Dane, and within an hour, this guy kills him and takes the letter. If he's not involved, then we have an even bigger mystery. Namely, what was his motive for killing Dane?"

"I see what you mean."

"Actually, there are a lot of unanswered questions here."

"I warned you."

"Here's another one: how did this guy know you two were meeting in San Francisco?"

"I'd like to know that one myself."

Kori was thoughtful for a moment and said, "Evan, you know your life is in jeopardy, right?"

"Of course. I don't believe for a second that whoever is behind this is content with Dane's death. I was the guy who had the letter in the first place.

Why didn't they just kill me, even before the meeting at the coffee shop? And what's to keep them from doing so now?"

"Unless they figured you'd drop the case once you delivered the letter. I mean, the threat is against the US, not Canada. Maybe they figured you wouldn't have discovered that Dane was killed. You'd have thought you did your job in passing along the information and go about your business never the wiser. Killing you in that case would have only brought more attention to the matter. When you stop and think about it, the only reason you did learn about the murder was because I contacted you with Dane's phone, which was something of a fluke. Johnny Gardner's mistake was not taking the phone when he took the letter."

"He wasn't as professional as we thought."

"No, maybe not. Of course, the other explanation is that he just never got the proper chance to kill you. Dane was walking alone, at night. Gardner had the opportunity. Either way, and whether Gardner is a professional killer or not, apparently he knew enough to try to cover his tracks. He must have revisited the scene of the crime, saw me talking with the police, and decided to follow me. I might never know his ultimate intentions. Maybe he just wanted to discover what I knew about the killing. But now, whoever is behind the plot knows that Gardner is in custody. They must know by now that you've contacted US authorities. They'll come for you, Evan. I'm sure of it. Most likely, they're having you followed."

"I've assumed so. I've been careful."

"I don't think you can be careful enough. It stands to reason that they were at the airport. If so, they're now following both of us. I appreciate that we're safe and secure here inside, but sooner or later, we're going to have to leave your little fortress."

Banks nodded. "I know. What do you suggest, Kori?"

"Is there a back entrance to this building?"

"Sure. There's a maintenance elevator that leads to a rear delivery door."

Kori looked at her watch. "If we're being followed, I don't imagine they'd think we'd be going anywhere at two o'clock in the morning. And not out the back door. Pack a bag. We'll turn the lights out as if we're going to bed. Then we'll exit out of the rear of the building. Leave your car here. We'll hoof it for a few blocks back from the main street into the neighborhood, then circle back to that old hotel I noticed down the street."

"The Sylvia."

"Yes. We can call for a cab there. We'll go to the airport where I'll take the first plane back to DC with this letter. Why don't you come along? I could use the company. And DC is pretty nice this time of year."

Banks smiled. "As much as I'd like to, Kori, I think I should do what you're doing. I should report to my headquarters in Ottawa. They need to be briefed on what's going on with our southern neighbor."

"Yes, I guess that would be best. Shame, though. I've enjoyed meeting you, Evan. A trip together could have been fun."

"Another time, I hope," Evan Banks said, and then he smiled again and the light caught his dimples so delightfully that Kori simply had to look away.

CHAPTER 7

They had no trouble getting to the Vancouver airport. As Kori suggested, they left out of the back entrance of Banks's building and walked a circuitous route to the Sylvia where they called for a taxicab. Then, to be certain, they had the cabbie drive a circuitous route to the airport. No one had followed.

The earliest flight to Washington was 6 a.m. and it went through Dallas, giving Kori a couple of hours to kill. Banks's flight to Ottawa was in another terminal and the two said their goodbyes shortly after arriving at the airport, both promising to keep in touch. **Two wonderful men, two goodbyes**, Kori thought. All in just a little over twenty-four hours.

She needed sleep but resisted the urge to nod off before getting on the plane. She normally had trouble sleeping on planes, but surely she'd be able to doze on the four-hour flight to Dallas once reclined in her customary first-class seat. Why nap on the uncomfortable chairs at the airport when you can nap in relative luxury on the plane? And so she stayed awake, filling the time at the airport eating snacks from a newsstand and sending a coded email through Rampart's secure servers to Eaglethorpe, advising him of her plans to come in and requesting a briefing session with the rest of the group. He'd see it first thing in the morning and would make certain that the DC contingent of Rampart agents would be assembled for her.

Finally, the plane boarded. Kori took her seat, leaned back, closed her eyes, and suddenly the plane was landing at Dallas/Fort Worth International. She felt like a new woman. During the layover, she had lunch and a cold beer at a barbecue restaurant near her gate. Now she felt even better. Another plane ride, this one three hours, and she was in DC, the evening shadows already starting to fall on the nation's capital. She grabbed a coffee in the concourse of Reagan National Airport and then met the car that Eaglethorpe had sent for her. A twenty-minute ride put her at the offices of Gladstone Conveyor. "Simply the Best," read the sign out front. Inside, was a small stark office—an open collection of metal desks and networked computers.

"Kori!" said Cooper who was sitting at the desk nearest the door, tapping away on his keyboard. "We've been expecting you. Welcome back." Cooper was lean but muscular, and with short, dark hair. He wore wire-rimmed glasses, which set him apart from his fellow technical geek, James Foster, who didn't wear glasses but otherwise could have passed for his twin.

"Hi, Coop. Good to be home." Kori looked around the room. "Where is everybody?"

"They're all in the conference room waiting for you. Chief said you have some important details for us. C'mon."

The two walked down the hallway and into a room with a long, heavy table and high-backed leather chairs.

"Agent Briggs," smiled Director Eaglethorpe. "Good to see you." Eaglethorpe, sixty-four years old was a black man with short, gray, bristly hair. Tall and thin, he had a kind face that often seemed incongruous with his serious nature. Then again, Kori had known Eaglethorpe to let his guard down at times and be anything but serious. She always felt like she wanted to hug him when she came back after an extended period away, but as much as she would have liked to, it never quite felt appropriate.

"Hi, Chief," she smiled at him. Agent Foster was there, too, as was Agent Gibson. Agent Vasquez, Kori knew, was en route at that very moment to Grand Rapids, Michigan to try to dig up what he could on Johnny Gardner, forklift salesman and apparent killer of Dane Reinhart.

"I've told them what I know, Briggs," said Eaglethorpe, "but why don't you fill us in on the particulars?"

"Well, fellas," Kori began, "it's like this. An agent with the Canadian Intelligence Service named Evan Banks has a contact who works at the Iranian consulate in Istanbul. An insider. A mole, if you will. Anyway, this contact came across a certain correspondence that was, in its essence, an order to attack the United States. Here it is." Kori pulled the letter out of her purse and laid it on the table.

Eaglethorpe picked it up, saw the Persian script,

and handed it to Foster. "You're our language guy," he said. "What's it say?"

"Plan of attack approved," Foster read aloud. "US to suffer, to feel our wrath. On its own soil. The Great Satan will fall to its knees. Proceed when reasonable to do so."

"Wow," said Cooper.

"Are you sure, Agent Foster?" asked Eaglethorpe.

"Well, I mean, with translating any language there are always difficulties," said Foster. "Not every word has an exact English match, but sure, that's more or less the gist of it."

"Okay," said Eaglethorpe. "Continue, Agent Briggs."

"Right. Well, as you can see, the letter is written on Iranian consulate stationery. We believe the writer was a high-level official in the consulate staff, the consul general, in fact. Banks's contact in the consulate swiped the letter from his desk and gave it to a Canadian Intelligence agent in Istanbul, too afraid of being caught to risk turning it over to anyone in the US consulate. The Canadian agent, in turn, delivered it to Banks. Banks, knowing this was an American matter, contacted Dane whom he'd worked with in the past. The two agreed to meet in San Francisco at a coffee shop where Banks handed over a copy of this letter. An hour later, well, we all know the rest. Dane's killer is a guy named Johnny Gardner from Michigan who's been arrested for the crime and is, as we speak, sitting in the San Francisco County Jail and saying exactly nothing."

"Yes," said Eaglethorpe. "Vasquez will be doing some snooping around in Grand Rapids where Gardner lives. We managed to track down his ex-wife and that's where Vasquez will start. Hopefully, we can discover the connection. Briggs?"

"Well," Kori continued, "that's really all we know at this point. Here's what we don't know: We don't know who the letter was for. We don't know the nature of the planned attack. Or when it is to be commenced. Or where. We can assume the intended recipient knows. We don't know who originated the plan. Was it the consul general? Is he writing that **he's** approved the plan, or is he writing to tell the recipient that approval has come from somewhere above? If the latter, how high above? Does this plan reach into the uppermost levels of the Iranian government? And on top of everything, as Chief said, who's this guy Gardner and how could he possibly be involved?"

"All relevant questions," said Eaglethorpe.

"But I don't understand something," Gibson

piped up. "Why put the note on official consulate stationery? Why not slip the recipient an unidentifiable scrap of paper, or pass along the message verbally? Why take the chance of incriminating the Iranian government?"

"For credibility," said Cooper. "Whomever this was meant for, they needed to be convinced that the order was real. They needed official permission."

"Makes sense," said Eaglethorpe.

"Or else the stationery is fake," offered Foster. "Maybe it's someone who's trying to make it look as if the Iranian government is involved when maybe they're not. A frame job."

"Or maybe they used official stationery because they just never imagined the letter would get pilfered," said Gibson. "I mean, if this mole is good, then the consul general probably had no reason to believe that any given item on his desk was at risk of being seen by foreign eyes."

"All possibilities," said Kori. "But I'm inclined to think Coop is right. The attack needed official sanctioning. I believe this goes pretty far up the chain of command."

"Why, Agent Briggs?" Eaglethorpe asked.

"Because someone is sure intent on making certain that the letter doesn't come to light. Dane was killed because he had it. The opposite would be the case if someone were trying to make people think Iran is contemplating an act of war against the United States when they're really not. We were never meant to see this letter."

"That seems like a reasonable conclusion," Eaglethorpe agreed. "But it's still based on speculation. We can discuss this for the rest of the night, but the fact is, we need some solid answers. Let's see, Agent Pratt is in Bulgaria, isn't that right, Agent Cooper?"

"Yes, sir," Cooper replied.

"He's the closest agent. I suppose I can have him fly to Istanbul and start nosing around at the source." Then Eaglethorpe threw a glance at Kori. "Unless anybody else wants to volunteer to go to Istanbul…?"

Kori smiled. "More air miles, Chief?"

"Well, Agent Briggs, you are sort of invested in this case now."

"I guess I am at that. Sure, Chief. I'm happy to go."

"Glad to hear it. Especially since I've already had Cooper make your flight arrangements. You leave for Istanbul first thing in the morning. Now go home and get a good night's sleep."

Kori's condominium was on the fourteenth floor of a high-rise building overlooking the Potomac with a balcony view of the Washington Monument. She was never able to spend much time on the balcony, but it was nice knowing it was there. Once home, she dropped her bags and then thought of how she'd have to pick them right back up first thing in the morning. At least she'd have the evening to relax and get a little laundry done.

The first order of business was dinner. Lunch at the Dallas/Fort Worth International Airport seemed like days ago. Fortunately, there was an Italian place around the corner that delivered and before long, Kori was settled into her cozy sofa with a warm plate of lasagna and a glass of cabernet sauvignon that she'd pulled out of the stainless steel wine cooler in her kitchen. Just a few bottles left. She made a mental note to restock whenever time would permit, but who knew when that would be?

The second glass of cab accompanied the order of tiramisu that the restaurant had placed into the delivery bag. She hadn't ordered it, but the restaurant knew Kori well and was always adding little things to her delivery orders at no charge. It didn't hurt that she was always very generous with her tips. Plus, she was pretty sure the chef, a young, broad-shouldered Italian man with jet-black hair had a crush on her. She knew she didn't need the dessert, but its coffee-flavored, cocoa deliciousness could not be resisted.

After dessert, she threw her clothes into the washing machine and dialed her mother.

"Hi, dear! So good of you to call. How was San Francisco?"

"It was great, Mom. I think we'll get the contract."

"Wonderful. And did you get to sightsee? Did you go to Fisherman's Wharf?"

"No, there really wasn't a lot of time for sight-seeing. I did take a ride on a cable car, though. That was kind of fun."

"Oh, that's nice. Well, I want to hear all about it. Are we still having dinner on Sunday?"

"I'm afraid not, Mom. They're sending me to St. Louis. There's an installation I need to oversee. No rest for the weary, I guess."

"Oh, that's too bad. When do you have to go?"

"First thing in the morning, I'm afraid. In fact, I

won't even have time to swing by my place. I'm headed straight there." Kori didn't dare tell her mother she was home. She needed the evening to herself. To relax. To reload. Her mother wouldn't understand and insist upon seeing her. Kori loved that about her, loved her affection and attention. But sometimes, she needed a little space. Above all else, Kori valued her alone time.

"Well, how long will you be gone?"

"Tough to say, Mom. Got to see how things are going down there. I'll call you in a day or so and let you know. How's everything with you?"

"Well, okay. I had a bit of a dustup with that Dorthea Stamper. You know, the woman in my book club?"

"Of course."

"Well, the rest of us agreed to read **The Liar's Club**, but Dorthea claimed she'd already read it. But I don't think she did. I asked her some questions about it and I could tell that she didn't know the first thing about that book and yet we've all decided to read the same books at the same time or what's the use of having a book club if you can't sit down and discuss the same book and I told her flat out that I thought she wasn't being honest with us and if she didn't want to read **The Liar's Club**, she should just come out and say so and then Melinda said…"

Kori's mom continued as Kori poured the last of the bottle of cabernet into her glass and smiled. She liked hearing her mother's voice, even if she didn't really listen to what she was saying. She found it comforting. It grounded her somehow.

Finally, after the two hung up, Kori filled her whirlpool tub, took the clothes out of the washer, tossed them into the dryer, and slipped into the tub, allowing the heat and the jets to relax her from head to toe. She put a terry cloth robe on, folded the laundry, packed her bag for the morning, then dropped the robe and slipped into bed, thinking about how nice it was to be home, if only for a few short hours.

CHAPTER 8

The flight to Istanbul was thirteen hours including a two-hour layover in, of all places, Frankfurt, from where Kori had flown to San Francisco just seventy-two hours prior. To Kori, it seemed like two weeks prior. She thought briefly of calling Shane. Ramstein Air Base was only an hour's drive from the Frankfurt airport. They could have a drink together. But then she thought better of it. What would be the point? To say goodbye all over again?

Istanbul was eight hours ahead of DC time so when she landed, it was early morning and the sun was just coming up. Kori's taxi took her through the old part of the city, down narrow stone streets and past historic mosques with tall minarets. The drive led to the Hotel Amira with a view of the Sea of Marmara.

The other direction from the airport would have ended on the shore of the Black Sea. Running between the two bodies of water is the Bosporus Strait, which the city of Istanbul straddles and which represents the divide between Europe and Asia. Istanbul, therefore, has the distinction of being situated on both continents. Northwest is Bulgaria. Southeast of Turkey is Syria, Iraq, and Iran. It's no wonder the city became such an important trade and cultural hub, as well as a melting pot of ethnicities. As Constantinople, the city was at one time the capital of the Roman Empire. In time, it would become the capital of the Ottoman Empire, eventually renamed Istanbul several years after Turkey declared its independence on the heels of the First World War.

At the hotel, Kori left her bag with the bell captain and went in search of breakfast. Her room wouldn't be ready until early afternoon, always a disadvantage of arriving somewhere too early in the day. But the city was alive now and she enjoyed strolling down the historic streets as they began to bustle with locals and tourists alike. About a mile from her hotel, past the iconic Blue Mosque, she spied a small restaurant advertising kahvalti and took an outdoor table. This was not Kori's first trip to Turkey and she knew kahvalti meant breakfast— but not just any breakfast. A Turkish breakfast typically includes simit, a circular bread that's something like a bagel. Jams and spreads, different kinds of cheeses, eggs, and a spicy, beef sausage called sucuk are also served. Kori couldn't resist. She ordered it all and then took out her phone and texted Eaglethorpe to let him know she'd made it safely. To her surprise, her phone rang right back.

"Chief," she answered, "it must be three o'clock in the morning there."

"Sure," said Eaglethorpe, "but who can sleep? I've been sitting here in my living room. You know, I have access to over 800 channels and I still can't find anything decent to watch? Especially at this ungodly hour."

"I hear you, Chief. It's a world gone mad, huh?"

"So, when's your meeting with Banks's guy?"

"This afternoon. At the Grand Bazaar."

"What do you know about him?"

"Evan, uh, Agent Banks said that Wallace Simon

has been with Canadian Intelligence for about ten years. He's been assigned to the Middle East for the past eight. It was Simon whom the consulate informant, a guy named Hajar, gave the letter to pass to Banks. And that's about all I know. Should be a good place to start, at least."

"Sure. But why don't we just interview this Hajar guy directly?"

"Agent Banks said he's a little skittish. Apparently, he's keeping a pretty low profile. And who can blame him? If the originator of that letter knew that it had been stolen, I can't imagine things would go too well for the guy who took it."

"No, I don't suppose they would."

"So, the plan is, I'll talk to Simon and see if he'd be willing to vouch for me and get me hooked up with Hajar. I'll assure him that our meeting will be held in secret and in the strictest confidence. Hopefully, Hajar will trust me enough to talk to me and give us some answers."

"Yeah, let's hope."

Kori's breakfast came and she raised her elbows off the table to allow the waiter to slide the plates of food in front of her. She looked at it hungrily, wondering how long her conversation with the Chief was going to last.

"So what's the word from Vasquez?" she asked, sticking a fork into the sausage, making the decision to proceed with breakfast despite the conversation.

"He met with Gardner's ex-wife yesterday morning. Pretty interesting interview. As it happens, Gardner's more than just a forklift salesman. He's got a little hobby."

"Oh, yeah?" Kori asked, trying not to sound completely incomprehensible with her mouth full of food.

"Yep. Get this. It turns out Johnny Gardner is involved with the Guardian Militia."

"What, the antigovernment, neo-Nazi group?"

"One and the same."

"Really? But I thought the FBI shut them down after their attempted attack on the United Nations Building in New York a couple of years ago. In fact, I assumed they were all doing jail terms."

"Not all of them. There were enough of them that couldn't be tied to the crime to regroup and form anew. Johnny Gardner is one of them. Apparently the Guardian Militia is alive and well."

"Wow, Chief. So Gardner is a neo-Nazi. But what's the connection with an alleged Iranian plot to attack America? The Guardian Militia and Iran? I mean, you talk about strange bedfellows."

"I know, Briggs. It's not making a lot of sense. Maybe it's a complete coincidence, who knows? Vasquez is still in Grand Rapids and he's going to nose around some more, maybe see if he can get one of the other members of the group to talk. You work on things from your end and let's see if we can find how this whole thing fits together, if it fits together at all."

"Right, Chief."

"In the meantime, I've called the president and informed him of what we know so far. In turn, he's notified Homeland Security. Everybody is on high alert. POTUS had a lot of uncomfortable questions for me about the presumed attack, Agent Briggs, that I didn't have answers to. Like 'where' and 'when.' We need to get the bottom of this Kori. Pronto."

"I understand, Chief."

"Call me when you know something. Anything. At any time, day or night. I'll be here."

"Roger, Chief. Hope you find something decent on TV in the meantime."

"Sure. And I hope you enjoy the rest of whatever it is you're eating."

Kori chuckled. "Thanks, Chief," she said sheepishly. "I was hoping you couldn't tell. Actually, it's

Turkish kahvalti. Breakfast, you know."

"Well, I'm sure it's delicious. I'll look forward to hearing from you soon, Kori."

"Right, Chief."

Kori hung up, finished her breakfast, and ordered a coffee. Turkish coffee is strong and made without the use of a filter; the Arabica beans are ground very fine, then the coffee is brought to a boil until it begins to froth. The waiter presented it in a small porcelain cup and Kori sipped the steaming brew slowly, first because it was hot, and second, because she had some time to kill before her meeting with Agent Wallace Simon and she had no hotel room to retire to.

Eventually, she finished the coffee, paid the bill, and walked off into the streets of Istanbul, heading in the general direction of the famed Grand Bazaar. Once there, the time went fast. She wandered the colorful passageways of the ancient market, under the arched columns, past stores with multihued ceramics and Turkish lamps, showrooms of rich and vibrant kilim rugs, artisan craft shops, and shops with Turkish teas and soaps and candies. She watched shoppers haggling with shop proprietors. At one point, she fell in with a tour group that was strolling around and listened to the tour guide recite the basic facts of the Grand Bazaar, how it had originally opened in 1461, how it currently housed over 4,000 shops, and how it was spread out over 61 covered streets.

Ultimately, she noted the time and peeled off, finding her way to a particular café that sold kebabs. This was the place that had been described to her. In the corner sat a man matching Agent Wallace Simon's description. Medium height, sturdy build, dark crew cut, fortyish.

She walked up to his table and spoke the code phrase. "Excuse me, but is the food good here?"

"It is if you like Turkish food," the man replied, looking up from his plate.

"And if you don't like Turkish food?"

"Then it's even better."

Kori smiled. "Hello, I'm Briggs."

"Simon," the man said, holding out his hand. "Please, sit. Want some of this? Chicken and beef. They give you way too much here. How am I supposed to eat it all?"

"No, thanks. It looks great, but I had a big breakfast. Although the next time they come around, maybe I'll order some baklava. Something sweet might hit the spot."

"Done." Simon waved to an employee who

came right over. "Murat, can you get my friend here some of your tasty baklava, please?"

"Of course, Mr. Simon," said the employee and off he went to retrieve the dessert.

"I eat here all the time," said Simon. "Good people and good food. So, Evan Banks told me about your fellow agent in San Francisco. I'm very sorry. When you lose an agent, it's hard not to take it personally."

"Thank you. Yes, it's an assault on all of us, isn't it?"

Simon nodded. "Well, I'm sure you want to talk about the letter. Obviously, it represents a very real threat. It's fortunate that our informant was able to snare it. My hope is that you guys have the time to figure out who the intended recipient is before the attack, whatever it is, gets launched."

"And do you have any ideas as to whom it was intended for?"

"Not really. We know the sender was most likely Arash Nasirian. Ah, here's your baklava. Thank you, Murat."

"Yes, thank you," said Kori, digging into the sweet pastry. "Yes, Agent Banks mentioned the consul general."

"Yep. That's Nasirian. The letter came from his

desk. Our guy on the inside spotted it and took it more or less impulsively. It was in an envelope marked 'confidential.' He routinely looks for such correspondence. Perhaps Agent Banks told you about Hajar's relationship with us."

"He did."

"He's been helpful with little bits of information before, but nothing like this. Needless to say, he did not expect to come across a letter of such gravity."

"No, of course not. I'd like to talk to Hajar if I could."

"I'm sure. Unfortunately, that might be difficult, Agent Briggs."

"Yes, I know, Hajar is fearful of being found out. I can certainly understand his reluctance. But I can make our meeting a safe one. He'll have no reason to be afraid."

"Well, it's not just that. You see, Hajar has been missing for at least the past two days."

"Missing?"

"Yes. I tried to contact him the day after he had handed me the letter. I was on my way to Vancouver and I called him from the airport. The call went to voicemail. I didn't think much of it, but then I tried to call him later that day, on my way back. And the next day. And this morning. Same result each time. Before my meeting here with you, I went by Hajar's apartment. It was dark. Then I disguised my voice and called the consulate and asked for him."

"And?"

"And nobody there has seen him."

"I see," Kori said, frowning. "Is there anywhere else he might be? A relative's or friend's house? Maybe some place he goes to get away from things?"

"Not really. In fact, the person who answered the phone at the consulate seemed surprised he wasn't there. He hadn't spoken to anybody at the consulate in the time that he's been missing and he told nobody of any plans to go anywhere."

"That doesn't sound good."

"No, it certainly doesn't."

"You mentioned his apartment. Did you go in?"

"No, and I'm afraid I can't, Agent Briggs. It's out of my jurisdiction, I'm afraid. The Turkish authorities, as you might imagine, take a rather dim view of foreigners breaking into the homes of visiting diplomats and their staff members. Not to mention the way it would reflect on my country if the Iranians discovered I broke into the home of an Irani national. I have good contacts with the Turkish police, but I have no authority. It's not like I can request a warrant."

"I see what you mean," said Kori. "Then would you mind giving me the address, Agent Simon? I have no such restrictions."

Simon raised his eyebrows. "Really, Agent Briggs? I can't imagine things would reflect any better on the US if you got caught breaking into Hajar's apartment."

"True. Perhaps restrictions was the wrong word. I suppose I should say I have no qualms."

"And why not?"

"Because I don't intend to get caught breaking in, Agent Simon."

Agent Simon smiled, appreciating the brashness, and gave Kori the address.

CHAPTER 9

Hajar's apartment was a fifteen-minute walk from the Grand Bazaar through crowded streets that wound past small shops and cafés. Kori was grateful for the directional app on her phone. The apartment was on the top floor of a four-story building that spanned half a city block, with a travel agency, laundromat, and tiny market on the first floor with a big Coca-Cola sign out front. Across the street was a café with outdoor seating. The wonderful aromas wafting in the air from the café were enough to make Kori forget she'd had breakfast and baklava.

She stopped into the café and ordered a bottled water from the counter from where she could get a good viewing angle of the apartment building.

"Something for lunch, Miss?" asked the man behind the counter in broken English, taking Kori's money.

"Just the water, thanks," said Kori, looking beyond the man, sizing things up across the street.

The man frowned. "We have open tables and great food."

"Yes, I'm sure you do. Thank you, perhaps later."

The man shrugged, handed Kori the water, and went off back to the kitchen. From Kori's vantage point, she could see a door between the travel agency and the market, and the windows above it revealed a stairwell. The doorway was obviously the entrance to the upstairs apartment units. But the door had an electronic lock. With nobody around, Kori would have had no problem getting past the lock, but several people were standing just outside the market and there were other pedestrians strolling along the street. Maybe nobody would notice her. Then again, maybe somebody would.

Kori walked down a block, crossed the street, and then walked a block to a deserted alleyway that led behind the apartments. She scurried down the alley to the back of the building where she spied a rear entrance with a simple keylock. It was always this way. Front doors always had the most security. Back doors were treated as afterthoughts by the owners of buildings, as if nobody would ever think to gain access via the rear of a building. Kori pulled a lockpick out of her purse and was inside in seconds. She hesitated for a moment at the bottom of the back stairwell, listening. Hearing nothing, she treaded softly up the steps to the fourth floor. She looked up and down the hallway and saw nobody. Then she scampered two doors down to Hajar's apartment, picked the lock, and made her way inside.

The apartment was small. One bedroom, a small living room, a cramped kitchen, and a tiny bathroom. Kori wondered what kind of expense accounts Iranian consulate workers were given. Then again, apartments in this part of Istanbul weren't cheap.

Kori looked around, not entirely sure what she was looking for. The apartment was neat and tidy and everything seemed in place. There were no signs that a struggle had taken place and no signs that anybody had broken in. Family pictures rested on an end table next to the sofa. The near wall was adorned with a montage of classic Persian miniature paintings. Next to a chair, Kori noticed a briefcase. Opening it, she found various notes and files but nothing that told her anything. No doubt this was Hajar's day-to-day briefcase, filled with the typical items a person working in a consulate office might be expected to have. But then again, that told her everything. Why was this briefcase in the apartment and not with Hajar? He hadn't been seen in days. The people he worked with had expected him to report to work and he hadn't. And wherever he'd gone, he'd left behind a briefcase of information vital to his work.

Kori searched the bedroom. Dresser drawers were filled with clothes. A closet of hanging clothes seemed undisturbed. Two suitcases sat empty on the floor of the closet. Hajar clearly hadn't planned on going anywhere. If this were the United States, Kori's next action would have been obvious. Canvas the building, ask the other tenants if they saw anything suspicious, if they noticed any strangers coming up to Hajar's apartment, or heard any odd noises in the night. But this wasn't the States. Kori wasn't supposed to be there. Wallace Simon was right; an American intelligence agent being disco-vered breaking into an Iranian citizen's apartment in Istanbul, Turkey, would no doubt create an international incident.

Then Kori heard some commotion coming from downstairs. She sidled up to the front window of the apartment and looked down to see two Turkish police cars parked in the street, blocking the traffic. Had someone spotted her breaking into the building? Impossible. Nobody had seen her pick the back lock. Plus, the police had arrived too quickly. This had to be a coincidence, but why were they there?

She heard footsteps coming up the stairwell. In a flash, she exited the apartment, locking the door behind her. She dashed down the hallway to the opposite end where a window led out to a fire escape on the side of the building. She slid the window open and stepped up and through, out to the fire escape. She ducked down and then carefully peered back through the window. Three police officers were lumbering down the hallway toward Hajar's apartment. She watched as they tried the lock, then one of the officers kicked open the door and all three entered.

Kori looked down toward the street from the fire escape hoping nobody had noticed her up there. Luckily, it was the side of the building away from the café. Down below she noticed a couple of passersby, but from four floors down, they didn't see her. She waited until they were out of sight and then she climbed down as far as the metal fire escape led, several feet above the ground. From there, she dropped and rolled and then regained her feet. Then, rather than walk in the opposite direction from the apartment building, she walked in front of it. Kori knew that had someone seen her clambering down the fire escape, and assumed she was a burglar or worse, they would not have believed her so bold as to stick around. A guilty person would have run off in the face of the police presence.

In fact, Kori made for the café.

"I've changed my mind," she said to the man behind the counter. "I think I'll take a table after all. Maybe that one, toward the street?"

From her table at the café, looking back over at the apartment building, Kori watched as the police officers began stringing crime scene tape around the entrance. Soon, another police vehicle stopped by, this one a van.

"Excuse me," Kori said to a waiter. "Do you speak English?"

"Yes," the waiter nodded.

"Can you tell me what it says on that police van

across the street?"

"Yes, Miss, it says 'crime scene investigation.'"

"Thanks very much."

"Something to eat?"

"Oh, um, yes, the shawarma wrap, please." Kori wasn't especially hungry, but she needed the vantage point of the table. What were crime scene investigators doing in Hajar's apartment? She knew they'd find nothing there. Nothing, that is, but Kori's fingerprints. Had she known the place was going to be searched by the police, she would have been more careful.

She thought for a moment and then pulled out her phone and called Wallace Simon. "Agent Simon, you said you had contacts with the Turkish police."

"Sure. Why, what's going on? Did you get into Hajar's apartment?"

"Well, that's just it. I searched the place, but couldn't find anything except evidence that Hajar had not intended to go anywhere. His briefcase is still there, clothes, toiletries, suitcases, everything. If he took a vacation, it certainly wasn't planned. But here's where it gets interesting. Right now I'm sitting at a café across the street and watching while Turkish police are searching the place themselves."

"The police?"

"Yes. In fact, they brought out a crime scene investigation unit. I barely got out of the apartment myself before they came storming in."

"What would a CSI unit be doing there?"

"That's what I was hoping you could tell me."

"Okay, sit tight. Let me make a phone call and see what I can find out."

"Thanks, Agent Simon. I'll be here waiting on your call."

Kori's wrap arrived and she chewed on it while watching the activities across the street. The police cars soon pulled away, leaving only the CSI van. Finding no immediate threat, the police presence was no longer needed. Now it was up to the investigation team to investigate…what exactly? What crime did the police believe occurred in Hajar's apartment? What would have made them decide to enter the residence of an Iranian consulate employee? Shortly, Kori's phone rang and she had her answer.

"They found Hajar this morning," said Simon. "Dead."

"Oh, no."

"In fact, worse than dead. He'd been tortured. Several of his fingers were broken. There were cigarette burns on his body, too."

"Good God. Where did they find him?"

"On the outskirts of the city. He'd been dead for several days."

"Well, that explains the police activity at his place."

"Yes. They're looking for clues no doubt."

"I don't think they'll find much. There was no sign of a struggle or anything. If someone came by to nab him, he must have gone with them voluntarily."

"Or perhaps at gunpoint."

"Yes, perhaps," said Kori. "Either way, it seems pretty clear who killed him, doesn't it? Now we have our answer as to how the Iranians put it together that you had the letter and that you'd delivered it to Agent Banks."

"They tortured it out of Hajar."

"Looks that way."

"Damn."

"His fears came true. They knew about him. They knew he'd been operating as a spy for the West and it cost him his life."

"Yep. Well, I guess I'd better get a hold of Agent Banks and tell him the news. Damn shame. Hajar was a good man, just trying to do the right thing."

Kori thought of Evan, distraught over the loss

of his American friend Dane Reinhart. And now, just a couple of days later, he'd be hearing about the death of an Iranian agent he'd often worked with.

"Be gentle," said Kori. "It won't be easy for him."

"Of course. Tough racket we're in, huh? So what are you going to do now, Agent Briggs?"

"Well, I'm going to finish my wrap and then take the next logical step in my investigation."

"And what might that be?"

"I only wish I knew, Agent Simon. I only wish I knew."

CHAPTER 10

Actually, Kori did know the next logical step. It came to her before she finished her lunch at the café across from Hajar's apartment. The consul general. Arash Nasirian. That's the man whose desk the letter had come from in the first place, the man who knew the details of the plan to attack the United States, the man Kori needed to investigate. And the man who knew how high up the order to implement the attack went. Did he create the plan? Did the plan come from his boss at the embassy in Ankara? From Tehran? From the supreme leader of

Iran?

Kori looked at her watch—3:30 p.m. Istanbul time. In Washington, it was 8:30 a.m. She pulled her phone out and called Director Eaglethorpe.

"Agent Briggs," he said, "what have you learned?"

"Not much. The informant was tortured and killed. So we know how it is that the Iranians learned of our discovery of the letter. The informant must have spilled the beans about giving the letter to Simon and of his handing it to Banks. The Iranians most likely tracked Banks to San Francisco and then had Reinhart killed once he acquired the letter."

"By an American neo-Nazi?"

"Yeah, I know, Chief, that part still doesn't make much sense. Well, you asked what I'd learned and, in my defense, I started out by saying 'not much.'"

"True."

"What about Vasquez? Has he turned up anything more?"

"Not really. He's identified a few more names of Guardian Militia members, but none of them seem to be around. And apparently Johnny Gardner isn't saying anything at all from his cell in San Francisco."

"Well, I'm going to start following the consul general, Arash Nasirian. He's the key, after all."

"Good idea. But be careful, Kori. These guys are

playing for keeps."

"I will, Chief. In the meantime, can you get Cooper to run a profile on Nasirian? Any information from our computer database would be helpful."

"Absolutely. I'll have him text you everything we've got."

"Thanks, Chief. And I'll call as soon as I learn something here."

"Please do, Agent Briggs. Let's see if we can increase our level of knowledge at least a step or two above 'not much.'"

"Roger that, Chief."

Kori hung up, threw a few lira down on the table as a tip, and then made her way back to the Hotel Amira where her room was finally ready. Time was of the essence, but she desperately needed a shower and, more importantly, a change of clothes. She knew she looked too much like an American. She needed clothes that were more subdued. Istanbul was a fairly liberal city by Middle Eastern standards, but if she wanted to follow an Iranian official around, she didn't want to stand out in any way. Anticipating this possibility, she had packed a long skirt and a loose blouse. She decided that she'd put her hair up, too, and cover her head with a scarf.

The hot shower felt good. A power nap would

have felt even better, but Kori was anxious to get started. The room had a coffee maker and the caffeine would have to substitute for the nap. In the meantime, Cooper had texted a secure link that led Kori to a dossier on Consul General Arash Nasirian. It was scant, a basic description and some general details about his background. There was a photograph, too, so at least Kori knew what he looked like. Nasirian had a long beard and was tall—six-five, and slender.

She dressed and was soon back out on the streets of Istanbul, this time walking toward the Iranian consulate. Fifteen minutes later, she was standing across the street from it. **Now what?** she thought.

The building, a stately neoclassical structure that looked more like something one would see in Washington, took up most of the block. The property was surrounded by a security fence and Kori noticed the requisite cameras. She walked lazily and inconspicuously around the block and decided the back entrance was most likely where Nasirian would exit. That seemed to be the employee entrance, while the general public, anyone who had business with the Iranian consulate, entered and exited through the front.

It was now late in the day and before long, Kori

observed employees of the consulate leaving the building. She sat on a bench across the street from the rear of the building and watched as they passed. A half hour went by. Then forty-five minutes. Nobody who looked like Nasirian had left. An hour and a half later, people stopped coming out altogether. Had she missed him? Was there another exit she hadn't noticed? Was he working late? Kori waited one more hour, until the building looked empty. **Damn**, she thought.

In Cooper's dossier, there was information about Nasirian's home in Tehran, but there was nothing about where his residence was in Istanbul. Kori had no idea where to look for him next. Tossing the matter around in her head, she finally came to the conclusion that her only hope would be to talk to Nasirian's counterpart in the American consulate. Certainly, they would know of Nasirian. Maybe they could shed some light on his where-abouts. But the American consulate would be closed now too. Kori was stuck at a dead end for the day.

Now there was nothing left to do but trudge back to the hotel for dinner. Not the worst thing in the world. The hotel had a rooftop bar that overlooked the Marmara Sea. If she hurried, she could make it in time for sunset.

Along the way, her phone buzzed with a text message: **Thinking about you. Hope all is well in Istanbul. Agent Simon called to fill me in and he told me about Hajar. Be careful, Kori.**

Evan Banks. Kori smiled. It was nice to know she'd been in Evan's thoughts. She'd had a few passing thoughts about him, too. **I will,** she texted back. **Sorry about Hajar. Hope you're doing well.**

I'm okay, came the reply. **But please keep me posted.**

I will, Kori promised. **Let's stay in touch. Okay?**

I'd like that, Kori. Very much.

Me, too, Evan, Kori texted back. **Very much.**

Kori finally made it to the rooftop bar for dinner and a drink, where it occurred to her that the view of the sunset was even better than she had imagined it was going to be.

The next morning, Kori was in the lobby of the US consulate just as it opened. She'd called Eaglethorpe the night before, who'd called his contacts at the

State Department. The US consul general was expecting her visit.

"Hello, you must be Ms. Briggs," said the consul general coming out to greet her in the lobby. "I'm Marsha Rose." Marsha Rose, in her early forties, was a curvy woman with ash brown hair and a kind smile.

"Hello, Ms. Rose. Thank you for seeing me."

"Not at all. Please call me Marsha. Come on back to my office, won't you?" She ushered Kori down the hallway to the far corner office and gestured to a chair in front of her desk. They both sat down. "Now, what can I do for you? It's not often we get a call from as high up in the State Department as the one I got first thing this morning. You can imagine my concern. What's the situation and how can I help?"

"Well, to be honest, Marsha, we have a bit of a security threat that we're investigating."

"Oh, I see. And I'm sorry, who did you say you were with? The CIA?"

"Well, something like that. I'm with a US-based intelligence agency."

"And what can you tell me about this...security threat? Something here, in Istanbul?"

"No, actually, we believe the US homeland is at

risk from some sort of attack."

"Oh, my."

"Yes, but, you see, we think the source of the threat is here. With the Iranian consulate, in fact."

"The Iranians?"

"Yes, possibly, although we don't know how high up the ladder it goes. All we know is that the consul general, a man by the name of Arash Nasirian is involved. Do you know him?"

"Well, yes, I know **of** him. As you might guess, we don't often socialize with members of the Iranian consulate. Nevertheless, there are get-togethers from time to time between consulates. Some formal, some informal. Sometimes we have business with another consulate. Naturally, there are receptions and dinners and the like. The foreign service world is kind of a small one, as you may imagine. We bump into each other from time to time. We're all away from our homes, of course, and we all have that much in common if nothing else."

"Of course. Well, can you tell me anything about Nasirian? Where he lives. Where he goes. Where he eats. Anything at all would be helpful. We need to follow his movements. I need to know who he's in contact with, who else might be involved in this scheme we've uncovered."

"I see."

"I might even need to take him into custody and question him."

"Oh, my," said the consul general, suddenly looking alarmed. "Take him into custody, did you say? Ms. Briggs, I must say, that's a pretty bold plan. You'd need permission from no less than the secretary of state. Maybe even the president. Even if you could to it, I don't exactly see how you could get the consul general to cooperate with any kind of questioning. In fact, Ms. Briggs, I think Iran might consider that an act of, dare I say, war!"

Until now, Marsha Rose seemed interested and cooperative. Kori realized that she might have gone too far with the mention of taking Nasirian, but she needed to impress upon the consul general how serious the matter was. And, truthfully, taking Nasirian into custody was not a strategy Kori had ruled out. She could do it because Rampart operated in the shadows. Nobody would be able to legally tie an abduction of the consul general to the US because by any outward appearance, Rampart didn't exist. Kori Briggs was not an agent of the United States, she was the senior VP of Gladstone Conveyor. There would be a lot of questions asked and accusations made, but the legal grounds for war would be missing. From a practical standpoint, that didn't matter, of course. Wars start without legal grounds all the time, but in the court of world opinion, perhaps necessary for the building of a coalition of allies, deniability was paramount and the US would be able to deny they knew anything at all about the unfortunate seizure of the Iranian consul general.

"Rest assured," Kori said, "that if it came to that, Marsha, America would not be implicated. I would be acting on my own authority."

"Ms. Briggs," said the consul general in a very serious tone.

"Kori."

"Ms. Briggs, I have to advise you as your official government representative while you're here in Istanbul, that I cannot let you harbor such ideas. You're going down a very dangerous road, it seems to me. My role, among others, is diplomacy. I am the ambassador's representative here in Istanbul. As such, the cordial relations between foreign countries and ourselves is of the utmost importance to me. Not to mention one of my top responsibilities, in a very legal sense, mind you. Truthfully, based on what you've just told me, it's probably within my power to detain you. If it weren't for the fact that you were sent here by the State Department, I'd be tempted to do just that!"

Kori smiled as warmly as she could. She needed the cooperation of Consul General Marsha Rose. "Please don't get the wrong idea, Marsha. It's not my intention to violate any international protocols. I appreciate your position and I'm not here to ruffle any feathers. Did I say, 'take into custody'? Perhaps, that was a bit strong."

Marsha Rose looked only slightly relieved.

Kori needed to make her understand. "Marsha, may I read to you the letter that we intercepted that came from Nasirian?" She pulled a copy out of her purse and recited the directive: "Plan of attack approved. US to suffer, to feel our wrath. On its own soil. The Great Satan will fall to its knees. Proceed when reasonable to do so."

"Oh, my," said the consul general.

"Do you see, Marsha? I'm interested in cordial relations just as much as the next person. But if anybody is flirting with an act of war, it's the Iranians. But it's not just an **act** of war. What they're proposing, Marsha, **is** war."

"My goodness. How did you come by that letter?"

"It's a long story. But two people are dead because of it. Nasirian no doubt knows the letter was intercepted and has certainly sent another. Whomever the order was intended for is even now working toward carrying it out. And it could come at any time." Kori leaned forward. "I need to find Nasirian. Can you help me, Marsha?"

Marsha Rose softened. "Well, of course, I'll do what I can. Obviously, the letter puts a different slant on things, doesn't it?"

"Indeed it does."

"It's Kori, yes?"

"Yes."

"Well, Kori, for starters, I doubt you'll find Nasirian on the grounds of the consulate building."

"No?"

"No, you see they run their consulate a little differently than we run ours. Consul general is considered kind of a plum position by the Iranians, more so than we regard it. Such positions typically go to well-connected people. And, I should say, specifically, to well-connected men. Women aren't too highly regarded in Iran, as you probably know. The positions you and I hold? They'd be filled by men. Did you know that women represent less than 20 percent of the Iranian workforce?"

"I figured it was probably something like that."

"Well, anyway, the positions come without

much of a workload for the consulate officers. The day-to-day stuff is considered beneath them. They delegate practically everything. Nasirian probably makes a consulate appearance once or twice a month."

"I see. So if I won't find him at the consulate, would you happen to know where he resides?"

"No, but I can probably find out. Let me think…" Marsha looked off into the distance for a second and then continued. "How about this? I can call the consulate and ask for Nasirian's home address, telling them that we're sending out personal invitations to some reception that we'll be hosting next month. I'll say the occasion is for some visiting dignitary or something. It really won't matter. The Iranians never attend these things anyway. But I'll bet they'll give me his address."

"That sounds excellent, Marsha. Would you do that, please?"

"Are you really going to kidnap him, Kori?"

"No, Marsha, I don't think so. I'll start with some basic surveillance. He won't even know he's being followed."

"Well, I know you have to do whatever you have to do to keep our nation safe, but I must admit it's a relief to hear that. When I joined the foreign service, it was never my intention to get dragged into a dangerous diplomatic crisis. Truthfully, I just wanted to see other parts of the world."

"Of course."

Marsha reached for the phone and punched a button for her secretary. "Could you put me through to the Iranian consulate, please?" In a few moments, she was conversing with the receptionist there, exchanging pleasantries and then asking for Nasirian's address for the bogus reception invite. "Oh, I see," she said. "And you have no idea when he'll be back? Okay. I understand. Well, thank you very much." Marsha hung up.

"Nasirian's gone?" Kori asked.

"Yes, I'm afraid so. He's been ordered to the embassy in Ankara. It came rather suddenly and the receptionist made it seem as if the move might be permanent."

"Interesting."

"What do you suppose it means, Kori?"

"Well, my hunch is that it means the plot goes higher up than Nasirian. The embassy is closer to the top in the governmental hierarchy than the consulate. It also means I'll be taking the next flight to Ankara." Kori rose and offered her hand. "I appreciate your help, Marsha."

"Of course. Good luck to you, Kori."

"Thanks, Marsha. I have a feeling I'm going to need it."

CHAPTER 11

Kori went back to her hotel, packed a small bag, and took a taxi to the airport. Ankara was an hour flight from Istanbul on Pegasus Airlines. While waiting in the gate area, she called Eaglethorpe and briefed him on the latest.

"Well, obviously, the right move is surveilling Nasirian," Eaglethorpe said, "no matter where he goes. But how, Agent Briggs? How are you going to locate him? And what exactly are we hoping to find?"

"Good questions, Chief. To which I'm not sure

I have answers. I guess I'll stake out the embassy and follow him from there. Maybe I can break in after hours and—"

"Break into the Iranian embassy in the capital of Turkey?" Eaglethorpe interrupted.

"Well…sure."

"Kori, why don't you just fly to Kentucky and break into Fort Knox?"

Kori chuckled. "So you're saying it would be difficult, Chief?"

"That's what I'm saying."

"Well, then maybe I'll find where he's staying. Look, the thing is, we know that Nasirian is somehow affiliated with this crazy, American, neo-Nazi group, right?"

"That's the working theory, preposterous as it seems."

"Well, then, I guess what I'm looking for is a name. There's got to be someone he's in contact with. The intended recipient of the letter. Presumably, an American who is, somehow or other, affiliated with the Guardian Militia."

"Agreed. But that letter comes with its own set of problems. For example, have you thought about why Nasirian used a letter as the means of communication in the first place?"

WE'LL QUIT WHEN WE'RE DEAD

"Sure, what Cooper said. For credibility. To provide an official sanction to the attack."

"Well, that's why the message is on official government letterhead, but that doesn't explain sending a letter. Why not email? Why send a letter 5,000 miles around the world from Istanbul to Grand Rapids, Michigan?"

"Email is too easy to hack. There are a lot of servers that an email has to bounce through to get that far. Or...," Kori started.

"Or what, Agent Briggs?"

"Well, I was just thinking, Chief. Iran keeps a pretty tight lid on the internet. It's not easy for the Iranian people to access very much, mostly just government-sanctioned sites. I'd bet they extend those restrictions to their government employees, except maybe for the real higher-ups. Consul general in a foreign city is a nice position, I'm sure, but let's face it, Nasirian isn't exactly a member of the Parliament or the Guardian Council. Let alone a member of the supreme leader's inner circle. He's just a cog in the wheel."

"So what are you saying?"

"Well, Nasirian knows his electronic communications are most certainly monitored, right?"

"Sure."

"So he didn't send the directive via email, because he didn't want his superiors to know about it."

"Because they're not involved," Eaglethorpe said, finishing the train of thought.

"Exactly. Nasirian is a loose cannon, Chief. This isn't an Iranian plot after all. Nasirian must represent some outside faction."

"Well, that would be nice to think. Nobody wants to go to war with Iran. But we can't afford to jump to that conclusion just yet. We have to consider all possibilities. You might have been right when you said that Nasirian would have been concerned about getting hacked from someone outside of Iran. Hell, he knows our CIA has the capability of doing that."

"True."

"But here's another question. Let's say the letter was, in fact, meant for someone with the Guardian Militia. Was Nasirian really just going to send it through the mail? What, drop it off at a Turkish post office? Put it in a Federal Express envelope? Send it all the way to Michigan?"

"Yeah, that seems kind of inefficient, Chief. And risky. What if it got lost somewhere along the line?"

"Maybe he was going to hand it off to someone.

Someone locally who would personally carry it to its destination. That would make more sense."

"Right, Chief. Or someone locally who's off the grid, or at least operating under the radar. Someone who could relay the message back to the States electronically without having to worry about their communications being monitored or hacked. Heck, they probably could have sent it on to its final destination via text message."

"Then that's the contact you need to find, Kori. That local person, whoever he is."

"Right. The thing is, he's probably here in Istanbul where the consulate is and where Nasirian was, at least up until very recently. But I would have no idea how to find him. I'm going to have to go to Ankara, locate Nasirian, try to somehow find the name of his contact, and then come back here to Istanbul. Good thing I kept my hotel room. Chief, when I get home I'm going to need to talk to you about a raise."

"I'll keep that in mind. But your sentiment is not without merit. Your job won't be easy, Kori. And it might be dangerous. I don't like the idea of you investigating Nasirian and his potential contact all alone. I'm going to send you some help. I'll have another agent rendezvous with you in Ankara."

"Chief, that's not necessary. I've got this. Really."

"No arguing, Agent Briggs. You need backup."

"Well, who are you going to send?"

"I don't know. I'll think about it and let you know. Now get on that plane. Time is wasting."

"Roger, Chief."

"And Kori?"

"Yes, Chief?"

"Be careful."

"Yes, Chief."

After touching down in Ankara, Kori took a cab to the Lugal, an upscale hotel a mere seven-minute walk from the Iranian embassy. It was luxurious plus convenient, and Kori appreciated the former every bit as much as the latter. She dropped off her bag in her room, realized she needed sustenance, and went looking for lunch. She didn't have to look far. The hotel's restaurant served a lamb loin in a plum sauce. Kori washed it down with an Efes Pilsen beer, a Turkish number that hit the spot.

Afterward, she walked to the embassy, a four-story structure that resembled a modern office building, but the crash bollards and security fencing indicated it was more than that.

It was hot and dry in Ankara, the sky a deep, cloudless blue. Kori circled the embassy a few times hoping, by some remote chance, that she'd spot Nasirian coming or going. At one point, she received a text from Eaglethorpe advising her that a Rampart agent would rendezvous with her at the Lugal in three hours. He didn't say who, but Kori was sure it would be Agent Pratt out of Bulgaria. She tried to remember what she knew about him. She'd met him only once, three years before on a case in Montenegro. Decent enough agent, but a bit overbearing, as Kori recalled. He liked to call the shots. She was going to have to remind him that this case was hers. She'd followed it from San Francisco to Vancouver to Washington to Istanbul to Ankara. She didn't need anyone jumping in as quarterback at this point.

Deciding that Nasirian's sudden appearance at the embassy would be something of a miracle, she decided to kill some time before Pratt showed up. Once he arrived, she would organize some sort of surveillance plan for the two of them. If he was going to tag along, he might as well be useful. The embassy had front and rear exits. An agent could be stationed at each. But there was nothing to be done now, so she flagged down a cab and took a drive to the oldest part of Ankara.

Ankara was a vibrant, urban capital city. As cosmopolitan as Istanbul, if not more so, it was a richly cultural city. There were a lot of art museums and theaters, and the Presidential Symphony Orchestra made its home there. But it was also an ancient city. Archaeological sites were commonplace. Kori's cab ride went from modern highway to stone road, ending at Ankara Castle, a historic fortification built by the Phrygians in the eighth century BC and resting on a rocky hilltop with panoramic views of the city. Kori idled away a couple of hours at the castle, wandering around the small village within its walls, checking out the shops, and then climbing the ancient stone steps to the top of the castle to take in the view of the city below and all around.

Eventually, she took a cab back to the Lugal for her meeting with Pratt. It was now late in the day. In the lobby bar, Kori ordered another Efes Pilsen to quench her thirst from the afternoon and waited for a text telling her where, exactly, Pratt would meet her. She picked up the bar menu, thinking that an appetizer might be in order. That was just about the time she heard a familiar Russian voice behind her.

"Ah, my American friend," the woman's voice said. "I knew I would find you at the bar."

CHAPTER 12

"Anya!" said Kori, embracing the petite but taut, athletic blond.

"Hello, Kori," smiled Anya Kovalev, Russian-born Rampart agent stationed in Moscow. The two had recently worked together and had quickly become close and trusted friends.

"You? You're the agent I'm to rendezvous with?"

"Yes. I got a call from Director Eaglethorpe and raced to the airport. Turkish Airlines has a three-hour direct flight that I was able to jump on. Director Eaglethorpe suggested that my arrival here might make for a nice surprise."

"It sure does. You're a sight for sore eyes. I was thinking I'd be working with our guy who operates out of Bulgaria. I much prefer you, my Russian friend."

"And for my part, I know that if it is a case that Kori Briggs is involved with, it is certain to be an exciting one. Perhaps too exciting? Yes, probably. But this is a risk I am willing to take."

"Well, pull up a barstool and let me fill you in. First round on me. Beer?"

"Hmm…no, I believe I am in the mood for a raki."

"Raki?"

Anya waved over the bartender. "Two rakis, please." The bartender nodded. "Do you remember the araks we had in Tel Aviv, Kori?"

"I do indeed."

"Raki is a similar drink. It is made of twice-distilled grapes and anise. It is Turkey's national drink, you know."

"As a matter of fact, I did not know."

"You Americans," Anya said, smiling and shaking her head.

Kori laughed. "Okay, so maybe I don't know as

much as you about the alcohols of the world, but I do know how to drink them."

"Agreed. That I would not argue with, my friend. So tell me about this case."

"Love to. But what do you say we order something to eat first, to go along with the rakis?"

"No objection from me. I am famished. Nothing was served on the plane, of course."

"Of course. Well, I see they have wood-fired pizza here. Mediterranean style. One with Eastern Anatolian cheeses and fresh local mushrooms."

"Then why are we not eating it?" smiled Anya.

"Why, indeed? Oh, sir? We'll have your pizza. The one with the cheeses and the mushrooms. Oh, and you might as well bring two more rakis, if you'd be so kind."

Over pizza, Kori filled Anya in on everything from Reinhart's murder to Nasirian's presumed presence at the Iranian embassy.

"But the connection with the American neo-Nazi group," said Anya, "this is puzzling, no?"

"Yes, it sure is. Strange partnership, huh? We still can't be sure that it's not some crazy coincidence."

"So what is the plan from here?"

"Well, I figure just good old-fashioned surveillance. Gumshoe stuff."

"Sorry?"

"An old American expression for detective."

"Ah."

"Anyway, we'll camp out at the embassy. You can observe the back entrance, I'll observe the front. We'll get there first thing in the morning and watch for Nasirian, make sure he goes in. Then we can tail him when he leaves. We'll follow him to wherever he's staying. Then, hopefully he'll leave his place for dinner or something and we can search it. Or we'll search it after he's gone to sleep. We need to find the name of the contact. The person Nasirian delivered the letter to. That contact is either the American who's at the center of this strange partnership, or the person who relayed the letter to him. Either way, it gets us a step closer to unraveling this thing."

"Sounds good, my friend. And I suppose there is nothing we can do tonight?"

"Sure there is."

"And what is that?"

"Finish this pizza and order another round of rakis."

Back in her hotel room, tired and in need of sleep, Kori nevertheless knew she had no choice but to call her mother. It was early evening back home and she would no doubt be wondering how Kori was making out on her trip.

"How's St. Louis?" Joan Briggs asked in a smiling voice.

Kori did a quick check on her weather app. Eighty-six degrees in St. Louis. Thunderstorms in the vicinity. "It's a little warm here, Mom, and it looks like it might rain. How are things there?"

"Warm here, too, honey. How's the installation going?"

"Oh, you know, same old stuff. The normal glitches. Nothing ever really seems to go smoothly. But I guess that's why I'm here, after all."

"You sound tired, dear."

"Do I? Well, I suppose I am a little tired." She checked her watch: 2 a.m. in Ankara. "I think I'll probably turn in early tonight."

"That sounds like a good idea."

"Is anything new there, Mom?"

"Not really. Tomorrow is book club. Nancy called to tell me that Dorthea told her that she might not be coming. Can you believe that? Isn't that just like Dorthea? She made some excuse to Nancy, but I think it's because she's just not the team player that I think we need in the club. Well, she can miss all the book club meetings from now on, as far as I'm concerned."

Kori let her mother ramble until her eyes started to close. Finally, she shook herself awake enough to say, "Mom, listen, I think my boss is trying to call me. I better hang up now. Could be important. I'll call you in a day or so."

"Okay, dear. And do get some rest."

"I will, Mom. Love you. Bye."

Then Kori hung up and let herself fall into a deep sleep.

First thing in the morning, well-rested on a few short hours of slumber and having downed a cup of black Turkish coffee, Kori met Anya in the hotel lobby and the pair walked to the Iranian embassy.

"Remember, Anya," she said along the way, "tall, thin guy. Long beard."

"Right. I have his photo. But my concern is getting close enough to make out his face. The embassy is very secure, is it not? I am sure we cannot just loiter at the doorways."

"Concern yourself no more. Here." Kori pulled an eyeglass case out of her purse and handed it to Anya. "Try these."

Anya opened the case. "Sunglasses?"

"Not quite. Try them on."

Anya put the glasses on. "Okay. Sunglasses."

"Now press the little button on the side."

"Aha! Binoculars!"

"Yep. A little something Cooper and Foster conjured up. There are three settings with that button, each one bringing things another ten times closer."

Looking off into the distance, Anya played around with the button. "Wow. Impressive."

"And here. Take this little brooch."

"Oh, thank you. A turquoise butterfly. How thoughtful."

"Don't get carried away, Anya. I have one too. It's a microphone and receiver. We can keep in constant contact with each other. It's good for several hundred yards."

"Nevertheless, it is quite charming in its own right."

"Isn't it? Butterflies are my favorite. It's another Cooper and Foster creation. But they wanted it in

WE'LL QUIT WHEN WE'RE DEAD

the shape of a frog. Can you imagine?"

"Men."

"I know, right?"

"And you thought to bring two pairs of sunglasses and two brooches with you to Ankara?"

"I was a Girl Scout, Anya. Our motto was 'be prepared.'"

"Good motto."

The two split up with Kori heading to the front of the building, Anya toward the rear. Across the street from the front entrance, Kori found a small grassy rise and sat beside a tree that gave her a decent view and a little cover. Across the street that ran along the rear of the building, Anya found a small coffee shop and took a table with a window view of the embassy's back entrance.

Kori tilted her head down toward the brooch. "Anya, do you read?"

"I read, Kori. You are coming in perfectly."

"How's your view back there?"

"Very good. I am at a coffee shop that looks over at the back entrance."

"Coffee shop? Damn. I knew I should have taken the back entrance."

"They have scones here, too."

"Of course they do."

Before long, embassy employees began filtering into the building, some in through the back door where the parking was located. Most, however, entered through the front door. Kori noticed the entrance was just fifty yards or so from a bus stop.

"Anya," said Kori, "I think regular staff members go in through the front. There's a bus stop close by. The higher-ups, with vehicles or drivers, probably access the rear where the parking is."

"Yes, I think you are right," came Anya's reply. "Nasirian is probably one of those who will come my way."

"Yes, I would assume so."

Sure enough, fifteen minutes later, a black Mercedes SUV bearing a pair of Iranian flags on the hood pulled into the back parking lot and cruised up to the rear door. Sliding out of the back seat was a tall, thin man with a long beard. Through her binocular sunglasses, Anya could make out the face.

"It's him," she said.

"Nasirian?"

"Yes, his car just pulled up."

"Okay. Well, now we know he's here at least. You continue to keep your eye on the back entrance. I think I should remain here in case he comes out of the front for some reason."

"Yes, my friend, but the man is not on foot. If we are going to eventually follow him from here, won't we need a car, too?"

"Indeed, Anya. I'll make a phone call and get us hooked up."

"Do you happen to know Turkish?"

"Sadly, I'm afraid that's not one of the languages I speak. You?"

"No. Sadly. Better ask for an English-speaking driver."

"Good thinking."

When the taxi pulled up to Kori's side of the street ten minutes later, she handed the driver 400 lira, a seemingly exorbitant number that nevertheless added up to around fifty American dollars. "Just hang out here, would you? I don't know how long I'm going to be. I'm waiting for…a friend. I'll be sitting over there, by that tree."

"Yes, madam," the driver said, a young man with a round friendly face and light goatee. "But for how long?"

"Indefinitely. Don't worry. I'll make sure you're well compensated for your time. What's your name?"

"Asim."

"Here ya go, Asim." Kori handed the young man

another 200 lira.

"Thank you!" he smiled.

Kori went back to her spot but barely sat down before she heard Anya's voice: "Kori, he's on the move. He just left the building and is getting in the car with some others."

"Wow, he didn't stay too long did he? Okay, I'm coming around for you. Look for the cab. Keep an eye on Nasirian. Don't lose him, Anya!"

Kori raced to the taxi and slid into the backseat, saying, "Go around the embassy building, Asim. We're picking up my friend in front of the coffee shop. Quickly, please."

The taxi pulled around the building and stopped when the driver saw Anya at the curb waving. "Is this your friend?" he asked.

Kori didn't have time to answer before Anya threw herself into the car, pointing ahead and saying, "Follow that Mercedes."

"Yes, madam," Asim said.

The Mercedes pulled out of the embassy lot. It was the same SUV that Anya had seen pull in, but she noticed that now the diplomatic flags had been removed. The windows were darkly tinted and it was impossible to see the car's occupants. The Mercedes took a few turns before finally getting on a main road heading first south, and then east. The taxi followed as the Mercedes drove farther and farther from the city, turning onto roads that grew progressively more rural. Before long, houses were few and far between. The landscape was dusty and hilly and mostly barren, but for some dry grass and the occasional bay laurel or olive tree. The traffic was equally sparse.

"He'll notice us following him," said Anya.

"Asim," said Kori, "drop back. Keep your distance, okay? But don't lose him, whatever you do."

"Sure. But may I ask why we are following this car?"

"Can you keep a secret?"

"Sure."

"We think the people inside of it are involved in an international terrorist plot."

Asim chuckled. "No, really, madam."

"It's true, Asim."

"Really?"

"Really."

"Wow. Who are you?"

"Oh, just a couple of gals looking to keep the world safe," said Kori.

"Look, he's turning," said Anya. About a hundred yards ahead of them, the Mercedes turned right onto a lonely dirt road, traveled fifty yards or so, then came to a stop behind a small grove of trees, the dust from the road settling behind it.

"Asim, pull over right here," said Kori. The taxi came to a stop on the side of the main road, perpendicular now to the Mercedes. Kori put on her binocular sunglasses. "Even with these, I can't see what's going on. Why in the heck would they stop there? C'mon, Anya." Kori tossed another couple hundred lira to Asim. "Sit tight, kid."

"Right."

Kori and Anya got out of the taxi and sprinted parallel to the dirt road, staying fifty yards or so from it. Closer to the Mercedes, a small hill rose up, giving the agents a decent perspective from slightly above and to the rear of the car while helping to ensure their concealment. They scrambled up the hill and lay flat, peering over the other side and down toward the SUV.

"Anya," Kori whispered, "I can't see anything through those trees. Can you?"

"No. And the car's dark windows don't help."

"Why would they come out to such a desolate place? What can they be doing?"

A moment later the back door of the Mercedes opened and something large slid out of the seat, landing awkwardly on the ground. The door closed, the Mercedes drove several yards forward, then turned in a U and began going back the way it had come, toward the main road. When it was out of sight, Kori rose up and could now make out what had slid out of the car. It was the tall, thin body of a man with a long beard, silent and very still.

CHAPTER 13

"Cripes, Anya," said Kori as the two stood over the body of Arash Nasirian. "They slit his throat."

"Should we go back to the taxi and continue the pursuit?" Anya asked.

Kori looked back toward the main road to see the Mercedes speeding off in the distance, back toward the city. "I don't see why," she replied. "It's an embassy car. It's probably going right back to the embassy. Although it would be nice to see who gets out of it. But I wouldn't be able to identify whoever it was, anyway. All we can know, or at least surmise, is that Nasirian was killed by people higher up than he was in the hierarchy."

"And so the attack plot goes higher up."

"Indeed it does."

"This is not good."

"No. So much for hoping Nasirian was a rogue element working on his own. Things just got a lot more complicated."

"So what now, my friend?"

"I don't know, Anya. I guess we'd better call the Turkish police, let them know there's a body out here. I'll call anonymously. The last thing we need is to get ourselves involved in a murder investigation. Why don't we go back to the hotel? I'll call the chief and we can regroup and figure out our next steps."

The pair returned to the taxi. "Back to the city, Asim," said Kori as she and Anya slid into the backseat. "Our pursuit has come to an end. Hotel Lugal, please."

"Yes, madam. So what happened back there?"

"You don't want to know, kid. Believe me, you don't want to know."

Sea bass was the fish of the day in the hotel restaurant and Kori and Anya both ordered it for lunch, along with a couple of Efes Pilsens. Kori was on the phone with Eaglethorpe, filling him in on the murder of Nasirian.

"Chief, you've got to get us more information on him. Something. Anything. We're at a dead end. The trail clearly goes higher, but that's not helping us get to the American contact. Somebody in the embassy knows something, but who? And how do we get to them? Nasirian was our only real lead. He's obviously not talking anymore, but there's got to be somebody connected with him. Somebody who can provide us the answers we need."

"I hear you, Kori," said Eaglethorpe. "I'll get Cooper and Foster back on it. I'm sure there's a thread somewhere we can have you pick up on. I'll call you as soon as we find it."

"Thanks, Chief."

Kori hung up and looked down at the plate the waiter had placed before her. "You know, Anya, I can just never get used to the way they serve fish over here."

"Why? What's the matter with it?" said Anya.

"Well, it's still got the head and tail attached."

"So?"

"So…nothing, I guess. Anyway, the chief is going to have Cooper and Foster see if they can find something on Nasirian that can help."

"Good."

"So, Anya, why do you think Nasirian was killed?"

"Incompetence? It was off his desk that the letter was taken. He is the one who let word of the attack slip."

"Yes, I think you're right. These Iranians don't mess around. You screw up with them, and it costs you your life. Anyway, I guess that confirms the idea that when they tortured Hajar, he told them where, and from whom, he got the letter."

"Yes. Thereby sealing Nasirian's fate. But Kori, Hajar was tortured in Istanbul, right?"

"Yeah, why?"

"Well, I wonder why Nasirian was brought to Ankara. Couldn't the same people who killed Hajar have taken care of Nasirian? Why bring him here to the embassy? Why not just do away with him in Istanbul?"

"Good point. Somebody in the embassy obviously wanted to do the job themselves. Nasirian was a pretty important piece of the puzzle. Hajar was just an informant. They probably didn't want to take any chances."

"So whoever ordered Nasirian killed wanted to be there when it happened."

"Looks that way. It does make you wonder how high up the plot really goes, doesn't it?"

"I suppose so. But I am not sure it matters, Kori."

"Seriously? Why do you say that?"

"Well, not to us, that is. How high it goes is a political question. An interesting one, and relevant to foreign policy, no doubt, but we have to...how do you say?... keep our eyes on the prize."

"How do you mean?"

"You and I are paid to protect. If you are about to get stung by a bee, you do not take the time to wonder where the bee came from. You move out of the way. Or you try to kill the bee. Surely, you do something to avoid the sting. Yes?"

"Of course."

"Somebody out there has been given an order to commence an attack on the United States. It could come at any time. It could come this evening, for all we know. Or tomorrow. Or six months from now. But the attack is imminent. Later, there will be time to follow the trail to the attack's true originator. Although, even then, I suspect we may never know."

"Why not?"

"People in leadership positions make it their business to insulate themselves from the potential fallout of serious authorizations like this one. They will take credit if it works. They will deny it if it does not. In fact, that's how clever leaders often end up being leaders in the first place."

"I see what you mean. Well, Anya, you're right, of course. The politics of all of this isn't our department. So, the trail runs in two directions. It runs up to the person or persons who have originated and sanctioned the attack, and it runs down to the person or persons who will carry it out."

"Yes, and the interest for you and me is the latter."

"Agreed. That's why they pay us the big bucks."

The two ate their fish and ordered a couple more beers, both silently thinking over the situation as it stood.

At last, Anya said, "Perhaps we should revisit the San Francisco connection, Kori."

"You mean Johnny Gardner?"

"Yes."

"Well, the problem is, he's not talking and it doesn't look as if he's going to. I let the San Francisco police department take him into custody. Probably a mistake. Now he has all the luxuries of our Bill of Rights. If I had taken him into custody myself, I could have beaten the information out of him."

Anya frowned.

"What?" said Kori.

"I do not disagree with your sentiment, my friend, but isn't your Bill of Rights, in essence, what we are seeking to protect? Your way of life? The freedoms that your Constitution guarantees its citizens? Due process for all?"

"Ah, but Anya," Kori smiled devilishly, "that's a political question, is it not? Ours is to protect. You said it yourself. How comfortable do you want to make life for the bee that is about to sting you? Are you going to take the time to read it its rights when it lands on your nose?"

"I see your point, Kori," said Anya, chuckling. "Nevertheless, there has got to be a better way."

"Maybe, but if it were up to me—wait, my phone's ringing. It's the chief. Chief? What's the word?"

"The word is you're going right back to Istanbul," Director Eaglethorpe replied to Kori.

"Really? Why?"

"Because we just discovered that Nasirian has a brother there."

"No kidding?"

"No kidding. Foster just uncovered a name."

"That's great, Chief. How?"

"He has a contact in the Foreign Service of the State Department. The contact had spent some time in Istanbul several years ago and on a whim, fueled more by desperation than anything else, Foster called him up. As it happens, the contact was in Istanbul when Nasirian made his debut as consul general. He remembered him. Apparently there was a reception for Nasirian, and the contact recalled that his younger brother was with him. He moved to Istanbul with Nasirian to enroll in the university there. Evidently, he's still there because we managed to locate him. His name is Farzad. I'll text his address to you."

"Excellent, Chief. Nice work. Tell Foster to take a little something for himself out of petty cash. Agent Kovalev and I are headed to the airport."

Kori hung up and turned to Anya. "Finish your sea bass, my friend, we've got to go."

"But I did finish."

"Really? Looks like you left the head and the tail."

Sitting in the plane waiting for its departure from Ankara to Istanbul, Kori pulled out her phone, deciding to text Evan. **Just thinking of you**, she tapped. **Hope all is well.**

Seconds later: **All is well. How is Turkey?**

We're making progress. Following leads to see where they go. Or don't go, as the case may be. Nothing I can discuss, of course.

Of course. I'll look forward to hearing all of the details when you solve the case!

And I'll look forward to filling you in.

A full minute went by before Evan texted again: **Maybe you can come visit me in Vancouver…?**

Then the announcement was made that the plane was ready to take off. **Sounds nice**, was all Kori could text. It was a short conversation, but it made Kori smile, something Anya, sitting beside her, noticed but decided not to explore. Maybe later. Instead, she closed her eyes for a quick nap.

The agents arrived in Istanbul early in the evening, took a taxi to Hotel Amira where they dropped off their bags, and began walking to Farzad's apartment, a twenty-minute hike toward Istanbul University. Farzad lived three blocks off campus above a shoe store.

"Kori," said Anya as they walked, the old city streets now busy with people beginning to fill the restaurants and bars for the evening, "once the Turkish police identify Nasirian's body, they'll contact the consulate, which will most likely contact Nasirian's brother, correct?"

"Sure, I would think so. I assume he doesn't have any other family here."

"So Farzad will probably make a beeline for Ankara where his brother's body is, no?"

"Cripes, Anya, you're right. We probably should have just stayed there. For all we know, we passed him in the air."

"Except that we'd have no idea how to find him in Ankara."

"We could have contacted the Turkish police."

"But we have no guarantee that they would have given us any information on Farzad."

"True. And then they'd want to know why we were asking and how we were involved."

"Right. Better to keep clear of any police investigation. Plus, there is no guarantee that Farzad will go to Ankara. He might just take straight off for Iran. His family might send for Nasirian's body. Have it brought back to Iran for burial."

"So, you're saying that Farzad is either headed to Ankara or directly to Iran and he's not going to be here. And he might have left already."

"We have to hope he is still here. But either way, something might turn up in his apartment that can help us. Maybe some sort of clue."

"Let's hope so. We'll turn the place upside down."

"But if he is there, Kori, that brings about a bigger question."

"Which is?"

"What do we do with him?"

"Hmm…I don't know, Anya. Truthfully, I hadn't thought that far ahead."

"We have to assume he'll be sympathetic to his older brother's cause. The two were apparently close. You told me that Foster said Farzad followed Nasirian here to Istanbul."

"Yes, you're right, Anya. Unless, of course, Farzad knows that it was the Iranians that killed his brother. Then he might be less sympathetic. Perhaps even cooperative."

"I doubt he will know who killed his brother. The Turkish police will probably never discover Nasirian's killer. Without knowing what we know, they would have no reason to suspect anyone from the Iranian embassy. We'll have to explain it to Farzad, Kori."

"Yeah, but there's no way he'll believe us, Anya. No, I think we can assume that Farzad will be hostile. We need to apprehend him and question him. And he won't be very willing. It could get ugly."

"Well, we will do what we must do. We need to know what he knows."

Kori grinned. "What about the Bill of Rights?"

Anya grinned back. "Well, my American friend, if **you** don't mind bending them, why should I? I am Russian. And this is Turkey. And Farzad is Iranian. Ah, but we must be getting close to his apartment. This is the street here, correct?"

Kori looked at the map on her phone screen and nodded. The agents turned down the street where Farzad lived and spotted the shoe store a block away.

"Look, a light is on in the apartment," said Kori as they approached. "We might just be in luck."

"How should we do this?" Anya asked.

"Let's go around back and scope it out."

Kori and Anya walked around the rear of the two-story building but there was no back entrance.

"Not even a fire escape," observed Kori. "We'll need to enter from the front, but we're going to have to be damn quiet."

The agents walked back around to the front of the building, passing the window of the shoe store to get to the door that led to the building's interior stairwell.

"Anya, what do you think of those?" Kori said, pausing at the window and pointing at a pair of Badgley Mischkas.

"Cute. A little pricey though, no?"

"Maybe. But I just love the color."

"Too bad the store is closed. Oh, and of course that other thing. The fact that there is a man one floor up who might have information concerning an imminent terrorist attack on your country."

"Okay, okay, point taken. Still, it's a nice pair of heels."

"Come on. Unlock this door."

Kori took her lockpick out of her purse and soon the agents had gained access to the stairwell. Kori peered up the steps.

"His apartment is right at the top," she whispered. "The door has a peephole. We'll need to crouch down so he doesn't see us. I'll get to the right of the door, you get to the left. But it looks to be metal. I don't think we're going to be able to break it down, not without a lot of effort and noise. And even then."

"What do you suggest?" Anya whispered back.

"Well, I can't pick the lock. He'll hear it. I don't see any other choice; we're just going to have to knock."

"Knock? And say what exactly?"

"I don't know. Use that sexy Russian voice of yours. He won't trust my American accent, that's for sure. Just get him to open the door an inch. I can take it from there."

"Right."

The pair stepped gingerly up the steps. When they reached the second-floor landing, Kori ducked down and moved to the right of the door. Anya followed, ducking down and moving to the left. They straightened up, keeping their backs flat against the wall. Anya looked at Kori and Kori nodded. Anya knocked loudly on the door.

"Who is it?" came a deep voice from within.

"I have a delivery," said Anya. "For Farzad Nasirian. From the university." Anya moved in front of the door, in view of the peephole and produced her friendliest smile.

"What is it?"

"Uh…research notes."

"What? Research notes? I'm not expecting anything. Who are you?"

Kori whispered, "I don't think he's buying it."

"I'm a student," Anya continued. "I was given a package for this address from Professor Topal. Are you Farzad?"

"Yes, but I don't know any professor named Topal. Just leave it at the door."

"Topal is new. And I'm afraid you need to sign for it."

"Okay, okay, just a moment."

Kori heard the door being unbolted and as soon as she saw a sliver of light between the door and the door jamb, she thrust her body against the door, shoving it wide open. Anya rushed in and took the stunned Farzad down to the floor face first, kneeling on his back.

"Who are you?!" Farzad cried.

"United States intelligence agents," Kori declared.

Then Farzad smiled, what Kori could tell was an obvious smile of relief and, perhaps, even… gratitude? What he said next was even more surprising.

"**Alhamdulillah!**" he exclaimed through tears that were beginning to well up in his eyes. "Praise be to Allah that you are here!"

CHAPTER 14

"We didn't exactly think you'd be happy to see us, Farzad," said Kori. She had pulled her Glock out of her purse and was pointing it at the man who lay prone on the floor under Anya's knee. He was tall, like his brother, but beardless and obviously younger. An open, half-packed suitcase rested near the sofa of the small studio apartment.

"They have killed my brother," Farzad said. "They have killed Arash."

Anya took her knee off Farzad's back and stood.

"Yes, we know," she said. "When did you learn

of it?"

Farzad rose to his knees. "An hour ago. The Turkish police were here. They told me Arash had been murdered outside of Ankara. I have to fly to Tehran to break the news to our mother and father. It will not be easy."

Kori could tell Farzad had been crying. In his current state, he certainly didn't seem to be a threat, but she kept her pistol trained on him just the same.

"What do you know about your brother's work?" she asked.

"He was trying to stop a terrorist attack on the US," Farzad replied. "I am sure that is why he was killed. The police said they didn't know who the murderer was, but I know."

"Who?"

"The ambassador, no doubt. Or one of his henchmen. Of course the police won't be able to trace the killing to them. Or they will be reluctant to do so. Right now, Iran and Turkey enjoy a close relationship. Even if the Turkish police could prove the killing, they will be stopped from investigating by those on the Council of Ministers. But I know in my heart that Arash was killed by our own country-men."

"You're right, Farzad," said Kori, slipping her

gun into her purse. "We were there. At your brother's murder."

"You saw Arash being killed?" Farzad's eyes welled up again. "How…how did it happen?"

"It was in an Iranian embassy staff car on a dirt road. Like the police told you, about an hour outside of the city."

"It was quick," Anya added.

"I see," Farzad said quietly, his eyes looking down toward the apartment's worn carpeting. "Bastards," he whispered.

"We're very sorry," Kori said softly. She pointed to the sofa and said, "Please, sit and tell us what you can."

Farzad moved over to the sofa while the two agents pulled up a couple of stools from the kitchen.

"I'm Agent Briggs," said Kori. "This is Agent Kovalev. Sorry about the rude entry. As you can imagine, we assumed you weren't going to give us a very cordial invitation to enter."

"Because you assumed my brother was part of the attack plan."

"Yes. He wasn't?"

"Look, Agent Briggs, we are good Iranians, my brother and I. We are loyal subjects to our supreme leader. And we are faithful Muslims."

"Of course," Kori nodded.

"We love our country. It is for this reason that Arash decided to expose the plan. It is not an Iranian plan, you see."

"It's not?"

"No. It begins and ends with the ambassador, Arman Golzar. Golzar is a radical, masquerading as a centrist. He is intent on dragging Iran into a war with the United States. He has wanted it for quite some time. It's been nothing less than a dream of his. From the embassy in Ankara, he has been operating as the head of a faction of extremists, surrounding himself with those of similar belief, handpicking his staff members and creating a cabal of those loyal to his cause."

"How did your brother get involved with him?" Anya asked.

"Arash was an extremist, too. At one time. So was I. Maybe this seems confusing to you, but you must understand that we were made to hate the US from a very early age. And I confess to you even now that I still question your nation's values and your role in other country's affairs."

"Noted," said Kori.

"Be that as it may, war between our countries is a losing proposition for us both. Especially for us.

It would be long and drawn out and cost millions of lives. In the end, I fear my country would not survive it. We can dislike your country, it seems to me, and still remain at peace."

"I'd like to think so."

"But Golzar was intent on not only starting a war, but bringing it to your soil. I cannot emphasize enough that he has been operating strictly on his own. His superiors in Tehran have no idea of his plan. If they did, I have no doubt that Golzar would be summarily executed for actions that are nothing less than treasonous. Our government leaders are not stupid. They know of the consequences of open hostility toward America. But Golzar…well, my brother began to see him for what he was: unstable. And dangerous.

"You see, my brother went along with him for quite a while. He knew him well in Tehran and initially appreciated his political stance. When Golzar became ambassador to Turkey, he brought my brother with him, making him consul general of the Istanbul consulate. Golzar figured that he could operate more freely here in Istanbul, farther removed from Tehran than Ankara, both geographically and politically. So my brother became the Istanbul extension of Golzar's work. The idea, as far as Arash knew, was to wage a war on a propaganda front, try to influence the thinking of those within the political structure of the US who may be sympathetic to Iran and who may be inclined to help our country's aims. But then Golzar started becoming more and more militant and fanatical. America was the Great Satan, he often said, and must be brought down. Finally, he started hatching a plan to start a full-fledged military war. Worse, the people he surrounded himself with at the embassy fell into line with him, including, to a point, my brother. He and I had many arguments about where Golzar's thinking was headed."

"Your brother spoke openly with you about Golzar?" Kori asked.

"My brother and I were very close, Agent Briggs. We talked about everything. We got together quite often…" Farzad paused, struggling to regain his composure.

"Please," said Anya, "take your time."

Finally, Farzad continued. "We talked about politics frequently. Arash told me of Golzar's fanaticism, yet argued to me on his behalf. But I could see that Arash was only trying to rationalize beliefs that he could not bring himself to fully embrace. I told him he needed to distance himself from Golzar.

And then about two weeks ago, Arash came here, to this apartment, and told me of this attack plan. We talked late into the night about it. I could tell he was struggling with the idea. I told him he needed to do what he could to stop it. Ultimately, he agreed. He knew then that I was right, that Golzar was going off the deep end and had become a danger to our nation's future."

"Why didn't he just take his concerns to Tehran?" asked Kori. "Let them know what their ambassador to Turkey was planning?"

"He didn't think he'd be believed. Golzar is a master manipulator. The leadership in Tehran believes he is loyal and competent. He has many friends there. That's why he was appointed in the first place. And it is considered disgraceful to go over your superior's head. So Arash did the only thing he could think to do. He allowed a staff member to intercept the order of attack."

"Hajar."

"Correct."

"How did he know what Hajar would do with it?"

"He didn't. But Hajar had come under suspicion. There was a belief by some that, for quite a while, Hajar had been passing along secrets to someone in the West. Can I now presume that suspicion was correct, and that the someone was one of you?"

"Well, sort of," said Kori. "Truthfully, he was passing along secrets to an old acquaintance of his who worked for Canadian Intelligence. But the letter ordering the attack eventually came to us."

"That is what Arash had hoped. And that is why I was so glad to see you."

"So your brother purposely left the letter for Hajar to take?" Anya asked.

"Yes. That way, he would have deniability."

"That explains the envelope being marked 'confidential,'" Kori remarked. "Probably made it more tantalizing. More likely to be picked up by Hajar."

"Yes."

"Well, then, who killed Hajar? Forgive me, but until your brother's death, I assumed he did it."

"No. My brother would never kill in cold blood. Golzar has a couple of staff members who are nothing more than paid assassins. They flew here to Istanbul to torture Hajar and then kill him. Arash knew of the plan, but of course, there was nothing he could do to stop it without casting suspicion on himself. He thought about warning Hajar in some way, but it was too late. One day, Hajar was just gone. These assassins are probably the ones who killed Arash, too, but Golzar apparently wanted it done in Ankara. He probably wanted to supervise it himself. Obviously, my brother underestimated Golzar's wrath. And overestimated his relationship with him. Last night, Arash called me to tell me that Golzar had requested he come to Ankara. I told him not to. I had a bad feeling."

"Why did he go?" asked Anya.

"What else could he do? He could not disobey a request from his superior. Plus, he felt it would look worse if he didn't go. It would seem suspicious. Besides all that, I'm sure he assumed he might get a stern lecture from Golzar at worst. Perhaps a demotion. Maybe even sent back to Tehran. He could not have known that leaving the letter for Hajar would cost him his life."

"Golzar isn't messing around," said Kori. "You're right to call him dangerous."

"He has become crazed with the idea of war," said Farzad. "Now, whether he knew of Arash's true intentions or just killed him because he was angry at his ostensible carelessness with the letter, I do not suppose I will ever know. Not that it matters. My brother is gone."

"Of course," said Kori. "Can you tell us anything about the plan itself?"

"Nothing, I'm afraid. Arash purposely kept me in the dark as to its details. It was his way of protecting me. Of protecting his little brother." Farzad bit his lip and looked down at the floor once again.

"Do you have any idea whom the letter might have been meant for?"

"All I can tell you is that he was to have it couriered to a person here in Istanbul. I don't know who. Someone who had apparently been enlisted by Golzar to help carry out the plan."

"Do you know anything about this person?" asked Anya. "Their nationality, maybe?"

"I'm sorry, no. Nor do I know where the order was headed from there. I'm sorry I cannot be of any more help."

"It's okay," said Kori. "You've been a great help. Tell me, where did your brother live?"

"In an apartment not far from the consulate."

"We'd like to search his place for clues. We promise not to disturb anything."

"Of course. I'll give you the address. I have a copy of his door key, too. But it is rather a nice place. There is a doorman you'll have to get past."

"We'll figure it out," said Anya.

"In the meantime, we'll leave you to your packing,"

said Kori. "Please accept our condo-lences. I'm sure your brother was a fine man."

"Thank you. Please do what you can. My tragedy is a personal one. A much bigger one awaits if you cannot stop what has been put into motion. Nothing less than the future of both of our countries is at stake."

Arash Nasirian's apartment was in a block-long, five-story building with a covered entrance. True to Farzad's word, a doorman stood sentinel at a valet stand in front of a set of double glass doors. It was night now, but the entrance area was bathed in light from the building's exterior floodlights. From across the street, Kori and Anya could see that there would be no slipping past the doorman without being spotted.

Kori took a lira coin out of her purse. "Heads or tails?"

"Heads, I guess," said Anya.

Kori flipped the coin in the air, caught it, and opened her hand. "Tails, my friend. Sorry. I'll search the place. You keep the doorman occupied."

"I knew I should have said tails," Anya grumbled.

The two walked down a block, then crossed the street and started for the apartment building. Kori hung back and slipped behind some shrubs, watching as Anya approached the entrance. In front of the doors, Anya stopped, staying out toward the street about twenty yards from the building.

"Hello!" she called out to the doorman, a short, pudgy man with a bulbous nose and receding chin. "Can you please help me? I am so lost. Do you know this neighborhood?"

"What is the matter, Miss?" the doorman called back.

"I am supposed to meet my friends in front of the Topkapi Palace. My directional app says it should be right here. But this doesn't look like much of a palace. And I am afraid my phone is running low on power."

"This is an apartment building, Miss. But you are not that far away from the Topkapi Palace. It is three blocks from here. In that direction," the doorman said, pointing.

"In what direction?" Anya said, squinting her eyes.

"That direction," he repeated.

"I'm sorry, my eyes are not so good. Where are you pointing? Can you come here and show me?" She drifted under a streetlamp and smiled prettily. The doorman smiled in return and walked out toward the street. Kori took advantage of the suddenly unmanned doorway and slid into the building, listening behind her as the doorman began making small talk with Anya about the direction of the famous palace and asking Anya creepy questions about what her and her friends were up to that evening, mentioning that he would be off duty in an hour. **Ugh**, thought Kori, making a mental note to offer to buy the drinks later as the very least she could do for winning the coin toss.

Nasirian's apartment was on the third floor. Kori entered and elected to use her phone's flashlight rather than flip on any lights in the apartment. It was possible the place was being watched and Kori didn't see any reason to advertise her presence. The apartment was much more upscale than Hajar's. Consul generals obviously did much better than regular staff members.

In short order, Kori found a desk with various papers scattered about, much of it in handwritten Persian script. On a shelf above the desk was a small photograph of Nasirian with his younger brother

Farzad. They were both smiling for the camera and Kori thought of Farzad, back at his flat getting ready to fly to Tehran to break the news to his parents that they had lost their oldest son.

Next to the photograph, Kori noticed a single slip of paper with numbers on it. The print was in Turkish, but the paper was clearly a bank transaction receipt, specifically a withdrawal note, dated ten days prior. Kori didn't need to understand Turkish to appreciate the number at the bottom: **$2,500,000 (USD).** Next to the number was a handwritten name. **Wyatt Davenport**. Hardly Iranian, thought Kori. Next to that was written: **1/2**.

She folded up the receipt and slipped it into her purse. Then she texted Anya. **If you're done flirting with the doorman, make your way back to the hotel bar. Drinks on me. I found everything we need.**

CHAPTER 15

Anya was working on a raki, but Kori had gone back to her normal scotch. It was close to midnight and besides the bartender, the lobby bar of the hotel was populated only by Kori and Anya and an American tourist couple who were sitting in the corner demonstrably more interested in each other than in the drinks that were in front of them. The agents sat at a high-top table along the wall and munched on a plate of falafel and an order of calamari.

Kori's phone rang.

"It's the chief," she said to Anya. "Let's see what

they found out. Briggs here, Chief."

"Kori," came Eaglethorpe's voice, "Foster was able to trace the bank account number you texted earlier."

"Excellent, Chief. So what's the scoop?"

"It's an account with Akbank. Akbank is the largest private bank in Turkey, headquartered there in Istanbul. The account is held by an Arman Golzar. Does the name mean anything to you?"

"It sure does. Golzar is the Iranian ambassador to Turkey. Nasirian's boss. He's the one behind the impending attack and likely the person behind Nasirian's murder. That's what Nasirian's brother told us. Chief, we've got to figure out who this Wyatt Davenport is, the name that was written on the bank slip. I'm thinking the attack must involve him in some way, right? Maybe that's where the $2.5 million went. I mean, why else would it be in US dollars?"

"Agreed. We'll run a search on him. Meanwhile, we've gotten some news from Vasquez. He uncovered something pretty interesting in Grand Rapids. And possibly disturbing."

"Oh, yeah? Do tell."

"Through a little sleuthing, he was able to compile a partial list of current members of the

Guardian Militia, the ones not serving time from the attempted UN bombing. About a dozen names."

"Nice work."

"Indeed. But here's the thing. Most of them live in Michigan. It's a pretty localized contingency. Right now, however, they're all missing."

"Missing?"

"Yep. Every single one of them. Vasquez has enlisted the help of the local authorities and none of these guys are where they're supposed to be. They're not at their homes, they haven't shown up for work, and nobody has seen them. The only common denominator is that their vehicles are all gone."

"So, they've taken off?"

"Yes, but we can't determine to where. They've left no paper trails behind. No plane tickets, no hotel reservations, not even a fuel purchase. Apparently, wherever they are, they're paying for everything with cash."

"What about spouses and kids? Friends and neighbors?"

"We've canvassed everyone. These guys have been masterful at keeping everyone in the dark as to their plans."

"How long have they been gone?"

"It seems as though they all took off about nine days ago."

"Chief, that would be the day after the bank withdrawal."

"Yep. Coincidence?"

"Unlikely, Chief."

"Right. Well, listen, you and Agent Kovalev get yourselves a good night's sleep. It must be late in Istanbul and I don't think there's much more you can do tonight. We'll keep working on our end. I'll have Cooper and Foster do that search on Wyatt Davenport and have a complete report for you in the morning."

"Thanks, Chief. Sounds like a plan." Kori hung up and popped a falafel into her mouth. "Vasquez turned up the names of the members of the neo-Nazi group that Johnny Gardner belongs to," she said to Anya.

"That's great. Where are they?"

"Well, that's the problem. They're all on the move somewhere. But nobody knows where."

"The scene of the attack, no doubt."

"I'm afraid so."

"What about the bank account?"

"It belongs to Golzar."

"Interesting." Anya downed her drink and motioned for the bartender to bring another. "But, Kori, why do you think Nasirian left that note out where it could be so easily found? Along with the name?"

"Isn't it obvious, Anya? He wanted it to be found. It's the same thing he did with the letter ordering the attack. He hoped Hajar had found a way to get the letter into the right hands. He had no idea who we were, but he hoped someone like us would start following the scent. Before he left for Ankara, he jotted Davenport's name on the bank receipt and placed it in an obvious spot. In a sense, he left it for **us**, Anya. He was trying to do the right thing. I just hope we're not too late."

"And Nasirian in possession of the bank receipt must mean that he had access to Golzar's account."

"Yes, it's an Istanbul account. As consul general, Nasirian probably had authorization to withdraw funds from it. The funny thing, however, is that it's not an embassy account. It's a personal account in Golzar's name."

"And it is a lot of money," mused Anya. "That amount of money isn't put into an account without a purpose. You do not leave $2.5 million in the bank for a rainy day."

"So let's think this through, Anya. But of course,

to properly do so, I'm going to need another scotch. Bartender?"

The bartender brought another couple of drinks over to the table as Anya finished off the last of the calamari.

"Okay," said Kori, "the bank account is a private one, right? Not connected with Iran or the Ankara embassy or the Istanbul consulate at all. That would seem to confirm what Farzad told us. Golzar's working on his own."

"Correct," Anya agreed. "If it was an account held in the name of the Islamic Republic of Iran, it would be a different story."

"Right. So there are two fundamental questions. Where did the $2.5 million come from, and where did the $2.5 million go?"

"Well, I think we can assume that Golzar probably raised funds for his plan. You heard Farzad. He had surrounded himself with people sympathetic to his cause against the West. And a man like Golzar, high enough up on the governmental ladder to be awarded the ambassadorship to Turkey, must have some pretty influential contacts."

"Exactly. Wealthy contacts."

"Right. So, Golzar raised the money, opened an account in Istanbul, instead of Ankara where he lived and worked, and left it to Nasirian to administer it."

"Yes. Still in his name, but an account operating remotely from where he was. Nobody would think to look for an account in Golzar's name in Istanbul when he's stationed in Ankara, thereby helping to ensure that the whole operation would fly under the radar."

"That's a lot of trust to put in Nasirian. It's a significant amount of money."

"Sure is. Well, that might explain his wrath when he came to realize that Nasirian possibly betrayed him by leaving the letter out for Hajar to find."

"Indeed."

"So, Anya, the second question: Where did the money go?"

"Nasirian withdrew it and, can we assume, gave it to this Wyatt Davenport?"

"I think that's a fair assumption. Why else would his name be written on the slip? Davenport's the inside man."

"How do you mean?"

"How would you attack the US, Anya? And on its own soil, which apparently is the goal? If you're a private concern like Ambassador Golzar's group, you can't very well just launch a military strike from the outside. Planes and bombs and missiles? No way. Even if you had them."

"So you launch an attack from the inside."

"Exactly. And that's where Wyatt Davenport comes in. Somehow."

"So Davenport was paid $2.5 million to…do what, exactly?"

"That's the $2.5-million-dollar question, Anya."

"Kori, Davenport must be connected to the neo-Nazis."

"Yes. I'll bet there's a link between Wyatt Davenport, Johnny Gardner, and the names that Vasquez uncovered."

"I don't know, Kori. It still seems strange. How do you get a group of neo-Nazis to decide to work with Islamic fundamentalists bent on attacking the United States?"

"Beats me, Anya."

"This thing is getting more confusing all the time. But based on what we know, Kori, it looks as though payment was made to Davenport, the Guardian Militia members go on the move right afterward, and then…"

"And then the letter authorizing the attacks gets sent. To Davenport, no doubt. He's the guy Farzad said the order was to be couriered to."

"Kori, let me see the receipt." Kori pulled the receipt out of her purse and handed it across the table. "What do you suppose Nasirian meant with this fraction? '1/2.'"

"Yes, what? One out of two … one-half … one over two …"

"Kori, maybe the number represents the first of two payments."

"Right, Anya! It's a deposit. Half now, half after the attack is successfully committed. Davenport is getting $5 million in total to pull off whatever the heck it is he's trying to pull off."

"Exactly. Certainly, if you're Golzar you don't pay the full amount up front."

"So one payment has been made. By the time the second gets paid, it'll be too late for us, Anya. The attack will have been committed."

"Yes, and it is disconcerting that the Guardian Militia members are already on the move."

"Indeed. They're probably already at their destination, wherever that is. This thing might happen soon, Anya. Very soon."

"We have to find Davenport, Kori."

"Yes. Let's hope Cooper and Foster have some answers for us after they research him. In the meantime, it looks as if our glasses are empty. Nightcap?"

"I have rarely needed one more."

Kori and Anya both slept restlessly, and over simit and jam the next morning at a sidewalk café down the street from the hotel, they awaited Eaglethorpe's call, hopefully with some answers. Chief among them, who was Wyatt Davenport?

"So, my friend," said Anya, seeking to give their minds some respite from the situation at hand, "you never told me how things went with the Air Force pilot."

"Shane? Well, there's really not much to tell, my Russian friend. We had a great time together in Heidelberg."

"How great a time?" Anya smiled.

"Pretty great," Kori smiled back.

"I see. And?"

"And what?"

"Will you see him again?"

"I don't think so, Anya."

"No? Wasn't that whom you were texting on the

airplane?"

"Huh? Oh, no, that was just…somebody…"

"What happened to Shane?"

"Well, you know how it is, Anya. It was just one of those things. I mean, I like Shane. He's a wonderful guy. And we got along really well. It's just that…"

"Just what, Kori?"

"How do I explain it? Every time I find myself getting close to a man, having real feelings for him, I just…"

"Just what?"

"Well, I—oh, it's the chief. Hold that thought." Kori pulled her ringing phone out of her purse. "Chief?"

"Good morning, Briggs."

"Good morning. Or night, or whatever it is over there. What can you tell us, Chief? We're on pins and needles here."

"Well, Wyatt Davenport turns out to be a pretty interesting study."

"Oh? How so?"

"Up until six months ago, he was a nobody. He runs a small travel agency in Lansing, Michigan. Davenport Tours."

"Aha! How far is that from Grand Rapids?"

"Not that far. Sixty-eight point two miles. I

figured you'd ask."

"So you're thinking what we're thinking. Davenport is connected to Johnny Gardner."

"It would seem so, although we can't prove a direct connection. What we do know is that in the past six months, Davenport suddenly became very active on internet sites that dealt with antigovernment, neo-Nazi, hate groups."

"Like Gardner's Guardian Militia."

"Exactly. He started posting on message boards and writing blogs. But he didn't use his own name. Cooper was able to determine who his internet provider is. He hacked into his account and was able to examine his online activity. Whenever Davenport posted something, he used the name Daniel Price. And in a short period of time, Daniel Price apparently built up quite a following by writing some pretty extreme stuff. But here's what's strange. There is nothing—and I mean nothing—in Davenport's past that would indicate any kind of future interest in this kind of stuff. In fact, he served faithfully in the Air Force, working as a technician. He grew up in a normal, middle-class household. His father sold insurance and his mother taught Sunday school. Davenport has no history of trouble as a kid. He got good grades and served on his high school student council. Played basketball. He went into the service after graduation, served with distinction, came out, and enrolled for a couple of years in community college back home. Then he started his travel business. Since then, not a single brush with the law. Not so much as a parking ticket."

"That sure doesn't fit the profile of the guys we see who get involved in antigovernment groups, Chief. And no history of racist activity?"

"None whatsoever."

"How odd."

"Yes, but here's the really interesting thing: When he was in the Air Force, he was stationed at Incirlik Air Base."

"Here in Turkey."

"Right. Apparently, he liked Turkey. As it happens, his travel business seems to specialize in Middle East guided tours. He goes there quite often and the tours always go through Istanbul and Ankara."

"Wow. So that explains how he might have met Nasirian or Golzar."

"Yes, I would think so. But listen to this, Kori. He's on a tour there right now. According to the itinerary posted on his travel company website, he's in Istanbul for another three days."

"Of course! It's the perfect cover. He can come here and do business with the Iranians and nobody will suspect a thing. It's no coincidence that he's here now."

"Exactly. Now listen, the tour group he escorts always stays at the Vogue Hotel. Do you know it?"

"Sure, I know it. It's about ten minutes from where we are. Close to the Hagia Sophia mosque."

"Well, what are you waiting for, Agent Briggs? Get there. I'll have Cooper send you a photo of Davenport in the meantime. Find him, Kori."

"Yes, sir. We're on our way."

Kori hung up. "C'mon, Anya," she said, getting up and laying some lira down on the table for the breakfast bill.

"Where are we going?" Anya asked, stuffing her mouth with the remaining simit.

"I'll explain on the way."

"Will you finish explaining about Shane, too?"

"Sorry, Anya. No time."

"Will you at least tell me who you were texting on the plane?"

But Kori was already ten yards down the street.

CHAPTER 16

In the tastefully appointed lobby of the Vogue Hotel, Kori turned to Anya and said, "Follow my lead."

The two strode briskly to the front desk.

"Can you please help us?" Kori asked breathlessly to the young man working the desk. "We're afraid that we're late. Did our tour group leave already? Davenport Tours?"

"Davenport Tours?" the young man said.

"Yes," said Anya. "We were supposed to meet them here. But we lost our way coming back from breakfast this morning. I knew we shouldn't have wandered out on our own! Did the tour start without us?"

"Oh, I hope not!" Kori moaned. "We've spent so much money to get here. We were supposed to tour the Grand Bazaar today."

"Yes, the Grand Bazaar!" cried Anya. "And some mosques. Please, can you help us?"

"Ladies, ladies," the desk clerk said, smiling. "You can relax. If I am not mistaken, that is your group right outside the door there, is it not? You must have walked right past them on the way in." Beyond the double glass doors behind them, Kori and Anya could see a group of ten or twelve people standing outside.

"Oh, what a relief," Kori said. "How did we miss them? My, my, we're just so frazzled."

"I believe your guide must be running late," said the desk clerk. "I don't think I see him among them."

"Mr. Davenport?"

"Yes, Mr. Davenport."

"Do you know him?"

"Oh, yes, Mr. Davenport's tour groups always stay here. He has been a loyal customer of ours."

"How long has the group been waiting for him?" Anya asked.

"It seems to me that people started to gather outside probably more than an hour ago. So, I presume Mr. Davenport will be here shortly. He's probably still in his room. Why don't you wait with the others?"

"Of course," said Kori. "Thank you so much."

"Not at all."

The two walked back outside and lingered next to the group and soon found themselves over-hearing some grumbling among the members.

"Excuse us," Kori interrupted, "is this where Davenport Tours is supposed to meet?"

"Yes," said a middle-aged woman with charcoal gray hair and a frown. "**Supposed** to. The problem is, we're missing our guide. He was to meet us here an hour ago."

"Wyatt Davenport?"

"Yes. Do you know him?"

"When was the last time any of you saw him?" Anya asked.

"Two days ago," said an older, heavy man with a Kansas City Royals' cap. "Our tour ended rather abruptly that day. Wyatt took a phone call and then said he needed to meet with someone. Then he suggested that we all take a day to ourselves, which was yesterday, and then we were to meet up again here this morning."

"But he's not here," said the woman. "And he's not answering his phone!"

"Frankly, we're feeling as though he's abandoned us," came another voice from the group.

"Right," someone else chimed in. "I mean, what's the deal with the day to ourselves yesterday? We paid for a guided tour."

"Yes!" someone else called out. "And now he's late for today? Really?!"

"And nobody's seen him!" said the man with the baseball cap. "I'd sure like to know what the hell is going on."

Other voices piped up. "We spent a lot of money!" "I saved for a year for this trip!" "What are we supposed to do now?!"

"Does anyone know Wyatt's room number?" Anya asked, but nobody knew.

The grumbling became louder and Kori and Anya both saw that the group was starting to resemble more of a mob.

"Listen," said Kori, "I don't know where your guide is, but I should tell you that, unfortunately, I wouldn't be surprised if he took off. Don't ask us how we know this. My advice would be to try to find another guide service. Or try to tackle the city of Istanbul on your own. You never know what adventures you might find. I have always found the people here friendly and helpful. And in the meantime, if you have any problems while you're here, don't hesitate to contact the American consulate. Ask for Marsha Rose. Tell her Kori Briggs sent you.

"Now, this is very important: if you happen to come across Mr. Davenport, please contact me immediately. Here." Kori pulled out a stack of her **National Bureau of Criminal Investigations** cards and passed them around, eliciting some small gasps as the group began to realize that whatever Wyatt Davenport was involved in, and for whatever reason he was failing to materialize that morning, it must be pretty serious.

"Miss," said the woman with the charcoal hair, "what did Mr. Davenport do exactly?"

"Nothing yet, ma'am," said Kori. "And we're trying to keep it that way. But, listen, this man might be dangerous. If you see him, contact us and let us handle things." Then, turning to Anya, she said, "Come on."

The two marched back into the lobby to the front desk, leaving the group outside dazed and asking each other questions nobody had answers to.

Kori knew her card would pull no weight with the desk clerk. She had no jurisdiction in Turkey, and Davenport was a valuable customer to the hotel. Besides, how could she even begin to explain the situation? She tried another tack instead. "Excuse us," she said, "but our guide doesn't seem to be coming. Nor is he answering his phone. It seems as though I've been elected by the rest of the group to go knock on his door, but I've forgotten his room number. Can you help me? They're getting a little restless outside."

"Oh, I'm sorry, ma'am," said the clerk. "We don't give out the room numbers of our guests."

"Yes, but we're with his tour."

"I understand, but it's policy, you see."

"Can you ring his room for us, at least?" suggested Anya. "To let him know the group is waiting for him?"

"Yes, I can do that." The clerk tapped at his computer, retrieving Davenport's room number and then dialed it from the desk phone. After several moments, he hung up, saying, "I'm sorry, ladies. There seems to be no answer. Perhaps he has gone out for breakfast."

"Perhaps," said Kori. "Well, thank you anyway. I guess we'll go wait in our rooms."

With that, the agents turned and headed for the elevator. Once inside, Kori asked, "Did you see the number he dialed?"

"Yes, of course," Anya answered, pushing the third-floor button. "Davenport's room is 313."

But when they got there, to neither agent's surprise, 313 was empty. The "Do Not Disturb" placard was hanging on the knob. Once inside, the two women saw no sign of Davenport. No sign of any guest at all.

"Are you sure he dialed 313?" Kori asked, looking around the room.

"Sure I'm sure. He probably left two nights ago."

"Yep. That phone call he took. Probably to set up the meeting he mentioned to the group. And I'll bet that meeting was to get the official letter from Nasirian authorizing the attack. Or a copy of it, that is, since the original was pilfered, thankfully for us."

"Right. And then he told the tour group to meet him two days later, thereby giving himself plenty of time to get lost."

"But to where? Back to the States?"

"I doubt it, Kori. Remember, there is another $2.5 million that still awaits him here."

"Right. He could give his neo-Nazi guys the green light from here. But certainly, by now he knows about the lost letter and Gardner getting nabbed. He must suspect someone's on his tail."

"Right. So he checked out of here and is laying low somewhere, waiting for the completion of the attack so he can collect the balance Golzar owes him."

"Exactly. All we have to figure out is where exactly he's laying low."

"Istanbul is a big city. And with Nasirian out of the picture, he might now be dealing directly with Golzar. Meaning he might have even gone to Ankara."

"Yes, Anya, but that would be risky for Golzar. He set up a bank account in Istanbul specifically to avoid being associated with any kind of plot like this. My hunch is that Golzar will make payment right here, away from Ankara where too many people know him."

"So how do we find Davenport?"

"Anya, my friend, you have a maddening habit of always asking the difficult questions, don't you?"

"Do you know this man?" Kori was showing the

tour guide out in front of the Blue Mosque a photo of Wyatt Davenport that Cooper had just texted her. The agents had decided that the best way to track Davenport was to canvas the places he was sure to have been. According to the itinerary of Davenport Tours, the Blue Mosque was always one of the first stops. What were they hoping to discover? Neither knew. But both understood that sometimes a mere scrap of information can open the door to something more significant. Hopefully, somebody somewhere had the scrap they needed.

"Oh, yes," said the guide, an older, leathery faced man with a close-cropped pure white beard. "Yes, I know him. Mr. Davenport from the United States. He brings his tour group here quite often. Very nice man."

"Have you seen him lately?"

"Yes, two days ago. With his tour, as usual."

"Have you seen him since?"

"No, I can't say that I have."

"Do you happen to know anything about Mr. Davenport?" asked Anya. "Where he goes when he's here in the city? Where he eats? Where he hangs out? If he has any friends here?"

The man was thoughtful for a moment. "Hmm… if I'm not mistaken, I think he always stays at the

Vogue."

"Yes, we know, thank you. Might there be anything else you can tell us about him?"

"Is Mr. Davenport all right? Is he in some kind of trouble?"

"Well, the truth is," said Kori, "he's missing. His tour group expected him to show up this morning, but he hasn't made an appearance and his room at the Vogue is empty. We're American police officers. We promised the tour group we'd try to find Mr. Davenport."

"Oh, I see. Well, I don't know anything more, but if you ladies will wait here, I will go inside and ask the mosque's visitation director. He knows all the tour guides. He might know more than I do."

"Yes, please," said Anya. "That would be so kind of you."

"If you could bring him out for us to chat with him," said Kori, "that would be even better."

The man bowed slightly and then disappeared into the mosque.

"I don't know, Kori," said Anya. "This seems like a longshot."

"Agreed. Unfortunately, longshots are all we've got. In the meantime, Foster is pulling all of Davenport's credit information. The guys back in DC will start tracing any use of his credit cards. Hopefully, he checked into another hotel and we'll be able to nab him."

"Hopefully."

Kori looked around at the mosque. She'd walked by it a hundred times, but never bothered to take it in. "Look at this place," she said to Anya. "It's like a castle. It's beautiful. But why is it called blue?"

"Have you never been inside?"

"Afraid not."

"Thousands and thousands of blue tiles line the interior, even the high ceiling. It is actually quite exquisite. The tallest dome, incidentally," Anya said, pointing, "is 140 feet high. But there are five main domes."

"Geez, Anya, you could be a tour guide yourself. How old is it?"

"It was completed in 1616, if I recall correctly. Here is an interesting fact. Notice the six tall minarets?"

"Yes."

"Mosques normally only have one or two. Four at the most. It is believed that the sultan who ordered the construction asked for gold minarets. The Turkish word for gold in **altin**. But it is similar to the Turkish word for six—**alti**. The builder misheard. Hence the six minarets."

"Ha! So how come you know so much?"

"My father took me here a few times as a young girl. He would travel to Turkey often."

"Ah, yes. Nicholas Kovalev. The famous KGB agent."

Anya smiled. "One and the same."

"Interesting family business, Anya. The spy game. And should you ever have a child…?"

"He or she will be a teacher. Or an artist, perhaps. Maybe an architect. Doctor. Scientist. Poet."

"Anything but a spy, huh?"

"Anything but a spy."

Shortly, the guide returned. "I am very sorry, ladies. The director apologizes but is tied up at the moment. I did manage to speak to him briefly, however. I am afraid he knows very little about Mr. Davenport, but he did mention that there is a bar-restaurant where the director has seen him from time to time. That's not much to go on, of course."

"No, but anything helps," said Kori. "Where is this bar-restaurant?"

"It's just four blocks in that direction," the guide said, pointing down the main street in front of the mosque. "It's called the Faust."

"Okay, thank you. We appreciate your help."

"Not at all, ladies. I do hope you are able to locate Mr. Davenport."

The Faust was a cool, dark joint with a low ceiling, a long bar, and a dozen or so tables, most of them empty. Ten minutes after leaving the Blue Mosque, Kori was showing the Faust's bartender the photo of Wyatt Davenport.

"Yes, he comes in here," the bartender said in English, but with a heavy accent. "At the end of the day, usually. I think he is a tour guide. He always orders dinner and has a few beers. He was here last night, as a matter of fact. Can I get you two anything?"

Kori looked at her watch: 11:45. **Close enough to noon**, she thought. "Sure, why not? I'll have a beer."

"Make that two," said Anya.

The bartender poured a couple of drafts for the agents and then strolled down to the far end of the bar to refill another customer's glass.

"What do you think, Anya?" said Kori, sipping on her beer. "Would he really come back here? This seems to be his place. Not far from the hotel. Quiet. Dark. At the end of a long day of schlepping tourists around the city, he probably enjoys having a solid meal here and knocking back a few."

"But he's not—how do you say?—'schlepping' tourists around today."

"No, he's certainly not. Plus, if he knows he's being tailed, he's probably smart enough not to go to the same spots he usually goes to. That's why he checked out of the Vogue, after all."

"I suppose we could keep interviewing places along his tour route. But as far as that goes, Kori, there is an old Russian expression that I fear is appropriate. 'The game is not worth the candles.'"

"What's it mean?"

"It refers to poker players making only small bets. Such play is not worth the candles it takes to light the room where the game is taking place. It is a waste of effort. A waste of time."

"I'm afraid you may be right, Anya. The idea of running all over Istanbul hoping to bump into this guy isn't even worth one candle. But, listen, we're not the only ones working on this. Maybe the guys back at HQ have found something." Kori pulled her phone out and called Eaglethorpe.

"Chief, anything you can give us? Anything with Davenport's credit cards?"

"Nothing, I'm afraid, Briggs. Nothing is turning up."

"Well, we figure he left the Vogue two nights

ago. He should have checked into another hotel yesterday."

"If he did," said Eaglethorpe. "he didn't use his card. And if he ate anywhere or did anything that required money, he must have used cash."

"Good point. Hang on a second, Chief." Kori waved for the bartender. "Excuse me," she said, "but does the American guide usually pay cash when he comes in here?"

"No, never," said the bartender. "Always a credit card."

"And last night?"

"The same."

"Okay, thank you." Then speaking into the phone again, Kori said, "Chief, Agent Kovalev and I happen to be sitting in the bar where Davenport ate dinner last night. Bartender says he paid with a credit card."

"Well," sighed Eaglethorpe, "you know that means."

"I'm afraid so, Chief. It means he's probably got other forms of identification. Credit cards under an assumed name. Probably a false passport. He could be traveling under any name. Maybe the Daniel Price name that he posted on the internet with."

"Maybe," said Eaglethorpe. "But to acquire a

credit card, that would mean a different social security number, address, everything. It would be easier to use a stolen credit card. I'm afraid your job just got a little harder, Kori. Frankly, I don't see how we can help you track Davenport from this end."

"We'll just have to keep looking, I guess," said Kori. "In the meantime, what about the Guardian Militia members? Any better luck?"

"No so far. But we're working with Homeland and we've got law enforcement working to track down each member. So far, they've apparently all been quiet. They're laying low somewhere. And wherever they are, what they plan on doing remains a complete mystery."

"This is one strange case, Chief."

"That it is. In the meantime, all the normal precautions are in place here. Extra security at the airports, stadiums, etcetera. If we learn anything more, I'll let you know."

"Okay, Chief."

"Now, get back on it, Agent Briggs."

Before she hung up, Kori promised Eaglethorpe that she and Anya would continue their pursuit, but deep down was at a loss as to what to do next.

"How are we going to find Davenport in a city the size of Istanbul?" she asked Anya.

"It will take a **chudo**," said Anya.

Kori knew enough Russian to agree. Yes, it would take a miracle.

CHAPTER 17

Tackle the city of Istanbul on your own, the agent said. You never know what adventures you might find, she said.

Okay, why not?

Lola Jennings, a middle-aged woman with c harcoal gray hair, was wandering around the Grand Bazaar and enjoying the freedom that comes with solitary travel. There was something about the agent that inspired her. Both agents. They seemed... strong. Independent. Lola was these things, too, at least back home. Ask any of the sixty employees in her Pittsburgh staffing company. She was tough, practically fearless. And last year she was voted the city's Female Entrepreneur of the Year. You don't get to where Lola was if you're a scaredy-cat.

But…

But for some reason, foreign countries made Lola uneasy. Her Achilles' heel, she supposed. She felt out of her element and always had the idea that everyone else could tell she was an American tourist. She felt vulnerable and self-conscious, afraid to make a mistake, like ordering the wrong thing in a restaurant with a menu you couldn't make heads or tails of. Or taking the wrong bus or train and finding yourself lost, unable to get back to your hotel. She knew that what she felt was, for the most part, irrational, and she had finally decided that it wasn't a lack of courage on her part. She had something akin to a phobia. Phobias don't mean you're not courageous. Having a phobia just means that part of your brain doesn't always respond to reason.

Regardless, Lola loved to travel and she loved to meet people. And several years before, she had made up her mind that getting herself out of her element was exactly the thing she needed to do. She loved running her business, but there were times when she needed to completely reboot her mind. And she had discovered that there was nothing quite like travel for this task, nothing like yanking yourself out of your everyday existence and thrusting yourself into—literally—a foreign environment. Now, **that** takes courage. And whenever she did this—and so far she had taken trips to Paris, Rome, Amsterdam, Berlin, and Vienna—she always came away feeling like a new woman.

Lola always toured with a group and with a guide, however, thus mitigating the discomfort of being in a strange land. Why take chances? Plus, she didn't want to miss anything. Good tour guides know all the places to go and all the things to see. Maybe more than anything, besides the phobic discomfort, she didn't want to travel alone as a single woman. You take a couple of wrong turns in a foreign city and, just like that, you're in a dangerous neighborhood. This concern wasn't irrational fear. This concern was prudence. In fact, after the agents had left the hotel, she had tried to interest the rest of the group in seeing Istanbul together, but after the grumbling about Wyatt Davenport died down, everyone sort of drifted off in their own directions, some going for breakfast, some going back to their rooms. And that's when

Lola decided to brave the city on her own.

She used the directional app on her phone, made the fifteen-minute walk to the Grand Bazaar without difficulty, and was now strolling around all by herself, past a small shop with gorgeously colored ceramic vases and bowls and plates. She felt good about being out and about. This **was** an adventure, just like the agent recommended. It was high time she tried something like this. After all, she didn't become a successful businesswoman by shrinking from challenges. This could be fun.

But that didn't lessen the anger she felt about Wyatt Davenport. Just who was this guy, anyway? He was so highly recommended. The online reviews raved about him. All five stars. And she had to admit that until the day before, he'd been stellar. He knew his way around and seemed to know everything about the city of Istanbul. Plus, he seemed so nice. Charming, actually. Lola didn't even mind that Davenport suggested a day "to yourselves" yesterday. It was the third day of the tour and the first two had been something of a whirlwind. It had been go, go, go. Lola appreciated a day to unwind in the beautiful hotel. It had a pool, a bar, and even a spa. Plus, she was able to make a few phone calls and return some emails; just because she was on vacation, that didn't mean her business had stopped.

Still, it seemed strange to just break the tour off for a day. And then, when he didn't show up that morning? What could he possibly be involved in? Why were law enforcement agents looking for him? Lola eventually determined that it must have something to do with drugs. After the warning from the agents, she'd gone online and learned a little about drug trafficking in and through Turkey. The country was a significant smuggling route between Europe and Asia. Lola surmised that Wyatt Davenport, charming tour operator, was really a trafficker in heroin or cocaine. The presence of US agents must have meant that America was the ultimate destination for Davenport's drugs. They were there to cut off the supply at the source.

Lola hoped the agents would catch him and arrest him, but if they didn't, she was thinking about taking legal action of her own, and on behalf of the other members of the tour group. She was personal friends with one of the best attorneys in Pittsburgh and when she got back home, that was going to be the first phone call she'd make. She'd spent a lot of money for the tour and she'd be damned if that drug smuggling bastard Davenport was going to keep it.

If the agents couldn't catch him with the goods, she could at least sue him for all he was worth. And if they never found him, she could sue his company and take whatever assets it had, not that a travel agency would necessarily have a lot of assets. But that didn't matter. It was the principle of the thing.

Lola wandered around the Grand Bazaar for a while, thought about buying a small kilim rug, didn't, and then decided she was brave enough to go out into the streets to find a lunch spot. There were food places throughout the Bazaar, but that defeated the purpose of getting out and about in a foreign city. She'd been very careful in her trek around the Bazaar, a place she could tell was easy to get lost in, and was able to find the exit she wanted in pretty short order. According to her app, there was a café about ten minutes down the street. Sure, it was in the opposite direction from the hotel, but that was okay. The neighborhood looked nice and, besides, it was all a part of the adventure.

She strolled along the busy avenue and finally came upon the café. It had some outdoor seating, but the day had become hot. She figured maybe she'd get a table inside. A menu was displayed outside the door and she looked it over. Fortunately, the entries were in both Turkish and English, thus lessening the chances of ordering the wrong thing. **Worth a try**, she thought. She stepped inside the café, glanced around, and stepped right back out.

Davenport!

It was him. She recognized the mesh safari hat that he always wore. Had he seen her? No, it would have been impossible. He'd been looking down at his food and she had backed out of the door in a tenth of a second.

Lola crossed the street and walked down to the corner, wondering what to do. My God, she thought, a wanted drug trafficker! Right there in the café! A hunted man. A bad man. The agents had said he might be dangerous. Probably he carried a gun. A desperate man like that wouldn't think twice about using it. Who knows how many people he's killed in his life of crime?

She looked back at the café. There was just the one door. He would have to come out of it. Then what? She wondered how fast the agents could get to the café as she rummaged through her purse for the one agent's card. There it was: **Kori Briggs, National Bureau of Criminal Investigations**. She pulled out her cell phone and dialed, all the while keeping an eye on the door of the café.

"Miss Briggs? My name is Lola Jennings. We met this morning in the lobby of the Vogue Hotel. Yes, right. Well, listen, Miss Briggs—I found him! Him! Wyatt Davenport! He's in a café. The name? I don't know, it's in Turkish. The street? Um…oh, I can't pronounce it…Selim something. Selim Pasa, I think. Not far from a street called Ordu. Yes, I'll wait right here. I'll keep an eye on him, yes. Please hurry!"

Lola hung up. Agent Briggs had said she and the other agent were on their way. **My**, she thought, **if my little excursion wasn't an adventure before, it surely is now!** What a great story she'd have for the first staff meeting when she got back to the office. But, wait—there he was. Davenport was leaving the café. Lola slid back into a doorway and watched as he began walking in the opposite direction. **Now what do I do?** she wondered. **Why did he have to leave the café before the agents got here?**

"Corner of Selim Pasa and Ordu," Kori instructed the taxi driver as she and Anya jumped into the back seat. "And we're in a hurry, if you don't mind."

Lola Jennings's call had come as the agents were finishing off their beers at the Faust. It was a twenty-minute taxi ride and they hoped that Davenport would stay put.

"What do we do when we get there?" Anya asked.

"Arrest him, of course."

"But, Kori, we have no grounds. Think about it. The only piece of evidence we have on Wyatt Davenport, if it can even be called that, is his name scribbled onto a bank receipt. Everything else is conjecture."

"Damn it, Anya, you're right. Well, how about if we just take him behind the café and beat him senseless until he tells us what's going on?"

"Crude, but I suppose that's as good a plan as any."

"Let me know if you think of any other. Driver, can we go any faster? Please?"

The driver mumbled something in Turkish and Kori realized her English was lost on him. He hadn't understood the words "hurry" or "faster" and, worse, traffic was beginning to get snarled in the old city's narrow brick streets. Kori took a couple of deep breaths, trying to keep herself from becoming totally infuriated by the circumstances.

"Kori," said Anya, "why do you think Davenport is hanging out at a café?"

"Well, the man's got to eat somewhere. Obviously he's not going to be going back to the Faust. He knows he's being pursued."

"Nor will he go back to the Vogue Hotel."

"Right."

"So if we find where he's now staying, we'll find the $2.5 million, correct?"

"Sure, I would suppose so."

"But more importantly, Kori, we might find additional evidence."

"Like what?"

"Like evidence linking him to the Guardian Militia members. And evidence linking him to Arman Golzar. That would be good for us, of course, because we would have grounds to arrest him. But if Golzar really is operating without his government's approval, then I think the Iranians would want to know that. That might be the most critical consequence of proving the link at this point, do you see?"

"Sure. Good point, Anya. Yes, Golzar is about to get the Iranians into a war with the United States. They need to know what he's planning. Driver, can we get off this street, please? We're barely moving."

More mumbling in Turkish.

"Kori," Anya continued, "We may even be able to find some notes about the attack plan itself. Where it is to take place and when."

"So what are you saying, Anya?"

"Maybe instead of beating him up behind the café, we follow him to his hotel room, wherever that is. Let him lead us to the evidence that we need."

"Hmm…I guess that makes sense. So I don't get to beat him up?"

"Well, perhaps. When we break into his room, maybe he will offer up some resistance."

"I sure hope so. In the meantime, we're getting nowhere fast. Wait, that's my phone." Kori answered to hear the voice of Lola Jennings again. "Yes, Ms. Jennings? Left the café? Which direction is he headed? Okay, please listen carefully. It's very important that we know where he's going. Follow him, can you do that? Great. But try to keep your distance. Make sure he doesn't see you, but do not lose him. Yes, we're on our way. Unfortunately, the traffic is bad. Listen, stay on the phone with me, okay? Let me know what's going on."

"Yes, Miss Briggs, you can count on me." Lola looked up from her phone to see Davenport turning a corner. She turned the corner, too, following about twenty yards behind him. Soon, he turned another corner and Lola found herself on a busy sidewalk, shoulder to shoulder with jostling pedestrians. Lola was five feet four, in heels. And she wasn't in heels. Suddenly, through the maze of people in front of her, she lost sight of Davenport. She darted ahead, bobbing and weaving around the other pedestrians, but her efforts only led to more pedestrians blocking her view.

"I lost him!" she said into the phone. "The sidewalk is too crowded. I can't see around the people in front of me...I'm sorry, do what? Okay, hang on."

Lola quickly checked for vehicle traffic and then jumped out into the middle of the street and kept walking ahead. From this new angle, she could now spot Davenport's safari hat up ahead among the people over on the sidewalk.

"Got him!" she said. "He's just ahead of me."

The cars were moving slowly and she walked next to the line of traffic, maintaining enough distance from the sidewalk to give her a perspective that enabled her to keep an eye on the safari hat. Then the hat disappeared and Lola knew Davenport had turned down another street. She raced back through the pedestrians and across the sidewalk to see a narrow alleyway coming off the main street. Davenport was all alone in the alleyway, walking faster now.

"He's turned down an alley," Lola said quietly into the phone. "No, I don't know where. It came off a busy street…no, I don't know the name of the street. Let's see, he had taken a couple of turns from the café. The first turn was a right and then…no, I mean a left. Oh, Miss Briggs, I'm sorry, I don't know where I am. Yes, okay, I'll keep following."

Lola had been so intent on keeping Davenport in view that she'd paid no attention to where she was going. And it occurred to her with a start that she was exactly where she had never wanted to be. Lost in a foreign city.

"She's lost," Kori said to Anya, covering the mouthpiece with her hand. "But she's still got him in her sights and is still following. He's in an alley somewhere."

Meanwhile, traffic had come to a complete standstill. Kori leaned her head out of the window and saw a flashing of lights several blocks ahead.

"I think there's an accident or something," she said. "We can't be too far. At this rate, we're probably better off on foot. C'mon, Anya."

She scooted out of the taxi, tossing some lira behind her at the driver and soon she and Anya were running in the general direction of the café, Kori holding the phone up to her ear hanging on to the one hope they had of finding Wyatt Davenport—that Lola Jennings would not lose sight of him.

The alley ran past the rear of a block-long, three-story building that Lola surmised to be a second-rate hotel, maybe even third-rate. It was pale green in color but surely had been darker green at one time, before years of the Turkish sun had taken its toll. The paint was chipped and peeling in places. Several overstuffed garbage bags rested outside a rear door. The rooms' small window air conditioning units made a cacophony of noise and the alley smelled of rotting food and urine. **Not exactly the Vogue**, Lola thought.

Davenport turned at the corner of the alley and walked around to the front of the hotel. Lola followed. She could see the entrance now, at the far corner of the building, nothing more than a single glass door with a tattered awning above it. A neon light said **Hotel Ucuz**. Davenport entered. Lola hung back on the street, not daring to be seen. Into her phone, she said, "Ms. Briggs, are you still there? He's gone into a hotel called the Ucuz. Hang on, let me check." Lola walked down to the corner to read the street sign. "The street is Sarayici. Okay, I'll wait here."

Lola stood on the street corner and looked back at the hotel. **How are they going to find him in there?** she wondered. She counted the windows across the front of the hotel, figured there were rooms along the front and back side of the building, knew there were three stories, and calculated a total of forty-two rooms. **I should have followed him in**, she thought. **All the way to his room. What kind of an adventurer am I?**

She thought for a second, screwed up her courage, and marched into the hotel. The lobby, if one could call it that, was maybe twelve feet by twelve. A vinyl orange couch rested along the near wall with a fake plastic plant set in the corner, years of dust coating its leaves. In the other corner was a mostly empty vending machine. In front of Lola was a man seated at a desk in a small area enclosed by a security screen. The man was tapping away on a computer and barely looked up. Beside the computer was an open bag of potato chips and Lola could tell by the crumbs on the man's T-shirt that he'd been diligently working on them.

I've made sales calls on places worse than this, she told herself, trying to maintain her courage. She forced a smile. "Excuse me, sir," she said through the screen, "the man who just came in? With the safari hat? That's my husband. He has our room key and I'll be damned if I can remember our room number."

The clerk looked up at Lola with a blank stare and for a second, Lola thought he must not have understood her English. Then he reached into the bag of chips, grabbed a handful, mumbled, "104," and shoved the chips into his mouth before returning his gaze to the computer screen.

"Thank you, sir." Lola hung onto the forced smile,

looked down the darkened first-floor hallway, and then slowly backed out of the door into the street. She took a deep breath and raised her head to see a most welcome sight: two young women running toward the hotel along Sarayici. The cavalry was arriving.

CHAPTER 18

"There she is," said Kori. "And there's the hotel."

Kori and Anya made their way to Lola whose smile was no longer a forced one. "He's in 104!" she said excitedly. "I wormed the information out of the desk clerk. I told him he was my husband."

"Great work, Ms. Jennings," said Kori, catching her breath. "Now, listen, you stay out here where it's safe. Actually, it's probably best if you take a taxi back to the Vogue. We'll take things from here and I'll contact you later."

"Okay, Miss Briggs. But, please do let me know

how this turns out, won't you?"

"Of course. In the meantime, we thank you. The United States government thanks you."

Lola was beaming now. "Oh, well, you know, just trying to help. What any good citizen would do."

Kori's smile faded as she turned to face the hotel. She and Anya walked toward the entrance. Lola looked around the street for a taxi, but then decided maybe she'd wait just a minute or two in front of the hotel. She simply had to see how it was all going to play out. Besides, perhaps the agents would need her help again. She couldn't very well abandon them now.

As they entered the cramped lobby, Kori turned to Anya and whispered, "Looks like your plan of following Davenport to his hotel worked. Except that we didn't need to follow him. Someone did it for us."

"We should buy Ms. Jennings a drink later," said Anya.

"At least."

The two walked past the enclosed desk where Kori noticed a man tapping away at a computer screen with potato chips crumbs on his chin. He glanced up at Kori and Anya and then did a double-take. Beautiful women did not walk into his lobby very often. He straightened up and, in a brief moment of self-awareness, brushed the potato chip crumbs off his chin and shirt and smiled broadly at the agents. Kori smiled back as she and Anya continued through the lobby into the hallway. **Gross**, thought Kori.

The hallway was dimly lit and it took a second for the agents' eyes to adjust. Several doors down, on the side of the building that faced the street, they came across room 104. The door was wooden and cheap. Easy enough, thought Kori. She reached into her purse for her Glock. Anya reached into her purse for her Sig Sauer. Kori squared herself to the door, raised her foot, and kicked straight at the door just to the side of the knob, the weakest part of a wooden door. The door splintered and Anya drove her shoulder into it, forcing it to swing open. Both agents stormed in, guns pointed ahead of them.

"Freeze!" yelled Kori.

An older man was sitting on the edge of the bed with a younger woman, their eyes wide with alarm.

"We weren't doing anything!" the man cried out. "I swear! Who sent you? My wife? Did she pay you to follow me? This is Gina, my secretary. There's nothing going on between us. We're in the city on business! Good God, how did Marian even find me here? In Istanbul of all places!"

"Relax," Kori sighed, lowering her weapon. "We have the wrong room."

The man continued to look alarmed while the woman started to cry.

The agents walked back out of the room. "Sorry," Anya said, turning back toward the couple. She attempted to close the splintered door behind her, but it no longer fit the frame and wouldn't shut completely. She shrugged. "Again, our apologies. Please enjoy your day."

In the lobby, Kori went up to the security screen and said to the man behind the desk, "Excuse me, but a woman was in here just a few minutes ago and you told her that her husband was in room 104."

"Yes?" the man said, once again straightening up and breaking into a smile for the beautiful American woman.

"This man," Kori said, holding up her phone with the picture of Davenport that Cooper had emailed.

"Yes, 104," the man said.

"Are you sure?"

The man thought for a moment, then looked down at his computer, clicking his mouse a few times. "Oh," he said. "Very sorry. 106. But why do you want to know, miss? The owner says I am not supposed to give out room numbers."

"Your secret is safe with us," said Kori. "We won't tell him if you won't."

"Yes, but in the meantime," said Anya, "room 104 needs a new door."

The man blinked a few times, saying nothing.

Kori and Anya returned to the hallway and walked past room 104 to room 106. "Second door in as many minutes," Kori whispered as she pulled her gun and squared herself to the door. "You know, my record is five in one day. A case in Colombia a few years back. Remind me to tell you about it later."

Then she kicked again, Anya drove her shoulder again, and a locked door swung open again.

This time the room was empty. But not uninhabited. The agents noticed an open suitcase, some toiletries scattered on top of the dresser, and an unmade bed.

"Kori, the window," said Anya. Thin curtains were fluttering in the breeze coming in from the open window.

Kori crossed the room just as her phone rang: Lola Jennings. "He just ran past me!" she was saying. "I saw him jump out of the window! Are you two all right?"

"Anya, c'mon!" said Kori and the two ran out of the room, back down the hallway, through the lobby past the clerk, and out into the street. Lola was pointing in the direction Davenport had gone.

"Obviously, he heard the commotion in 104," said Anya.

"Let's go," said Kori and the two agents began running down the street where Lola had pointed. Kori thought she saw Davenport turning a corner in the distance, but by the time they reached the next intersection, he was nowhere to be seen. "Anya, you go up that way, I'll go this way."

"Right."

Anya turned left and ran up the cross street, while Kori turned right, both agents running for several blocks with neither seeing any sign of Wyatt Davenport. Finally, Kori called Anya on her cell.

"Anything?"

"Nope. You?"

"Nope. Looks like we lost him. We need to return to his hotel room, Anya, in case he double backs."

"Last one there buys the beers."

"You're on."

A couple of minutes later, the agents arrived

simultaneously, deferring, for the time being, the decision about who would be buying what for whom. Lola Jennings was still standing out front. "Did he get away?"

"I'm afraid so, Ms. Jennings," said Kori.

"Damn."

"It's okay. We'll find him."

"Well, I don't know it if matters, but I noticed that he was carrying a duffel bag with him."

"Really?"

"Yes, a black duffel bag. That's all I saw."

"Okay, thank you," said Anya.

"You've been a lot of help, Ms. Jennings," said Kori. "Now, please, for your own safety, I think you should return to the Vogue."

"Sure. But can you at least tell me something about Davenport and why you're after him? Is it drugs? It's drugs, isn't it? Heroin? Cocaine?"

"We're not really at liberty to say, Ms. Jennings," Kori said. "But I can at least tell you that it's not drugs. Believe it or not, it's worse. We think Wyatt Davenport is a potential terrorist."

"A terrorist! Oh, my. But he seemed like such a nice man. And the reviews he gets online for his tours!"

"Believe me, we know. It's a rather befuddling

case. We're still just putting the pieces together. And your efforts have helped make our job a lot easier. Now, there's a taxi. Let's get you back to the Vogue."

"Of course."

Kori waved to a cab drifting by. It pulled over and Kori handed the driver a wad of lira, saying, "Vogue Hotel for this woman, please."

"Oh, thank you so much," Lola said, sliding into the back seat.

"You're welcome, Ms. Jennings. We'll be in touch."

"Please. I simply have to know how this comes out. In the meantime, good luck!"

The cab took off and the agents once again went into the hotel, past the clerk, down the hallway past 104, where Kori glimpsed the couple inside packing their bags, and then into room 106.

"Kori," said Anya, "the duffel bag. It must have been the money."

"That's what I was thinking. Davenport had time to grab one thing and, naturally, he grabbed the $2.5 million. But there's his suitcase. Let's see what we can find."

"Looks like all his clothes are in here," said Anya, as the agents rifled through Davenport's personal belongings. "But with $2.5 million in American cash, I do not imagine he will have trouble replacing them."

"Which makes you wonder why he chose such a crappy hotel to stay in," said Kori.

"To keep a low profile. He wanted to get lost in the city until he could collect the second half of the money. How much more lost can you get than this place?"

"True." Kori unzipped the suitcase's inside pocket. "Look, Anya, an envelope." Kori pulled out a letter-size manilla envelope and undid the clasp. She slid a piece of paper out.

"What's it say?" asked Anya.

"It's a list. A list of names. An even dozen. Anya, I'd bet a bottle of scotch that these names coincide with the list Vasquez put together of Guardian Militia members."

"Yes, probably so," Anya said, looking over Kori's shoulder. "But look beside the names, Kori."

"American towns. Interesting. Macon, Georgia; Salinas, California; Salem, Oregon; Peoria, Illinois…"

"All small towns, yes?"

"Yes. Strange. Do you think these could be the places the members went?"

"Maybe. But why? Why different towns? And what damage could they do in these places?"

"Yeah, it doesn't make sense, Anya. What kind of terrorist attacks can you commit in a dozen small towns that would make America, as Nasirian's letter said, fall to its knees?"

"I have assumed an attack on one major target."

"Yeah, me too. What's one militia guy going to do in Peoria, Illinois? Take over a Walmart? We'd better call the chief. Let's go."

As the agents walked through the lobby, Anya, carrying Davenport's suitcase, turned to the desk clerk and said, "It looks as if you will also be needing a new door for room 106."

"Hey!" he called after them, but the two beautiful women were gone.

"Trivia question, Chief," said Kori into her cell phone as she and Anya sat at the bar back at the Hotel Amira. "Get Cooper and Foster on the line, too."

"Hang on," said Eaglethorpe.

Kori took a sip of the scotch in front of her. Anya had contemplated a raki, but chose to go back to her usual vodka.

"Okay," said Eaglethorpe. "I have Foster and Cooper on the line with me. Now, what's this about a trivia question?"

"The category is American geography," said Kori. "Ready? What do the following twelve towns all have in common? Macon, Salinas, Salem, Peoria, Providence, Scranton, Roanoke, Terre Haute, Abilene, Hattiesburg, Provo, and Daytona Beach."

"Easy," said Cooper. "Those are the locations of major electric-transmission substations."

"Say again?" said Kori.

"Power stations that are linked to the nation's power grid. They act essentially as distribution points. Why are you asking about them?"

"Because there's something else they all have in common."

"What's that?" said Eaglethorpe.

"They're the locations where we think the members of the Guardian Militia have all gone."

The line was silent for a moment, everyone contemplating the ramifications. Finally, Foster gave a low whistle and said, "Well that explains a lot."

"It sure does," said Eaglethorpe. "Pretty big piece of the puzzle, Agent Briggs. The Guardian Militia is poised to commit a terrorist act like no other. They're going to bring down the grid."

"Can they really do that?" asked Kori. "From just twelve stations?"

"Oh, yeah," said Cooper. "They sure can. It's our worst nightmare, outside of a nuclear incident. Those particular power stations are part of what holds the entire grid together. If someone were to sabotage all of them at the same time, this country would be plunged into darkness. Depending on the extent of the damage, we could be without power for months, conceivably even a year. It would be chaos."

"Then Nasirian characterized it properly, didn't he?" said Kori grimly, downing what was left in her glass. "America would fall to its knees."

CHAPTER 19

"Agent Cooper, how would such an attack work?" asked Eaglethorpe as the conference call continued.

"Well, it's like this," Cooper explained, "there are thousands of electrical substations around the country. These aren't power stations, per se. That is to say, they don't generate electricity like a power plant does. Generally, what they do is transmit the power. Electricity travels around the country at extremely high voltage. These substations transform the electricity into usable voltage and then distribute it to whatever geographic area they're covering. Or sometimes, they act as switching stations, basically redirecting the power to where it ultimately needs to go, maybe to the next substation. The point is, there are around a hundred or so substations that are **especially** critical to the system as a whole. And if you knocked out any eight or ten of these vital stations at the same time, it would create a domino effect on the entire grid. Everything is networked together, you see. It's like knocking out a couple of load-bearing walls in a building. The rest of the walls won't be able to handle the added stress. And the whole thing would come crumbling down."

"But how would you attack one of these stations, Coop?" asked Kori.

"Easy," Cooper replied. "This form of attack has been on our radar for a while. It's a known security weakness."

"You could conceivably do it with a couple of sticks of dynamite," Foster chimed in. "If you hit the right part of a substation, take out the right voltage regulator or capacitor, you'll cause the rest of the station to basically overload."

"Right," said Cooper. "It's like plugging too many things into the same socket. You'll blow a fuse and the power will stop. But in this case, it means the station stops transmitting electricity to the rest of the grid."

"Exactly," said Foster. "Now, the grid is configured in such a way that if a problem occurs at one substation, the power gets redirected to another, bypassing the nonfunctioning station. But like Coop said, if you knock out eight or ten of the most critical stations, the network will fold like the proverbial house of cards."

"Yes, and those towns you listed, Kori?" added Cooper. "Those definitely come under the heading of critical stations. Eight or ten would suffice. Twelve stations means these guys aren't taking any chances."

"How secure are these facilities?" Eaglethorpe asked.

"Not very," Foster answered.

"Hence the fact that we've been concerned about them," said Cooper. "Frankly, I'm surprised no one has tried something like this before."

"Well, there was one attack back in 2013," said Foster. "The Metcalf Transmission Substation near San Jose was fired upon by a group of gunmen. They shot at seventeen transformers, as I recall, doing about $15 million worth of damage. By sheer luck, the impact on the station's power supply was minimal. They never did find the culprits. Pretty professional job."

"Right," said Cooper. "Metcalf. Investigators believed it was an inside job, based on the knowledge of where, exactly, to shoot. These weren't ordinary vandals."

"But how can that happen?" asked Kori. "Aren't these places guarded?"

"Well, that's just it," said Cooper. "Power companies are privately run. Essentially, they're monopolies, sanctioned by local governments. In return, the local governments regulate the rates the power companies can charge their customers. But there's very little federal oversight. In fact, believe it or not, there are no federal requirements that power stations be secure."

"The only exception," added Foster, "is with nuclear plants. They're pretty heavily regulated, as you might imagine. But your garden variety electric substation? It probably has a chain-link fence around it and—maybe—some barbed wire."

"Right. Some of the substations aren't even manned," said Cooper. "Not so much as a night watchman. It's all computerized."

"Okay, so let's assume an attack," said Eaglethorpe. "How fast can a damaged substation come back online? You said months, Agent Cooper?

Maybe a year? Why so long?"

"The kinds of transformers and voltage regulators and miscellaneous elements that operate in these critical substations aren't exactly sitting on shelves somewhere," answered Cooper. "You don't just call your local electrical parts supply house and order a replacement if something gets damaged. The transformers themselves cost about a million bucks each and they're more or less made to order. Again, one or two would be doable, but a dozen transformers needing to be manufactured at the same time? Nobody's geared up for that kind of production."

"Good God," said Kori. "Can you imagine the chaos that would ensue if the country was dark for several months or a year? The economy would crash overnight. Communications would be nonexistent. No phones, no internet."

"It might be weeks before word even got around to people what had happened," said Foster. "In the meantime, everyone would be sitting in the dark."

"Everything runs on electricity," said Cooper. "Even municipal water plants and sewage treatment facilities."

"So the water will run out," said Kori.

"Yep. Even natural gas is distributed through a

system that relies heavily on electrical power to fuel compressors and pumping stations."

"The distribution of essentials would grind to a halt, too," said Foster. "Even the diesel fuel that runs the trucking industry is pumped via electricity. Food, medical supplies. Everything would become scarce. And there'd be no way to maintain refrigeration. So whatever might happen to be left in grocery stores would go bad, if it managed to remain on the shelves at all."

"Right," said Cooper. "I think we can assume that everything would be looted in pretty short order, leaving empty shelves and empty stores."

"There really would be very little of American life that wouldn't be affected," said Foster. "Maybe the lone hermit who lives in a solar-powered cabin in Montana and hunts for his food might not notice. But the rest of the population? We're talking starvation."

"But not before a heck of a lot of violence and mayhem," added Cooper. "People fighting their neighbors for clean water or scraps of food—"

"Okay, I think we get it," said Eaglethorpe. "An apocalyptic nightmare."

"Chief, let me put it like this," said Foster. "We'd be better off under a zombie attack."

"I always assumed a lethal raid on the grid would come by way of a cyberattack," said Kori. "A hacker, finding a way to shut things down."

"Yes, that's what most people think, including the operators of the substations," said Cooper. "To their credit, they've put a lot of effort into the prevention of cyber security breaches. But not so much effort into the prevention of a physical attack. It's now actually much easier to use good old-fashioned explosives than malicious computer code. It's back to the basics, I guess. Funny how things come full circle."

"Sure, but it's got to be coordinated," said Foster. "Had the Metcalf attack been successful, it would have affected much of Southern California, but it would have gone no farther. And it would not have lasted very long. With other substations fully functional, the grid would have found a way to pick up the slack in a matter of hours. But a coordinated attack like this one is an entirely different animal."

"Except for one thing," said Kori. "We know the locations of the substations these losers are planning to attack. That means that this doesn't have to happen. We can stop it."

"Exactly, Agent Briggs," said Eaglethorpe. "I'll call the president. I'll recommend that we mobilize

Homeland and probably the FBI. If we have to, we'll roll out the National Guard to surround the substations in question. We'll draw a perimeter. Nobody will get within a mile of the stations. And we'll stay in place until all of these guys are accounted for and arrested. But I have to say, I'm still confused by one thing. How in the hell did this band of misfits hook up with an Iranian terrorist group?"

"It's bizarre, Chief," said Kori. "But Agent Kovalev and I plan on answering that question just as soon as we find Wyatt Davenport."

"Then get to it, Agent Briggs. We'll take care of things on this end."

With the attack essentially thwarted, the urgency to find Davenport was reduced. Kori and Anya decided that he probably wasn't going anywhere, not with the second half of the $5 million still on the table. It might take a while before he would learn of the failure of the plan, and until then, surely he'd be hanging around Istanbul in anticipation of his big payday. The agents had a leisurely dinner and then agreed to meet in the morning for breakfast and to figure out the best course of action to find Wyatt Davenport.

Back in her hotel room that night, Kori decided it might be a good idea to call Evan Banks. Strictly for professional reasons, of course. He would no doubt be curious as to the progress the agents were making with the potential attack. After all, an attack of such scope would certainly affect the nation's northern neighbor. It was just common courtesy between two law enforcement agencies.

"Kori!" said Evan when he answered his phone. "It's so good to hear your voice."

Kori smiled at the warm reception. "Thanks, Evan. Good to hear yours, too. How are things in the Great White North?"

"Pretty quiet. Which is nice. How about in your neck of the woods? Are you still in Istanbul?"

"Yep. But, listen, I think we've figured the whole thing out."

"Really?"

"I can't give you details, but I think we just prevented an attack on the United States power grid."

"Oh, wow. A cyberattack?"

"Nope. A physical attack."

"No kidding? From Iranians?"

"Seems they somehow found a way to delegate the job. Strange set of circumstances. We're still trying to get to the bottom of it over here, but we'll figure it all out."

"I'm sure you will. Anything I can do to help? You say the word and I can call Ottawa and give you whatever support you need."

"Thanks, Evan, I appreciate that. I'll keep it in mind."

"Of course. Well, congratulations on the fine detective work, Kori. Maybe something good can come from Dane and Hajar's deaths."

"I can't get into the scope of the attack just now, Evan, but I can tell you that it's no exaggeration to say we owe our lives to those two."

"Wow. Well, I'd love to hear more. When will you be able to talk about it? I mean, no hurry. I understand all about ongoing investigations. And anything you ultimately tell me will, naturally, be regarded strictly as a confidential, official briefing between our two agencies. If you can tell me anything at all, of course."

"Evan, it was you who put us on to this whole thing. You deserve to know the story. I'll be happy to brief you, and I'm sure my chief would approve." Then, with a hint of playful flirtation, Kori added, "It should probably be in person, don't you think? I mean, for security reasons, of course. You know how it is."

"Yes, of course," Evan agreed, smiling to himself. "One can't be too careful. In person, face-to-face, **is** the proper protocol for something of this nature."

"Yes, indeed. Proper protocol."

"Probably the briefing should take place in some quiet, out of the way venue."

"Hmm, yes, that's what I was thinking."

"Low lit. Maybe even candlelight."

"Yes, that would only be prudent."

"Would you have any objection to the presence of a bottle of wine? You know how these briefings can go sometimes. It's always a good idea to be well fortified."

"Well, I don't see the harm. Perhaps we should consider some kind of dinner fare, as well. I mean, so long as we have the wine."

"Indeed. Italian okay?"

"My favorite."

"I think I know just the place. I'll make sure to have it all arranged, Agent Briggs."

"And I'll look forward to it, Agent Banks."

CHAPTER 20

Anya and Kori met for breakfast the next morning and then spent the day canvassing more places where Wyatt Davenport was known to have frequented—tourist sites, restaurants, shops—anywhere a lead from someone took them. They returned to the Faust. They revisited the Blue Mosque. They asked around at the Grand Bazaar. They went back to the Vogue Hotel and interviewed all the members of the last tour group, including Lola Jennings, who was thrilled to see them again, but sorry that she could be of no further help.

Nobody had seen Davenport.

The next day, they did more of the same, finishing the day back at the hotel's rooftop bar, completely exhausted of ideas.

"Let's face it, Anya," said Kori, over a dinner of spicy chicken Adana, "he's too smart to be found again. If he was keeping a low profile before, he's being even more careful now. It was something of a miracle that we found him the first time. If Lola Jennings hadn't spotted him…"

"America might be dark by now," Anya said, finishing the thought. "By the way, what have you heard from the chief?"

"Nothing since yesterday when he told us that all the stations were secure. But maybe I should call him and check in. I'm almost done with my chicken anyway."

"Call him before I order us dessert."

"What did you have in mind?"

"Ever have kunafeh?"

"Nope."

"It's a sweet, cheese pastry."

"I like every word you just used to describe it. Count me in."

Anya waved the waiter over while Kori dialed

Eaglethorpe.

"Agent Briggs," the director said, "I hope you're having better luck there than we are here."

"Frankly, we're striking out here, Chief. Davenport is nowhere around. But what do you mean? What's going on over there?"

"Nothing. And that's the problem. National Guard sentries are posted around the substations and police are patrolling the areas but all is quiet. The Guardian Militia members have seemingly vanished."

"Vanished?"

"Foster has been doing cyber surveillance, tracing credit card charges and so on. These guys must still be paying cash wherever they are. We've got APBs out for them, with descriptions and vehicle information. Nothing. Checkpoints have even been set up. And yet not one lead has surfaced, not one sighting. It's as if these guys have fallen off the face of the earth."

"Well, at least the substations are safe."

"Yes, at least there's that. And that's the main thing, of course. We can rest a lot easier now. Still, it's frustrating that we can't nab these guys."

"Well, Chief, I'm sure they'll turn up sooner or later. They can't hide forever."

"Right. Same thing with Davenport, I suppose. Speaking of which, what's your next move, Kori?"

"Well, I'm about to launch myself into a plate of something called kunafeh. After that? No idea, Chief. For all we know, Davenport might not even be in Istanbul anymore. Once he gets word that the attacks have been prevented, then there's no reason for him to be hanging around. It's not likely that Golzar is going to pay him for nothing."

"In fact, Kori, when you stop and think about it, Golzar would certainly want his $2.5 million deposit back."

"That's right, Chief! Davenport's life might be in danger if he stays here."

"Assuming he knows the attack has been prevented."

"Which depends on the level of communication he has with the militia members."

"Well, if they communicate at all, he'll know. By now, the militia members have surely seen the National Guard and the police presence."

"Right. So Davenport must know. And he's probably gone. He'll have taken his duffel bag of cash and left for God only knows where."

"Somewhere Golzar can never find him."

"Or us, so he would hope. Well, Chief, given all

that, what do you want us to do?"

Eaglethorpe sighed. "Well, I don't see any reason for you to continue chasing Davenport, do you? At least not in Istanbul. Why don't you come back to HQ, Kori? You can probably be of more help here, helping us track down the Guardian Militia members. We can worry about Davenport later. In fact, maybe one of the militia members will be willing to rat him out."

"Roger that, Chief. I'll head for the airport first thing in the morning."

Kori hung up, stuck a fork into the kunafeh, which had just been placed before her, and said, "Well, my Russian friend, I guess this is our farewell dinner. Chief wants me back home."

"Yes, I gathered. And I agree that Davenport is not likely to be in Istanbul anymore. It's no use us trying to find him here. But not to worry. Arman Golzar has 2.5 million reasons to look for him."

"Good point, Anya."

"Ironically, Golzar may end up doing our job for us. And I have a feeling that when Golzar finds him, he will not be treated as kindly as if we found him."

"You don't think Ambassador Golzar will read Davenport his rights?" Kori chuckled.

"Probably not," smiled Anya.

"But, you know, Anya, that brings up another point. Golzar. He cannot continue to operate. The Iranian government needs to know that they've got a loose cannon on their hands, someone who was almost successful in drawing America into a war with their country."

"Yes, of course."

"I'm sure the chief will notify the State Department. Through diplomatic channels, Arman Golzar's intentions will be brought to the attention of the supreme leader of Iran. I don't imagine he'll be treated any better than he would treat Davenport. Maybe even worse."

"Well," said Anya, "I'm sure everything will work itself out. We should be celebrating the fact that the attack was stopped."

"Indeed we should. Raki?"

"But of course."

"As always, it's been a pleasure working with you, Anya. I will miss you."

"And I you, Kori. Perhaps we will work together again very soon."

In her hotel room, Kori called her mother to tell her she'd be coming home. Everything in St. Louis had worked out fine. The glitches had been unglitched, the installation was almost finished, and Kori's presence was no longer needed. Joan was very glad to hear it. After the call, Kori turned in, slept soundly for a couple of hours, and then awoke with an anxious feeling. She tossed and turned for a while, but something unidentifiable was nagging at her, something about the case. Something wasn't right; she felt it in her bones.

Eventually, she sat up in bed and let her mind wander, giving up on the idea of sleep. She thought about her conversation with Director Eaglethorpe. The substations were safe. "We can rest a lot easier now," the chief had said. Then she thought about Cooper's description of how the grid worked. There were "a hundred or so" substations that were "especially critical." Meanwhile, nobody from the Guardian Militia had been seen around the twelve stations on Davenport's list. Davenport had to have known he'd left the list behind in his suitcase when he bolted out of the window of his room at the Hotel Ucuz. He hadn't had time to grab it. He'd taken a duffel bag, probably one containing $2.5

million in cash, and had disappeared, leaving the list of towns behind. And what was it that Anya was saying? Yes, Golzar would be out for blood at not only the loss of the money, but at the failure of the plan. Everybody agreed that Davenport had most likely fled Istanbul. But where would he be safe? Could he afford to fail?

A hundred or so substations that are especially critical.

Cooper's words kept echoing through Kori's mind.

Finally, with a sense of dread mixed with urgency, she placed a call to Eaglethorpe. "Chief," she said, "I'm afraid we haven't succeeded in thwarting Davenport's attack. We've only succeeded in redirecting it."

CHAPTER 21

Kori hung up with Eaglethorpe who planned an immediate call to Homeland. The protection of the grid was going to be expanded to encompass all the critical substations. But complete deployment was going to take time. Would it come too late? The only guaranteed way to stop the attack was to focus all efforts on the newly targeted stations. But which ones were those? Eaglethorpe and Kori agreed that even the members of the Guardian Militia might not know which sites. It was possible that each member knew only of his own target, just in case anybody got caught. You can't divulge what you don't know. Wyatt Davenport might have been the only one who understood the plan in its entirety.

Kori called Anya who surprisingly picked up on the first ring.

"I didn't wake you?" Kori asked. "It's three-thirty in the morning."

"I couldn't sleep," said Anya. "I fear we are not done with this case, Kori."

"That's why I'm up, too. Great minds think alike, my friend. I just got off the phone with the Chief. I believe we're protecting the wrong substations."

"Yes, precisely, Kori. That is what I have been sitting here contemplating. Davenport has too much to lose by giving up on the attack. He has to see it through. Losing the list was a wrinkle in his plan, but not a fatal one. No doubt he has sent his men to other substations. No wonder there were no sightings in the towns on the list."

"The militia members never arrived at those towns."

"Exactly. Kori, we need to find Davenport now more than ever."

"Indeed we do. Anya, you were hoping we'd be working together again soon. Is this soon enough for you?"

Kori jumped in the shower, dressed, grabbed a cup of coffee, and met Anya in front of the hotel, both agents ready to go.

But to where?

In all the rushing around to get back to the business at hand, neither agent had had time to think of the next move. It was still dark and now they stood on a sidewalk under a lamppost, an occasional car or taxi going past on the stone street that ran alongside the hotel. The morning was already warm but it would be at least a couple more hours before the city would come to life again.

The agents looked at each other.

"So what's the plan?" they both blurted out simultaneously, causing them to start laughing in spite of the situation.

"Anya, I thought **you'd** have the plan!" said Kori.

"No, no, this is the time for a Kori Briggs plan, I believe," said Anya. "I was sure that **you** would know our next step."

"I wish I did. The fact is, there are about 15 million people in the larger Istanbul metropolitan area. And we're trying to find one person."

"It is a—what is the expression?—needle in a bale of hay."

"Close enough. The point is, it would be hard enough to find Davenport if he **wanted** to be found. I don't even know where to start. We've interviewed everybody he ever comes into contact with in this city and gone to all the places he ever goes to. What are we supposed to do? Just start walking the streets? Hope we bump into him?"

"In an area that is roughly 2,000 miles square," Anya nodded. "We would need an army of searchers and we are only two."

"Yes, but you know, Anya, you've given me an idea. Maybe we can get a little help."

"From where?"

"Well, Farzad mentioned that the Turkish authorities would be reluctant to investigate an Iranian diplomat, given the close relationship the two countries have."

"Yes?"

"Well, we don't need investigatory help with an Iranian terrorist plan. We need help with a terrorist who is an American. An American who is in their country. Surely, the Turkish police can be persuaded to at least be on the lookout for someone of Davenport's description."

"Especially if they know what's at stake."

"Exactly. A blacked-out America isn't going to be good for anybody. They'd have to cooperate with us."

"So who do we talk to?"

"Well, I know someone to start with, anyway." Kori pulled out her phone and dialed the number of Canadian Intelligence officer Wallace Simon.

"Hello?" said a groggy voice on the other end.

"Agent Simon. Kori Briggs here." She looked at her watch: 4:30 a.m. "Sorry for the early wake-up call."

"It's okay, Agent Briggs. I'll assume it's important."

"It is."

"Having to do with the terrorist attack, no doubt."

"Good guess. We know who the ringleader is."

"Really?"

"Yep. An American. A guy by the name of Wyatt Davenport. And he's somewhere in this city. The problem is, we have no idea where. Can we prevail upon your contacts with the Turkish police to help us locate him?"

"I'll certainly do what I can."

"Thanks. I'll forward you a picture and a description."

"Do you have any idea where I should tell them to start looking?"

"Well, that's just it. We've been everywhere he usually goes. But, listen, whatever the Turkish police can do would be appreciated. I was thinking if they could just put out a…what do they call an 'All-Points Bulletin' here?"

"An All-Points Bulletin."

"Of course. Even if it's just an APB. Hopefully somebody doing their normal rounds spots him. It's a longshot, but we're kind of desperate."

"I understand. By the way, I'm glad you've identified the American. But where does the trail lead in the other direction? How high up does it go?"

"All the way to Arman Golzar in Ankara, Iran's ambassador to Turkey and Nasirian's boss. But we're sure it doesn't go any higher."

"Well, that's a relief, at least."

"And we believe Golzar is here in Istanbul now. Maybe you can tell your contacts to be on the lookout for him, too. Obviously, we don't expect them to take any action against him, but if they see him, maybe they can let us know where he is."

"Right, Agent Briggs. I'll get right on it."

"Thank you, Agent Simon. Stand by for that picture and description. And, again, sorry about the early hour."

"Not a problem at all. Terrorism never sleeps."

"Apparently not."

Kori hung up and texted Simon the information on Wyatt Davenport. "Well, at least we'll have a few more eyes out there," she said to Anya. "They'll be looking for Golzar, too."

"Good. But, Kori," Anya said thoughtfully, "maybe we're working to find Davenport in the wrong place."

"What do you mean? We've determined he'd probably stick around Istanbul, right? It's where he's expecting to collect the second $2.5 million from Golzar."

"Yes, no doubt. But, you see, we're looking for him here when, perhaps, we should be looking for him in Michigan. Or, I should say, more accurately, that we should be looking for him **from** Michigan."

"You lost me, Anya."

"Kori, somebody back in Michigan knows where he is, or at least how to contact him, don't you think?"

"I suppose..."

"A wife, girlfriend, partner. Parents, even. There is always somebody. Always."

"Hmm…I think I see where you're going."

"Our search should be there, not here. Not for Davenport, but for whomever it is that can connect us with Davenport."

Kori smiled. "Way to use the old noggin, Anya."

"Pardon?"

But Kori had already pulled out her phone and was dialing Eaglethorpe.

"Chief," she said when he answered, "what do we know about Davenport's personal life in Lansing?"

"Personal life? Not much. He's married, I'm pretty sure."

"Where's Vasquez? Is he still there?"

"No, he flew back here yesterday. Why?"

"Because somebody needs to interview Davenport's wife."

"Agent Briggs, do you really think Davenport would risk his operation by filling his wife in on the details of his plan?"

"No, Chief, but we don't need the details. We just need to know where Davenport is. Surely, he keeps in touch with his wife when he's on these tours."

"I suppose. But why would she give him up?"

"Because maybe she doesn't know what his plans are. Maybe she doesn't know the full scope. Heck, she might know absolutely nothing about what her husband is up to. Maybe she doesn't know her country is about to be plunged into darkness."

"And maybe she needs someone to explain it to her," Eaglethorpe said, grasping Kori's point.

"Vasquez needs to go right back there," said Kori, "and sit down with Mrs. Davenport and convince her to help us, for the good of all."

"The heck with Vasquez," said Eaglethorpe. "This trip I'm taking myself."

"Better hurry," Kori started to say, but Director Eaglethorpe had already hung up.

"It is frustrating, just sitting here," Anya was saying.

"Agreed," said Kori. "But there's nothing we can do now but wait—for the chief to get Davenport's whereabouts from his wife, or for the Turkish police to spot him somewhere."

Kori and Anya were now back in the hotel

having the Amira's continental breakfast—fresh-baked breads and jams, fruit, and coffee. Outside, the sun had risen on a new day in Istanbul. Kori spread some honey on a croissant, but neither agent could eat. Both were fidgety. Both felt helpless. Kori decided to try to get their minds off the current predicament.

"So how is Nikolai?" she asked.

"He is fine," Anya replied. "He has been talking about the future a lot lately. He wants us to get married."

"Really? That's wonderful, Anya! He proposed?"

"Well, sort of. Not officially. He talks about marriage all the time, but I try to change the subject."

"Oh, I see. Hmm…I thought you guys had a pretty good thing going. Sorry, I don't mean to pry."

"No, it's quite all right. Yes, we have an excellent thing going. We are both happy. But, Kori… marriage? How would it even work? In our business?"

Kori nodded. "I know, believe me. Does he still think you work for the Russian Commerce Agency, bringing business into the country?"

"Yes. Right now he thinks I am here trying to convince Turkish companies to bring their manufacturing to Russia. I do not like the dishonesty."

"I know. But it's what we signed up for. My own mother thinks I work for a conveyor company. Turkey's a little hard to explain, so I've been telling her I'm in St. Louis."

"It's difficult, no?"

"It is. But we don't have to do it forever, you know. Just until all the bad guys are put away."

With this, Kori could not suppress a smile and soon both were laughing.

"I suppose we have to keep our senses of humor," said Anya at last.

"Yep," said Kori. "Even if the humor is grim. So, what are you going to do about Nikolai?"

"I do not know," Anya sighed. "I love him, Kori. He is a wonderful, intelligent, sensitive man. But I have been thinking that it is not fair to tie him up. Perhaps it would be better for him to move on."

"But Anya, you can't let him go if you feel so strongly about him. You **could** always marry him, right? I mean, lots of agents are married. The chief is married. Foster is married. Blake is married, and he hangs out in Russia almost as much as you do. And none of their spouses are any the wiser about what their real jobs entail."

"I do not like the dishonesty," Anya repeated. "It

is not good for a relationship."

"I know, I don't like the dishonesty either. But what choice do we have? Rampart's success comes from its secretive nature. We can operate in the shadows like no other agency can. And we have full autonomy. We can spin and turn on a dime. And yet, we still have the ear of the president, giving us resources other agencies have to wade through levels of bureaucracy to get to. There's no intelligence operation on the planet that's more effective and efficient than Rampart. But if we're ever compromised, all that goes away. It only works because it's so clandestine."

"I know, I know. I hear everything you are saying and I cannot disagree with any of it. So, I suppose I will just have to get used to the idea of lying to my husband."

"Husband?" Kori smiled. "So, does that mean you are going to marry him?"

"Oh...did I say 'husband'?"

"You sure did."

"When?"

"Just now, Anya. You said you'd have to get used to lying to your husband."

"Hmm...I do not think I said such a thing."

"Clear as a bell, my friend. You said 'husband.'"

"Well, even if I did, I meant 'boyfriend.' I might have said 'husband' accidentally."

"Uh-huh. Well, you know, Jung said there are no accidents. I think that you and Nikolai—wait, that's my phone." Kori picked up her ringing phone and put it to her ear. "Briggs here. Yes. Yes, Ms. Rose, good to hear from you. You have whom? In your office? Now? Okay, keep him there, Marsha. We're on our way!" Kori hung up and turned to Anya saying, "I'm afraid we'll have to get into this whole marriage thing later, my friend. That was the consul general at the American consulate. Someone from the Iranian consulate is sitting in her office. He is seeking protection. He claims he has information about an impending terrorist attack on the United States."

"Excellent! Let's go."

As the two strode outside the hotel looking for a taxicab, Kori couldn't resist. "So tell me, Anya, are you thinking about a June wedding? I understand it's lovely in Moscow that time of year."

But Anya was waving down a taxi and if she heard Kori's question, she didn't let on. Before long, the agents were on their way to the American consulate. The time for idle chatter was over.

CHAPTER 22

In Lansing, Michigan, it was early evening. Rampart Director Richard Eaglethorpe had flown nonstop from DC and taken a taxi to the door of a middle-class ranch home on a suburban cul-de-sac. He knocked on the door.

A pair of blue eyes peered around the tiny curtains that covered the small glass window panels at the top of the door. "Yes?" came a woman's voice from within.

Eaglethorpe held up his National Bureau of Criminal Investigations badge. "Ma'am, my name is

Richard Eaglethorpe. I'm a federal agent and I have a few questions for you. May I come in?"

"Yes, of course." The door opened and a full-figured, middle-aged woman with shoulder-length, sandy blond hair motioned Eaglethorpe into her living room. "What's this about?" she asked.

"Are you Ann Davenport?"

"Yes."

"Well, I'm here about your husband, ma'am."

"My husband? Is he okay?"

"Yes, as far as we know. We're looking for him, you see."

"Looking for my husband? I don't understand. Whatever for? Is he missing?"

"Mrs. Davenport, may we sit down?"

"Of course, please." Ann Davenport gestured toward a chair where Eaglethorpe sat down. She sat on the edge of the sofa adjacent to him, her brow furrowed. Eaglethorpe glanced about the room. Middle-class home with middle-class decor. A big-screen TV sat opposite the sofa. Above the sofa was a painting of sailing ships. At the other end of the living room were built-in bookshelves and a small desk, and then a short hallway that led into the kitchen and dining room. In between, toward the near wall, was a stairway to the second-floor bedrooms. Eaglethorpe hadn't known what to expect, but this could have been any home in America.

"Agent...I'm sorry, what did you say your name was?"

"Eaglethorpe, ma'am. Special Agent Richard Eaglethorpe." Eaglethorpe noticed a large suitcase and a carry-on bag resting by the sofa. "Going somewhere, ma'am?"

"Why, yes, as a matter of fact, I'm off to the airport. I just called for a taxi and it's on its way. Agent Eaglethorpe, please tell me what this is all about."

"Mrs. Davenport, do you know where your husband is?"

"Yes, he's in Turkey. Istanbul, to be exact."

"And do you know what he's doing there?"

"Of course. He's hosting a tour group. My husband is in the travel business, Agent Eaglethorpe. Is he in some kind of danger?"

"Well, ma'am, I don't know quite how to put this, but yes, in a manner of speaking, your husband is in danger. He's in danger of helping to carry out a terrorist attack."

"What?!"

Eaglethorpe had a lifetime of experience learning how to read people. And in that moment, he knew that behind those disbelieving blue eyes, there was no way on earth that Ann Davenport had a clue as to her husband's real intentions. This was a woman who had been left utterly in the dark.

"I'm afraid it's true, Mrs. Davenport," he said. "And you have to help us stop him."

"But I don't believe it! A terrorist attack? Wyatt? What…what kind of attack? Why?"

"Your husband is planning an attack on the US power grid. If successful, he'll plunge the country into a darkness that will last months, at the least. And it could come at any time."

"No," said Ann Davenport flatly. "No, no, no, no. I do not believe you. Not my husband. I'm afraid, Agent Eaglethorpe, that you have made a mistake. I'm sorry you had to come here, but you have obviously confused Wyatt with someone else. My husband runs a travel business. Besides, how could he even commit such an attack? And from Turkey?"

"He's not planning on carrying out the attack himself. We believe that he's enlisted a cadre of terrorists from around the state."

"Wyatt?" With this, Mrs. Davenport laughed. "Wyatt doesn't know any terrorists. In the state? Here in Michigan? Terrorists?"

"Are you familiar, ma'am, with the Guardian Militia?"

"Sure. Wyatt joined them a few months ago."

Eaglethorpe paused at the revelation. "Well…do you know who they are?"

"Yes, Wyatt told me."

"He did?"

"Of course. You see, Agent Eaglethorpe, my husband and I do not keep secrets from each other. That is why I know he would not be involved in anything like what you're describing."

"Mrs. Davenport, what exactly did your husband tell you about the Guardian Militia?"

"Wyatt said it's a professional organization. Like a trade group. Sort of like Kiwanis or Rotary Club. He goes to the meetings hoping to drum up travel business. They're in Grand Rapids, not too far away. Oh, and he said they do charity work, too."

"I see. Have you ever thought to do an internet search on them?"

"No. Why should I?"

"Do you have computer handy, Mrs. Davenport?"

"Yes, over there on the desk."

"Can I ask you to humor me for a second, ma'am? I'd like you to get on your computer and do a search for 'Guardian Militia.'"

Mrs. Davenport hesitated and then stood and walked over to the desk. Eaglethorpe followed. Mrs. Davenport sat down, powered on a laptop and, with Eaglethorpe looking over her shoulder, typed "Guardian Militia" into the search box. A second later came the results:

Guardian Militia Members Found Guilty in Attempted Attack on United Nations.

Violent Guardian Militia Pledges to Regroup.

Behind the Guardian Militia: a Look at a Neo-Nazi, White Hate Group.

Besides other various news articles, counter-extremist sites were listed that mentioned the Guardian Militia, and a Wikipedia entry that detailed the group's radical political views. Mrs. Davenport sat at the desk chair in silence. Eaglethorpe let her take it all in.

Finally, she said, "Well, this must be a different group."

Eaglethorpe pointed toward an entry further down the page. "Click on that one, Mrs. Davenport. That's the website of the group itself."

Mrs. Davenport clicked. A blood red page filled the screen. In the middle of the page was a large white circle with a black swastika. "Learn More" read a link. She clicked on it and a page of "Truths" listed thirty or so grievances against ethnic and religious minorities. The list culminated in a call for a pure Aryan nation "by any and all means necessary." A contact address gave a post office box in Grand Rapids.

Eaglethorpe noticed the expression of Mrs. Davenport changing from surprise to the blank expression of the morbidly spellbound. Involuntarily, she navigated to a page of photographs from the Holocaust, along with photographs of lynchings and cross burnings. Finally, as if shaking herself awake, she shuddered and slammed closed the laptop.

"I think I'm going to be sick," she said.

"Take a couple of deep breaths, Mrs. Davenport," Eaglethorpe said gently.

She sat in silence for several moments and then softly spoke. "I had hoped it wasn't true," she said.

"You'd hoped?" said Eaglethorpe, lifting an eyebrow. "You mean you knew?"

Tears pooled up in Ann Davenport's eyes. "I found a pamphlet among Wyatt's things with similar stuff as the website. But it didn't make any sense that he had it. I guess I just…blocked it out of my mind. I didn't want to believe he would join such a group. Not Wyatt. I still don't believe it,

Agent Eaglethorpe."

"Of course. Let me get you a glass of water, Mrs. Davenport." Eaglethorpe retreated to the kitchen and opened a couple of cupboards before finding a drinking glass. He filled it and brought it back into the living room, dragging a small chair over to the desk and sitting down beside Mrs. Davenport.

"Here," he said, handing her the glass.

"Thank you."

"Of course."

"Why would Wyatt do such a thing?" Mrs. Davenport said, shoulders sagging and tears staining her face. "Why would he join this group?"

"That's what we're trying to determine, Mrs. Davenport. Has he ever held any of these racist views that you're aware?"

"Oh, no," Mrs. Davenport said, shaking her head. "Not at all. We're not like that. I have never heard Wyatt, even once, say anything bad about any race or religious group. And he loves his country, Agent Eaglethorpe. He served in the Air Force, you know."

"Yes, we're aware."

"I can't for the life of me imagine how he could have allowed himself to become involved with this group. I mean, if you ever met Wyatt, you'd know what I mean."

"Well, unfortunately, Mrs. Davenport, it seems he is more than just 'involved' with the group. Your husband now seems to be leading it."

"Oh, my…"

"And I'm afraid I can think of at least one reason. The oldest of them all."

"What's that?"

"Money. I can't tell you how we know this, but I **can** tell you that your husband stands to gain quite a lot of cash should the attack be pulled off successfully."

"But that doesn't make sense, Agent Eaglethorpe. There's no amount of money that would make my husband get involved with a terrorist attack on his own country."

"Well, there might be, Mrs. Davenport. Five million dollars, as a matter of fact. I have seen good men betray everything they believed in for much less."

Mrs. Davenport sat mutely, shaken to the core.

Eaglethorpe gave her a few moments to gather herself. Finally, he continued. "Mrs. Davenport, when was the last time you spoke to Wyatt?"

"Just yesterday," she answered faintly.

"Did he say where he was staying?"

"No. Just some cheap hotel, he said."

"And what was the nature of the phone call?"

"He said he had a surprise. He said he would be leaving Istanbul at the end of the week and flying to Costa Rica. He bought me a plane ticket. I was to meet him there. In fact, Agent Eaglethorpe, that's why I'm off to the airport. He is to meet me in San Jose in a couple of days. I have a room reserved there."

"So the surprise was a vacation to Costa Rica?"

"Oh, no, we've gone there several times. We can travel for cheap, of course. No, he said he would tell me the surprise when he got there."

"Well, I think we might be able to guess at it. Unless we can stop him, your husband will have a suitcase with five million dollars of cash in it, less whatever he plans on sending to the militia members for carrying out the attack. My hunch is that Costa Rica is the initial getaway spot. Who knows where he plans on taking the both of you after that? Could be anywhere in the world. He's a skilled traveler with plenty of cash. I'm afraid your future is one where you'll be spending most of your time on the run, Mrs. Davenport. You'll be wealthy, of course. Even more so when you consider that five million in US dollars goes a lot farther in places like Costa Rica than it does here. But we know about your husband. He'll be hunted, and eventually, of course, he'll be caught. And if you're with him..." Eaglethorpe let his voice trail off.

Mrs. Davenport buried her head in her hands and began to cry, faintly at first, then stronger. Soon she was trembling and sobbing uncontrollably.

Eaglethorpe put his arm around her shoulder and comforted her until eventually she stopped crying and sat still, looking down at the floor, an empty expression on her face.

"Mrs. Davenport," Eaglethorpe said, "we may not have a lot of time. Will you help us?"

CHAPTER 23

In a conference room in the US consulate in Istanbul, Kori and Anya and Consul General Marsha Rose sat on one side of a long conference table, while a haggard-looking, stubbled man with dark hair and narrow eyes sat on the other. Two guards stood outside the conference room door. The consulate itself was on security lockdown and US Marines patrolled the perimeter.

"And what were your responsibilities at the Iranian consulate?" Kori asked the man.

"Translator," the man answered. "I am fluent in

five languages, including, as you can tell, English." Indeed, Saman Miri, thirty-five, had been working at the Iranian consulate as a translator for the past six years. Originally from Qarchak, about twenty miles outside of Tehran, Miri had worked his way up through the government ranks and had leaped at the chance to serve in Istanbul as the official consulate translator. He loved Istanbul and he loved his job. Had you told him just a few weeks earlier that he would be sitting in the American consulate divulging the secrets of his superior—Ambassador Arman Golzar—and, in fact, seeking protection from him, he would have judged you mad.

"And you say that you knew Arash Nasirian?" Kori asked.

"Yes. Arash was my friend."

"And Hajar?"

"Also a friend."

"We're sorry for your loss," Marsha said sympathetically.

"Thank you."

"And I must say it took guts to come here today," she added.

"No, madam, not really," Miri said. "You see, I had no choice. As you can probably tell, I have not slept in days. Ambassador Golzar is purging those whom he has deemed disloyal to his cause. I fear I was next. He is losing support as the gravity of his plan is becoming more apparent to everyone, and he is lashing out. Golzar is a radical, you see. And he is trying to orchestrate a full-blown war with the United States."

"So we've been told," said Kori. "But we're confused about something. Why the Guardian Militia?"

"I'm sorry? The who?"

Kori and Anya exchanged glances. "The Guardian Militia," Kori repeated.

"I do not know who that is."

"The American antigovernment, neo-Nazi group?" said Anya.

Miri looked at them blankly.

"Wyatt Davenport's group?" added Kori.

"I had assumed Davenport's group were mercenaries. He had told Golzar that he had put together a paid army skilled in terrorist tactics."

"So…Golzar doesn't know the group is a white hate group?" said Kori.

"No. Neither did I, until this moment. That is interesting. But, I suppose it would not matter to Golzar, as long as this militia group you speak of could carry out the task."

"Yes, I suppose you're right," said Kori. "One terrorist group is as good as another. So how did Golzar ever get with Davenport in the first place?"

"With his travel business, Davenport was a frequent visitor to both Istanbul and Ankara. He met many people here. At some point, he became friends with an Iranian consulate employee here in Istanbul name Farid Tajik. Soon, he was being invited to social functions at the consulate. He met Golzar at one of them. Golzar often travels between here and the embassy in Ankara. I do not know the exact chain of events from there. I know that Golzar was looking for an American to help him with his insane plan to attack the US. Someone on the inside."

"I knew it," said Kori, looking over at Anya. "The proverbial inside man."

"Correct," said Miri. "Golzar was intent on finding an American, someone seemingly harmless, someone who would not be suspected of orchestrating a terrorist attack and who, therefore, would remain under the radar of US intelligence. He talked often of 'buying' someone's involvement. 'In the US, everyone is for sale at the right price,' he would often say. 'All Americans care about is money.' I suppose at some point, he approached Davenport with an offer that was more than Davenport could resist."

"Did you and Nasirian ever talk about Golzar's plan?" Kori asked.

"A few times. It is kind of funny, really. Neither of us liked the plan, but neither of us felt comfortable criticizing it in front of the other. I did not know for certain where Nasirian's loyalty lay and I suppose he did not know where my loyalty lay. Both of us were reluctant to put our cards on the table, but on the few occasions the plan would be mentioned between us, I could see in Nasirian's eyes that he was not comfortable with it. By the time I knew for sure that Nasirian was against the plan, he was dead."

"Were you aware that he left a note to be found in his apartment?" asked Anya. "A bank receipt with Wyatt Davenport's name handwritten on it?"

"It does not surprise me. I think, like me, he was looking for a way to let the world know of Golzar's plan without appearing as a traitor. And that, I take it, is why you know so much about Nasirian and Golzar and Davenport."

"Correct," said Kori. "Nasirian left a pretty good bread crumb for us to follow."

"He was a good man."

Kori drew the bank receipt out of her purse and

placed it in front of Miri. "Would we be correct in assuming that the $2.5 million is a 50 percent deposit on the full payment?"

"Yes, that was my understanding."

"Where was delivery made?"

"Nasirian met Davenport at a pub he frequented."

"The Faust?"

"Yes, I believe that was the name. My understanding is that he gave him the $2.5 million there, along with a letter authorizing the attack. Golzar has promised to deliver the balance himself, after the attack."

"Whose idea was it for the attack to be on the power grid?" Anya asked. "Davenport's?"

"No, that was Golzar's idea. He had it all figured out. He has been researching it for years, in fact. I would guess that he knows more about the power grid of the United States than your own secretary of energy."

"But I don't understand something," said Kori. "What is Golzar's end game? He's clearly not stupid. He cannot possibly believe an attack on the US would come without consequences to your country. Disastrous consequences. Iran cannot win a war against the United States."

"Golzar believes that if the US is provoked to

attack Iran, then our ally Russia will be drawn into the battle. Russia has strategic interests in Iran and has pledged to defend her."

"Wow," said Kori. "Pitting the United States against Russia. That could mean all-out war. **World** war."

"Oh, yes, that is Golzar's plan," said Miri. "Make no mistake, Agent Briggs. Golzar wants a war that he believes will end American supremacy once and for all. In his view, nothing less than a global conflagration will bring that about."

The room was silent for a moment. Finally, Marsha Rose said, "Agents Briggs and Kovalev, is there anything else you wish to ask Mr. Miri?"

"No, I don't believe so," said Kori. "Agent Kovalev?"

"No, I don't believe so," said Anya.

"Thank you Mr. Miri," said Kori. "You've been very helpful."

"What will become of me?" asked Miri.

"You will have our protection, of course," Marsha replied. "You have my word." She rose and crossed the room. Opening the door, she spoke to one of the guards in the hallway. "Please escort Mr. Miri to the anteroom outside my office. Make sure he's comfortable. Mr. Miri?"

Saman Miri stood and walked toward the door, turning as he exited the room to say, "Thank you all for your time and attention. I hope you will do what you can to stop Golzar's madness."

Marsha sat back down at the table after Miri left, taking a seat across from the agents. "Ladies?" she said, with a grave expression, "what do we do now?"

"Well," said Kori, "Miri didn't tell us much we didn't already know. Up until that little nugget about Russia, that is. Good lord. Arman Golzar's a real nut job."

"Yes, but ingenious in his own way, Kori," said Anya. "I believe he is right in his supposition that Russia will come to Iran's aid in case it is attacked."

"Russia and the US," mused Kori. "All the other countries of the world will line up, I suppose. Choosing which side to be on."

"World War III," said Anya.

"My, this is frightening," said Marsha.

"Yes, well, it doesn't have to happen," declared Kori. "We can stop it. Marsha, you need to contact the State Department in DC. No less than the secretary."

"Well, I probably ought to go through the proper channels. My direct boss is the American ambassador to Turkey in Ankara. I'll call him."

"Call him afterward, Marsha. There isn't time to waste. When he realizes what's at stake, he'll understand why you called the secretary of state directly. Communications with the Iranian government have to be opened immediately. They need to know about their ambassador to Turkey and his plans. Actually, I would be surprised if my boss hasn't already done that. But it wouldn't hurt for State to hear from you. After all, you heard it here yourself this morning. You're a witness to what is about to unfold. If we let it, that is."

"Certainly," Marsha nodded earnestly. "I'll place the call."

"In truth," Kori continued, "you probably won't be telling him anything he won't already have been briefed about. And from the top. By now, I would guess that my boss has been in touch with the president."

"The president?" Marsha said, eyes widening.

"Of course. Should Davenport's group of crazies bring down the grid, our government has to know that the attack came by way of a rogue element and not the Iranian government itself. That's how we can derail Golzar's plan for World War III."

"Yes, Kori," said Anya, "but that leaves us with

stopping the attack itself."

"Well, let's hope the chief is having some luck in Michigan talking to Davenport's wife."

"That's where I'm lost," said Marsha. "Who is this Wyatt Davenport and what is his motivation?"

"Great questions," said Kori. "So far as we know, there's nothing in his past to indicate any kind of contempt for his country. He's been a fine, upstanding citizen with a legitimate travel business. A hard-working entrepreneur. And so I'm left with only one theory that makes any sense at all. The money. He's doing it for the money."

"I simply cannot believe that," said Marsha. "I can't believe anyone would sell out their country like this."

"Marsha, I've been in law enforcement and intelligence for quite some time," said Kori. "You'd be surprised at what people will do when money is at stake. And five million ain't chicken scratch."

"Yes, but still…"

"I know. Unfortunately, nothing surprises me anymore."

Marsha sighed. "How do you keep from getting cynical, Agent Briggs?"

"Well, I know that for every bad guy, there's a thousand good guys," Kori replied. "Maybe ten thousand. That's why the good guys always win, Marsha. The odds are stacked in our favor. And they always will be."

"Well, I hope you're right, Ms. Briggs. Right now, the bad guys seem to have our backs up against the wall. I mean, it appears to me as if the plan of attack is already in play. From what you have told me, the blackout could come at any time, yes?"

"True," said Kori.

"I mean, even if you find Davenport, it might be too late for him to call it off."

"Well, yes, that might be correct. But until we actually find him—"

"Kori!" Anya interrupted, half rising out of her chair. "Something just occurred to me."

"What is it, Anya?"

"Miri had no idea that Davenport's gang is a neo-Nazi hate group, right?"

"Right. He'd never heard of them before. Apparently, neither had Golzar. So?"

"So Davenport's gang probably hasn't ever heard of Ambassador Arman Golzar, either. Or Nasirian. Or anybody involved over here. They probably have no idea that Davenport is connected to an Iranian seeking to drag the US into a world war."

"Anya, you're right! Wait—except for Johnny Gardner, the guy who swiped the letter from Dane."

"Yes, but Kori, the letter was in Persian, yes?"

"Right! Gardner probably had no idea what it said."

"Indeed. It seems unlikely that such a man would know how to read Persian."

"Well, excuse me," said Marsha, "but what does all this matter?"

"Think about it," said Kori. "What if Davenport's guys knew who they were **really** working for? What if they knew they were getting their direction from an Islamic fundamentalist bent on destroying their country? I mean, whether they love or hate America, they sure as hell wouldn't sign up for that, right? They're being played. They think they're stirring up a revolution from within but they're really stirring up a war from without. They're being used as pawns in a bigger game. The very idea would probably make a Guardian Militia member blow a gasket. Brilliant, Anya."

"I'm using my noggin, yes?"

"Yes," Kori laughed. "And now we know how it was that two such disparate groups came together for a single cause."

"Because they don't know about each other."

"Right. They're not strange bedfellows, Anya. They're complete strangers. The only thing they have in common is Wyatt Davenport."

"I wonder if the Guardian Militia members even know about the money he's being paid," said Anya.

"Good point, Anya. I would guess not. They're orchestrating the attack solely for the greater glory of...well, whatever it is they believe in. Imagine if they knew that their leader was collecting five million smackers. Heck, they probably don't even know who Davenport really is—the fact that he owns a tour company and travels to the Middle East."

"Everything you're saying makes sense," said Marsha, "but what good does this revelation do for us? You can't find these neo-Nazis, right? So how are you going to let them know about Davenport and Golzar and the true plan?"

"Well," Kori said thoughtfully, "we don't have to find all the neo-Nazis. We just need to find one. I'm sure they're in communication with each other. They'd need to be in order to coordinate the attack. Timing is critical for them."

"Then we need to find one," said Anya.

"As it turns out, Anya, we already have one. We just talked about him. Johnny Gardner is sitting in a jail cell in San Francisco. Maybe he can't single-handedly stop the attack, but I'll bet he can clue us in to the whereabouts of his fellow neo-whackos. He probably even knows their phone numbers."

"But, Kori, we're running out of time. Who's going to go to San Francisco to talk to him?"

"I don't know, Anya." Kori stood up and began pacing around the room. And then it struck her. "Mack Walton!" she exclaimed.

"Who?"

"Mack Walton. He's the San Francisco detective assigned to the case." Kori pulled Walton's card out of her purse. "I knew I kept this for some reason." She grabbed her phone and dialed. **Please pick up**, she thought.

"Walton here."

"Detective Walton! Agent Kori Briggs here."

"Ah, Miss Briggs. From that mysterious intelligence agency. I wondered if I'd ever be hearing from you. What's the good word? You know our murder suspect still isn't talking."

"I'm not surprised, but I might have a way to change that."

"Oh?"

"Listen, detective, I can't get into all the details because there just isn't time. But suffice it to say that

Johnny Gardner is working with a neo-Nazi hate group out of Michigan called the Guardian Militia."

"Sure, we know all that, Agent Briggs."

"Well, what you don't know is that the Guardian Militia is working with an Iranian terrorist stationed in Ankara, Turkey, a terrorist bent on attacking the power grid of the United States, hoping to draw America into a war." Kori realized how preposterous it all sounded even before she said it out loud.

"Oh, is that so?" Walton said.

Kori could practically see his eyes rolling. "Yes, Detective."

"And why would a neo-Nazi white supremacist organization be working with an Iranian terrorist?"

"Simple. Because they don't know they're working together."

"Uh-huh. Look, I'm sorry, Ms. Briggs, I'm really not following."

"Well, it doesn't matter. I'm going to forward you a few things that you just need to get in front of Gardner. First, a translated copy of the letter he stole from Dane Reinhart. Then, I'll send you a link to a travel website for Davenport Tours. There's a picture of the owner there. Gardner needs to know that Wyatt Davenport is the real name of the guy his group is working with."

"I thought you said they were working with an Iranian terrorist."

"Yes, through Wyatt Davenport."

Walton sighed. "Look, Agent Briggs—"

"Detective, please just listen. Do you want a confession from Gardner or not?"

"Okay, Agent Briggs. I'm all ears."

"Tell Gardner that we're on to him. We know his group is planning an attack on the grid. Tell him that Davenport is not who he thinks he is and show him the website pics. Tell him Davenport is getting his orders from an Iranian ambassador named Arman Golzar and show him the translated letter. Then—are you getting this all down, Detective?"

"I'm getting it all down, Agent Briggs."

"Then tell him that with the murder of Reinhart and with his participation in a terrorist act from a foreign extremist, he'll be facing the death penalty if he doesn't cooperate. I think you should get your confession."

"California doesn't have the death penalty."

"Yes, but we're talking about an armed insurrection against the US government. This will become a federal case, Detective, make no mistake. And the crime is punishable by death. Now, if Gardner decides to play ball, we can leave it with you guys and a lifetime sentence in the comfort and care of the California Department of Corrections. I'll bet Gardner would prefer Pelican Bay to lethal injection."

"Well, if all that you say is true, I suppose you'd be right."

"Of course I'd be right. But we need more than the confession, Detective Walton. We need him to get us in contact with the rest of the members of the Guardian Militia. Better yet, we need Gardner himself to get in touch with them and tell them to stand down. He's got to explain to his fellow militia members what's really happening. If he refuses to help us, then the deal is off the table."

"I don't know, Agent Briggs. I have to run this by the district attorney, you know. I'm not sure she'll buy it."

"She doesn't have to buy it. Neither do you. Just do what I say and see what happens. I promise you won't be disappointed. But you have to hurry, Detective Walton. If you believe nothing else that I have said, believe this: that attack on the power grid? It's coming. Anytime now, the lights are going to go out all over America. This will be no isolated power outage. We're talking coast to coast darkness. There's no time to lose. Do you understand?"

"Okay, Ms. Briggs. I still don't really know who you are or who you're with, you've thrown a completely wild-ass story at me, and, frankly, I have a stack of cases I need to attend to. But for some reason, God help me, I think I believe you. I'll call the DA right now and we'll pay a visit to Johnny Gardner."

"Thank you, Detective Walton."

"All in day's work, Agent Briggs." And then Walton sighed once more and hung up the phone.

CHAPTER 24

In a cheap efficiency apartment in a four-unit concrete building on a narrow Istanbul alleyway a person could easily miss, a tall man in a mesh safari hat was hunched over a stove, stirring soup. The day was hot and the efficiency had no air conditioning. Worse, the man did not feel safe opening up the curtains to let a breeze in. Not that the day was especially breezy. Indeed, the windows were open but the drawn, threadbare curtains covering them hung limp.

The man took off his hat, fanned himself a few

times with it, then set it down on the kitchen counter. Hot soup would not have been his lunch of choice on such a warm day, but the provisions in the efficiency were slim and the last thing he wanted to do was venture out in public. That must have been how they spotted him while he was staying at the Hotel Ucuz. Whoever **they** were. All he knew was that someone, presumably with a gun, had kicked open the door of the hotel room next to his and had shouted "Freeze!" In American English, no less. Somebody was on to him. How they found out, he had no idea. But one thing was certain. He would not make the mistake of going out for lunch again. Or anywhere, for that matter. Not until the job was finished.

And besides, it's not like this was how he was always going to live. He glanced over at the duffel bag and smiled. He poured the soup from the small pot into a bowl and sat down at a folding table. He sipped a couple of spoonsful of the soup and then decided to open the duffel bag just to take another look. This was something he could not stop himself from doing. Rising from his chair, he stepped over to the sofa where the bag was resting, unzipped the bag, and gazed at the contents. This is what made it all worthwhile. He had never seen so much money in one place before. Then again, who had? There were 25,000 one-hundred-dollar bills in the bag, organized in one-inch stacks of 100 bills each. Total: 250 stacks. And to think that that was only going to be **half** the total!

He and Ann were going to live well in Argentina, that was assured. He would meet her in Costa Rica. They would fly progressively south to Colombia, Peru, Chile, and then Argentina, spending a few days in Buenos Aires before finally getting to their ultimate destination—San Luis at the feet of the Sierra de Córdoba mountain range. Ah, the benefits of being in the travel business. He knew the best ways to bounce from one place to another. The ways of little visibility. He knew the small, local airlines that flew in and out of the lesser-known airports. He also knew the people who could provide the forged travel documents. Even if their trail was somehow discovered in Costa Rica, that's where it would forever run cold. Wyatt Davenport would never be found again.

Ann would love San Luis. It was a beautiful town with a charming main square and tree-lined streets. They would buy a house there. Nothing too extravagant. They didn't need anybody asking too many questions about how and where they'd made their money. They'd enjoy the local cuisine and Ann would spend time in the museums and art galleries. The mountains surrounding the town were gorgeous and not too far away was Sierra de Las Quijadas National Park where they would go hiking and take in beautiful views from reddish cliffs.

Ann deserved no less. Oh, she might be reluctant at first to leave their home in Lansing, but after she adjusted, she'd be happy, and grateful. Of course, he'd have to eventually explain where all the money came from, but she would understand. She was loyal. As loyal a wife as any guy ever had.

After flipping through the stacks of bills once more, Davenport regained his chair at the folding table and finished his soup. He leaned back and thought about how ingenious his plan had been. Hard to believe it was only a year and a half ago that the opportunity had presented itself. That reception at the Iranian consulate. He hadn't even wanted to go. But his new Iranian friend had invited him and wouldn't take no for an answer. Farid Tajik was a strange bird. Signed up for a tour of the Blue Mosque one day and kept asking questions all along the way. Then, he offered to buy the drinks afterward at the Faust. They met for drinks a few times after that. Davenport didn't have any close friends in Istanbul, so it was nice to have someone to sit down with over a few beers. Especially after a long day of guiding tourists around the city. Tajik always drank only soda water, but he was still a good guy to chat with.

After a few evenings at the Faust, Tajik had started asking questions about Davenport's political views. "I don't have any," he had told him. And it was true. Geopolitical issues bored him and he rarely followed the news. So long as nothing happened to hamper his ability to continue giving tours in foreign countries, he didn't care. "Things are going to happen one way or another whether I'm involved or not," he'd told Tajik. "I'm just looking out for myself. As far as I'm concerned, more people should do the same."

Not long after that particular conversation came the invite to the reception. And that's where Tajik introduced Davenport to Consul General Arash Nasirian, and Arman Golzar, the Iranian ambassador from the embassy in Ankara. For Iranians, they were surprisingly nice guys. They all chatted about travel and family and this and that. But then Golzar had started asking political questions, just like Tajik had. Davenport reiterated his neutral stance about the world's problems. At one point, Golzar took him aside and asked him if he knew anybody who could help him with a little project he'd been considering.

"What kind of project?" Davenport had asked.

"Oh, just a little something to get the attention of your fellow Americans," Golzar had replied.

"Attention? How so?"

"Well, Mr. Davenport, you have said you are not especially political, which I respect. I admire that, actually. For those of us pressed into political service, however, we find ourselves having to do the bidding of our countries, always looking for ways in which to further our governments' aims and make political statements toward those ends. It is a curse, really. A job without end. But such are the roles we have assumed. Be that as it may, lately, we have been formulating the production of such a political statement. A message, if you will, about our relative strength. The thing is, we need this statement to take place within the borders of your country. Consequently, we need an American to help us."

"You mean like a public relations kind of thing?"

"Yes, you could say that. Sort of like a public relations thing. But nothing so…verbal. We are looking to make more of a physical statement, actually."

"I'm afraid I don't understand, Ambassador."

"Mr. Davenport, let me ask you a question. What do you do to a bully?"

"A bully?"

"Yes, you know, a playground bully."

"Well, you stand up to him, I suppose."

"Yes, Mr. Davenport, very good. You stand up to him. In fact, sometimes the best way to handle a bully is to give him a punch in the nose, just to get the message across that he should no longer bully you, or anyone else, for that matter. Would you agree?"

"Well, sure, I guess so." Then it began to dawn on Davenport what the nature of the "political statement" was that the ambassador was proposing. "Ambassador, are you saying you're going to somehow physically strike the United States?"

"Well, I cannot get into all the details just now, Mr. Davenport. But can I tell you something that might interest you?"

"Okay."

"For the right person to help us coordinate our 'statement,' we would be willing to pay a rather handsome sum. One million dollars, as a matter of fact."

Davenport had whistled at the amount. "That's

a lot of money, Ambassador. But, although I might be apolitical, I do respect my country. I served in our Air Force, you know. And I run a successful business there. I don't think even for a million dollars I could do anything that would harm the country I was born and raised in, the country that has given me a chance to make a good life for myself."

"I understand, Mr. Davenport." Golzar had stroked his short beard and looked thoughtful for a moment and had then said, "Well, how about three million?"

"Three million?"

Golzar had chuckled. "Oh, Mr. Davenport, we are speaking strictly hypothetically. Do not worry. Nobody would ask you to do anything you would not want to do. But—hypothetically—would three million dollars make a difference to you?"

"Well, no, I can't say that it would."

Golzar had become very serious just then. In a low voice, he said, "How about **five** million, Mr. Davenport?"

Davenport's head had begun to swim. How many offers of five million dollars would he ever get in his life? "Hypothetically?" he said.

"Of course."

"Well then, hypothetically, for five million dollars, I'd have to say I'd be a fool to at least not hear you out. So tell me more about this 'statement,' Ambassador."

And that's how it had all started. Deep down, Wyatt Davenport knew he would never betray his country, no matter how much he was offered to do so.

At least he thought he knew.

A funny thing happened as the days and weeks went by, however. The idea became less and less distasteful. When it got right down to it, what did the United States ever do for him? He'd served his country with his time in the Air Force. He didn't owe anybody anything. He needed to look out for number one.

Besides, he worked hard for his money and he paid his taxes faithfully. Truth be told, the travel business was struggling. Oh, he was able to afford a nice house for Ann and himself, but after his business expenses and the mortgage and car payments, there was little left over at the end of the month for any real extras. Of course, they could travel for cheap and that was a nice perk, but travel was his job. What he really wanted to do was settle down somewhere and relax for once in his life. Not have to worry about money.

Not have to always be concerned about the future. He perceived the wealth a lot of the people on his tours had. Some of them were filthy rich. They owned big companies or were big shot honchos working for even bigger companies. The worst were the ones who had inherited their money. You could always tell who they were. They were the people more prone to complain about something on the tour, always acting just a little more entitled. Either way, some people seemed to have everything while Wyatt Davenport had to work so damn hard all of the time.

Screw it, he finally decided. **Five million dollars is five million dollars**.

Golzar had kept in touch with him. It was easy to see why he had been chosen to be ambassador by his country. He was charming and persuasive. Not only that, he had the strike on America all figured out. It had to do with the power grid, he'd told Davenport. It would be simple. And not all that destructive. Americans would be without power for a couple of days, maybe a week at most, he had said. Just a "statement," he'd reiterated. Nothing more. Besides, Americans could stand a little hardship in their lives.

"You should see the way my people have to live

compared to yours," Golzar had said. All he needed was a select number of men to carry out his plan— American men already on American soil, their collective movements thereby free of suspicion from governmental intelligence authorities looking hard at foreigners.

"But if you cannot recruit such a group," Golzar had said on his last trip to Istanbul, "then I'm afraid the job will have to go to someone else."

Davenport had felt the opportunity slipping away at that moment. **It's now or never**, he thought. **Five million dollars or a life of continual struggle to make ends meet.** "Oh, don't you worry about putting a group together," he'd told Golzar. "I can tell you, Ambassador, that I have the men already lined up."

"Excellent! I am very glad to hear it. Then do we have an agreement, Mr. Davenport?"

"We have an agreement, Ambassador Golzar."

The two men shook hands. Two-and-a-half million up front, the balance after the strike.

Now all Davenport had to do was put the group together that he'd said he already had lined up. This was the genius part of Davenport's plan, although at first the thought had panicked him. **Where am I going to find a dozen American men to willingly**

carry out an attack against the United States? But Davenport was clever. It's why he was successful in business. He started thinking about the kind of men he'd need—men who already had a bone to pick with their country. Men who already held some animosity toward its government. The rest fell into place with surprising ease. Do an internet search for "antigovernment groups" and you've got your choice of dozens. All he needed was **one** group to get on board. How much easier than to search for twelve individuals!

Davenport told Golzar he needed six months to prepare "his guys." That was acceptable to Golzar. Golzar handed him what he described as a non-refundable, good faith deposit of $20,000. Davenport spent the next several weeks making something of a name for himself around antigovernment websites and message boards. Of course it wasn't **his** name. He chose an alias: Daniel Price. It had a nice ring to it and he liked the double meaning. Davenport **had** a price, in fact, and that price was $5 million.

He gave Daniel Price a backstory, too. Price was an Iraqi war veteran who'd seen terrible things during his service but had been treated shabbily by the Veterans Administration upon his return. He had a chip on his shoulder. But the chip had always been there. He had always mistrusted the govern-ment. And now, it seemed to him, everything was set up to make life difficult for the true inheritors of America—the white, Anglo-Saxon people. The nation was falling apart, crumbling at the edges and threatening to implode from the rise of colored people and immigrants, all taking jobs that belonged to the rightful progeny of the white Europeans who founded the country, the earth's true master race. And there was no easy, bloodless fix. What was needed was a revolution, a final battle between the races, between those with a divine right to the country, and those who, for years, had been no-good trespassers and leaches.

It was easy. Davenport basically parroted the stuff he read online. You didn't have to be parti-cularly bright to engage in political discourse with the people of the hate groups. In fact, when he posted material, he sensed the need to dumb things down a bit. The key was to make your points short and blunt. Nuance and subtlety had no place in this world. Soon, Davenport began his own website, complete with images of swastikas and burning crosses. He wrote a twice-weekly blog and in a short time, he had a following. And the following conti-nued to grow. It was actually disturbing to think that there were so many people out there who bought into the hate.

Before long, it became time to enlist "his guys." He found a group not far from his home called the Guardian Militia. He began to lure them in slowly, contacting them through their website and letting them know of his interest in their organization. Naturally, they checked him out. They examined his site and read his blogs and saw his online activity. He had written all the right things. Daniel Price certainly seemed like the real deal. They could tell that he was one of them.

Davenport sensed he was in when they invited him to a secret Guardian Militia meeting. That's all he needed. Wyatt Davenport had charisma and charm. He knew all he had to do was meet with these guys once and they'd accept him. Nevertheless, he took things very deliberately. He didn't speak much at that first meeting. He sat back and listened to the rantings of the group and nodded enthusiastically. He got invited back for a second meeting and then a third. The Guardian Militia met in secret once a week. He had to tell Ann he'd joined a civic organization to explain his absence every Tuesday evening. She'd asked which one, and he told her the Guardian Militia, knowing the name would mean nothing to her. It was a group of business people, he told her, but mostly a charitable organization—"guardians" of the rights of the underprivileged to participate in the American dream. That's all Ann needed to hear. She thought the charity sounded wonderful. And besides, she was never one to ask a lot of questions. She just went along with everything, God bless her.

Finally, Davenport began speaking up more at the meetings. One night, he made a long speech about how something hugely significant had to be undertaken by the group. The American government had let them all down and was on the path to ruin, he'd said. The militia had been recruiting well, gaining online followers at a pretty consistent pace. That was all well and good, but where was that going to get anybody? All they were doing, Davenport told them, was creating a bigger echo chamber of people with the same views. "We're just talking to ourselves," he had said. Didn't something more need to be done?

"We need to make a larger statement," he had declared, picking up on Golzar's phrasing. "Something big. Something that will get everyone's attention." Naturally, the group was a little skittish after that failed UN attack years prior. But that, Davenport noticed, was why there was a power vacuum in the organization. The brains behind that scheme were now in prison. The militia had soldiered on without them, but there was nobody, it seemed to Davenport, to properly lead the group. And that's where he came in. Not long after his speech, certain people in the group were making suggestions to Davenport that perhaps he should consider becoming the group's president. He certainly had the credentials and everyone in the Guardian Militia respected him.

The hook was set.

At the very next meeting, he laid out his plan. Or, that is to say, Arman Golzar's plan. Of course, nobody needed to know that little detail. Davenport came to the meeting with information about the substations and about the ramifications to the country's power grid of taking them out. The group listened raptly. He could practically feel them getting on board. He'd had it all mapped out, including the locations of the relevant substations and the equipment at each that needed to be disabled. Two of the members prided themselves on their knowledge of munitions and made the plan even more attractive by volunteering to set everyone up with the proper explosives. Davenport hadn't even expected that! How perfect. The meeting lasted three hours with a lot of questions for which Davenport had all the answers. Golzar had sure done his homework. By the end of the meeting, the group was positively rabid with excitement.

Davenport declared that he would start the attack himself. He'd travel to the substation at Niagara Falls and set off the first explosive. Within seconds, he'd contact everyone else, already dispatched to their assigned locations, and they would set off theirs. "And then—**bam!**" he'd said. "Good-bye, power!" This was met with wild applause.

They gave themselves a month to get all the explosives together, plus whatever food and supplies they'd each need for the week or so—Golzar's estimate to Davenport—that the country would be dark. In the meantime, Davenport told them he'd go on ahead to Niagara Falls. "We can't afford any kind of leak," he'd said. "Once I'm in place, I'll contact you each individually to let you know the exact date of the attack and your own assigned target. That way, nobody knows anything that can be accidentally spilled. And remember—no credit cards, no ATM withdrawals, nothing whatso-ever that creates a paper trail of your movements. On the day of the strike, once we're all in place, I'll make a group call one hour ahead of zero hour. That should give you enough time to get where you need to be to carry out the attack."

But Davenport didn't go to Niagara Falls. He flew to Istanbul instead. Of course, nobody at the Guardian Militia knew that. As far as they knew, Daniel Price was in Niagara Falls while they were all fanning out to their assigned substations to await his final instructions. Meanwhile, Wyatt Davenport, tour operator, was ostensibly attending to his tour group. In fact, he was awaiting the final instructions from Arash Nasirian, his main contact now. Arman Golzar remained in Ankara at the embassy, preferring to delegate from there.

But Davenport was no fool. "I need to see the order from the ambassador in writing," he'd told Nasirian. "I need the first half of the money, plus a written order from your office. If you guys don't hold up your end of the bargain, or if somehow things go sideways, I'm not taking the fall. In fact, put it in your own language and on your own stationery. That way, there will be no questions as to where this plan originated." Nasirian complied, almost right away, surprising Davenport. When the order came from Golzar to proceed, Nasirian met Davenport at the Faust with the money and a copy of the order just as Golzar had written it to Nasirian.

It was really going to happen!

But of course, there's always a snag. That stupid Nasirian. He'd left the original communiqué on his desk, and someone named Hajar had swiped it and gotten it into the hands of that Canadian agent who, in turn, had flown it to his fellow agent in Vancouver. Fortunately, Golzar had had a few goons in the Istanbul consulate who had been following Hajar and who had spotted him meeting with the Canadian. Somehow—who knows how?—they were able to get him to spill the beans on everything. Iranian contacts in Canada were able to follow the communiqué to the Vancouver agent.

And that's when Davenport received a direct call from Golzar. "You need to take care of a little problem, Mr. Davenport," he had said. Then he'd explained the little problem. The original letter was now in the hands of a Canadian Intelligence agent, thus threatening to expose the entire operation. The letter needed to be retrieved. "We cannot be involved in its retrieval," Golzar had said. "For obvious reasons. Please send one of your men to Vancouver immediately. I will give you the address of the agent there."

Well, this was quite a monkey wrench. How to get the letter without revealing to the Guardian Militia the Iranian connection to the plan? But Davenport was nothing if not a problem solver. First off, he knew just the guy to get it. Johnny Gardner, longtime member of the Guardian Militia, was an ex-Navy SEAL, skilled in weaponry and stealth. If he couldn't get the letter from the Canadian agent, nobody could. Second, the letter was in Persian script. Thank God for that. As far as Gardner was concerned, it could have said anything.

Davenport called Gardner, telling him he was in Niagara Falls, but that he needed Gardner to fly to Vancouver immediately for "an errand." Davenport had proof, he told Gardner, that the American government was in cahoots with a certain Middle Eastern country. There was a Canadian agent that had a letter—written in the language of that Middle Eastern country—that would blow the whole thing wide open. It was the kind of government conspiracy that, once made public, would help the cause of groups like the Guardian Militia.

"You have to keep this to yourself, though, Johnny," Davenport had told him. "Don't even tell the other guys yet. I want to make sure we have all our ducks in a row first. In the meantime, this won't derail our attack plans. Just go get the letter and come back as soon as you can. Nothing will happen until you're back at your assigned location." Gardner was eager to go, eager to please the man who was surely to become the new president of the Guardian Militia.

But now, Gardner was in a jail cell in San Francisco. Apparently, he'd followed the Canadian agent there and, in the process of retrieving the letter, had shot someone. **That** wasn't part of the plan. And now the letter was missing. Golzar hadn't been happy but agreed with Davenport that there was only one thing to do. "We need to step up the plan before it gets discovered," he'd said. "Forget the letter. Copies have probably been made by now anyway. Proceed regardless."

"No worries, Ambassador," Davenport had told him. "I will execute the plan without delay." But there were plenty of worries. Davenport had been discovered somehow. That letter must have put the intelligence community on high alert. So who were these people that had apparently discovered him? The CIA? And how did they do it? He'd barely escaped at the Ucuz, regrettably leaving behind that damned list of contacts and targets. Damn it all!

But the key in a situation like this is not to panic. You have to be able to react, to adapt. Everything was back on track now. Davenport had contacted

WE'LL QUIT WHEN WE'RE DEAD

everyone and had them move to alternate locations. Now, he was waiting for just one thing—word that Ann was safely out of the country and on her way to Costa Rica. As soon as she was on the plane, he was ready to make the call. The attack was imminent. And right after the attack, Golzar had promised to meet Davenport back at the Faust to personally hand him the second $2.5 million. Davenport would shake his hand, say, "Nice doing business with you, Ambassador," and head for the airport with his forged passport and his duffel bag twice as full as it was now. South America and a life of well-earned leisure awaited.

CHAPTER 25

With Eaglethorpe in Lansing using Davenport's wife to track down Davenport, with the Turkish police keeping an eye out for him and Golzar, and with Detective Mack Walton on his way to talk Johnny Gardner into giving up his comrades, there was nothing much Kori and Anya could do but wait in the consulate. Marsha had called out for lunch. Dönors—Turkish sandwiches of slow-cooked chicken and lamb wrapped in pita bread—were on their way.

Finding herself with a little time on her hands,

Kori had excused herself from the conference room to call her mother. Well, eventually. From the corridor outside the conference room, she first took the opportunity to text Evan. The last time she'd talked to him, she had told him they had already thwarted the attack. That now seemed like a long time ago.

Complications, she tapped out to him. **Attack still possible, but we're closing in.**

Evan replied right away, which made Kori grin. **Are you still in Istanbul?**

Afraid so.

Sorry to hear. Anything I can do to help?

Afraid not. But we're going to stop this thing, I guarantee it.

I know you will, Kori. Stay safe, okay?

I will. I'm going to hold you to that Italian dinner.

Looking forward to it. Please keep in touch.

Meanwhile, Joan Briggs had been under the impression that her daughter was coming home from St. Louis.

"Gotta stay a couple more days," Kori said when she got her mother on the phone.

"Oh, that's too bad, dear. What happened?"

"Well, some of the equipment failed. Just bad luck, I guess. We're having some new parts shipped in and I have to be here to make sure everything is up and running before I leave." Kori had become such a master at excuses that they rolled right off her tongue. Rolled like, well, conveyor, she imagined.

"I certainly hope they're paying you overtime, Kori."

"Yes, the boss said I'd be getting a little extra bonus for my time."

"Well, what are you going to do until the parts get there?"

"I don't know. Make some sales calls on some other distribution facilities, I guess. We have a vendor here, too, that I suppose I should go see while I'm in St. Louis." There. That sounded plausible. "But, listen, Mom, just out of curiosity, do you have flashlights and extra batteries in the house? Candles and stuff like that?"

"I think so. I guess I do. Whatever for, dear?"

"Oh, no reason in particular. Just wondering. I was watching the Weather Channel and they had a special on sudden storms and how quickly the power can sometimes go out. Remember that big thunderstorm a few months ago? Anyway, I just wondered if you were prepared for a power outage."

"I'm sure I am, dear."

"Yeah, but what about food and water, Mom? You know, canned food, stuff that won't spoil? And bottled water?"

"Kori, for heaven's sake you have to stop watching that Weather Channel!"

Kori forced a laugh. "Yes, I suppose so, Mom. I just worry about you, you know."

"I know, dear. But the forecast is clear and I'm sure if the power ever goes down for a day or so, Baxter and I will be fine."

"Sure, sure, of course. Well, Mom, I better go. Give Baxter a belly rub for me. I'll call when I get home. Love you, Mom."

Kori hung up. "A day or so," her mother had said. What about a week? What about a month? What about a year? It was too much to think about. Kori walked back into the conference room just as the dönors arrived.

"Lunch is served," said Marsha.

"They look good," said Kori. "Got anything to wash them down with?"

"Well, we have soda and iced tea. I think there's still some coffee left, too."

"Uh-huh. Actually, I was hoping for something a little stronger," said Kori.

Marsha thought for a moment, looked around,

and then grinned mischievously. "Well, let's see… we had a reception in here not long ago. Just a small one. More of a party, actually, for one of our staff members who was heading back to the States. But there might just be a bottle of something still around. I mean, it's a bit early in the day, but, well, these are extenuating circumstances, aren't they?"

"Quite so," Anya agreed.

Marsha fished in her purse for a set of keys and then unlocked a cabinet at the front of the conference room, revealing a full set of bar glasses and a couple of bottles of Beefeater London Dry. "Ah!" she said. "How about gin and tonics, ladies?"

"That'll work," said Kori.

"Yes, please," said Anya.

"What do you want me to do?" asked Ann Davenport.

The taxi had arrived to take her to the airport but she had sent it away. Now, Director Eaglethorpe was sitting in her living room, while she worked through a box of Kleenex.

"Well, as I explained, Mrs. Davenport, it's really very simple. All you need to do is call your husband. I won't have you ask where he is, precisely, because that might arouse suspicion. Instead, my people in Washington will triangulate the call."

"What does that mean, Agent Eaglethorpe?"

"It's a process by which we can track a cell call, basically by measuring radio signals between cell towers. It's how emergency services locates someone who has dialed 911. We can do it quickly, too, so it's best if you keep your conversation short. That way, your husband will have less time to sense anything is wrong."

"Okay. He's expecting my call anyway."

"He is?"

"Yes, he wanted me to call as soon as I was getting on the plane. He was quite adamant about it, in fact. He gave me a different phone number to call, however. He said his cell phone wasn't working and he had to buy another one."

"I'm not surprised. I'm sure he didn't want anybody trying to track his regular phone. If he's smart, he probably ditched it. At any rate, him wanting you to call him is perfect. Your call won't seem unusual. But, listen, Mrs. Davenport, you really have to try your best to sound as if everything is fine. I know it's going to be hard. This has been quite a blow, and I understand that. But it's important that your husband not get tipped off. If he does, if he suspects something is wrong, all that we have worked for will be lost. The country—your country, Mrs. Davenport—depends on us finding him."

"I understand, Agent Eaglethorpe. I'll pull myself together."

"I'm sure you will, Mrs. Davenport. I'll call my guys and let them know we're ready. Then we'll route your call through a special number. It's from there that we'll be able to trace the location of the phone your husband is using." Eaglethorpe pulled out his phone and dialed Cooper. "Agent Cooper? We're going to place the call. Are you all set? Okay, stand by."

The sandwiches were finished. Kori was toying with the idea of a second gin and tonic, but Marsha had made the first round pretty strong and Kori knew she needed to keep a clear head. Her cell phone rang and she saw that it was Eaglethorpe.

"Chief?"

"Agent Briggs, I need you and Agent Kovalev to be ready to mobilize."

"We always are, Chief. What's going on?"

"I'm here with Mrs. Davenport. She's about to call her husband. Agent Cooper is on the line with me."

"Hey, Kori," Cooper chimed in.

"Hey, Coop," Kori replied.

"Wyatt Davenport is expecting her call," Eaglethorpe continued. "Apparently, he was very insistent that Mrs. Davenport call him before her plane takes off."

"Her plane?" Kori said.

"It's a long story, Briggs," said Eaglethorpe, "but evidently, he was to meet her in Costa Rica. I guess that's where he was planning on making his getaway. She was, in fact, getting ready to leave for the airport as I arrived here this evening. Anyway, Cooper is going to triangulate the call and as soon as we get a fix on the location at the other end, you need to move."

"Understood, Chief."

"In the meantime, the White House has issued a security advisory. Every law enforcement agency in the country has been notified. We're ready to pounce on the militia members wherever they might be. Kori, it's imperative that you get the locations from Davenport."

"Roger that. We're ready."

Kori could hear Eaglethorpe in the background giving instructions to Mrs. Davenport. Soon, she could hear Mrs. Davenport on her cell phone talking to her husband, the man they'd been chasing for what seemed like forever.

"Yes, Wyatt," Kori could hear, "I'm on the plane right now…No, no delays, we're just about ready to take off…Yes, of course everything is fine…Well, I suppose I'm just a little tired…Yes, I'll do that. I'll get some sleep on the flight…Listen, Wyatt, the flight attendant is giving me a look. I need to hang up now…Yes, I'll see you there…I love you, too."

Mrs. Davenport hung up and all Kori could hear was sobbing.

Then in the background, she could hear the comforting voice of Eaglethorpe. "You did fine, Mrs. Davenport. Just fine." He spoke directly into his phone. "Coop, do you have it?"

"Got it," Cooper replied. "Kori, I'm texting you the coordinates now."

"Got 'em!" said Kori. "Thanks, Coop."

"Get going, Agent Briggs," commanded Eaglethorpe.

"On our way, Chief."

Kori rose from the conference room table and said, "Come on, Anya. Duty calls. Marsha, thanks for lunch."

"You're more than welcome. Can't you stay for another drink?"

"We'll have to take a raincheck, I'm afraid."

"Of course."

"Where are we going?" Anya asked.

Kori loaded Cooper's coordinates into her phone's map application. "Corner of Türksel and Namik. Looks like a small apartment building. About an hour from here. That's where Davenport is holed up. Let's go get him."

Halfway out the door, she stopped when her phone rang again. "It's Detective Walton," she said, glancing at her phone. "Detective?" she answered. "What's the good news from Gardner?"

"Unfortunately, not much, Agent Briggs. He's willing to take the deal. I've never seen a guy so dejected. You were right, I am forced to admit. Once I showed him who this Davenport guy really is and the translated letter, I thought he was going to cry. I've never in my life seen a guy so shocked and disillusioned. Took him a few minutes to get himself together, but then he was only too willing to help."

"Great. So what's the problem?"

"The problem is, his fellow militia members are incommunicado. They've been given strict instructions to stay off their phones. We gave Gardner his cell and he tried calling them. He called every single member and not one of them picked up."

"Well, I guess that shouldn't be surprising," said Kori. "By now, they've probably all been apprised that Gardner is in jail. Even if they were communicating with each other, they probably wouldn't take a call from him. Their best play is to act like they don't even know who he is."

"Right. And that's something that Gardner expected anyway, whether he was in jail or not. The fact, is they've been instructed not to take calls from anybody, save one person. Apparently, according to Gardner, now that the operation is under way, the only call they'll take is one from Wyatt Davenport."

"Damn," said Kori. "Then there's no way for us to locate them."

"Doesn't look like it. But Gardner did tell me this much, if it helps: The plan is that Davenport will make two phone calls to everybody. The first call will be a heads-up call, giving the members precisely one hour to get themselves into position at whatever power station they're assigned to. Apparently, you weren't kidding about this power grid attack, Miss Briggs."

"Nope."

"Anyway, the second call Davenport is supposed to make is the order to commence the attack. Davenport has an app on his phone allowing him to make a group call so that everyone will be notified at the exact same time."

"Why not just place the first call and then tell everyone to commence the attack one hour later? Why make a second call?"

"Just in case something goes wrong, I suppose. Maybe someone can't get in position in time, for instance. According to Gardner, Davenport is apparently a stickler for details, and something of a micromanager."

"Did Gardner have any idea when these calls were to take place?"

"No, it was all up to Davenport. The only thing Gardner could tell us is that he remembered Davenport mentioning to him that the first call would come after he took care of some personal business."

"Personal business?"

"Yep. No idea what that means."

"Good God, I think I know what it means, Detective."

"Yeah? What?"

But Kori had hung up. "Anya," she said, "how far away did I say those coordinates were?"

"About an hour."

"Then we have to go, Anya. We have to go **now!**"

CHAPTER 26

"Marsha, do you have a car we can use?" Kori asked.

"Well," Marsha replied, "I have a Toyota mini-van in the parking lot."

"That'll have to do," said Kori.

"Oh, but you see, it's not mine," said Marsha. "It belongs to the consulate. It's property of the US government. I'd have to fill out a special form to authorize its use to anyone else. Form 106-B, I believe."

"Marsha," said Kori, trying to keep herself from

jumping out of her skin, "here's the thing. Wyatt Davenport had exactly one thing he needed to do before ordering his men to their posts at twelve different power stations around the US. And that one thing was to hear from his wife to make sure that she was headed out of the country. Once he was confident of that—confident that she was safe and sound—he was going to call his men and issue the order. We can assume that by now he's already done that."

"Oh, my."

"Now, apparently he's going to place a second call one hour from the first, giving us just enough time to find him. If we're lucky. If we're very, very lucky. You see, with that second call, he's going to order the actual attack. His guys will set off their explosives, the grid will fall, and America will go dark. I'm afraid we don't have time for Form 106-B, Marsha, or 106-C, D, E, or F. Now, you could take the car and drive us there yourself, but I'm afraid with the time we've already lost, I would have to ask you to exceed the speed limits by quite a margin and engage in other activities that are probably not in your job description, but which, thankfully, fit nicely into ours."

"Of course," Marsha nodded. "I understand

completely. Screw 106-B."

"Thank you, Marsha."

Marsha dug into her purse and pulled out a set of keys. "Here, Kori. Do what you need to do. Godspeed."

"We appreciate it. And I promise to try to bring it back in one piece."

And just like that, the agents were gone.

Marsha took a deep breath, reached for the Beefeater, and poured herself another gin and tonic, this time without the tonic.

"Take a left here," said Anya, looking at the map on her phone.

Kori swerved left, came upon a car dawdling along the road, and then swerved hard around it, skimming the sidewalk for several feet and causing more than a few pedestrians to scurry out of the way.

"Sorry!" Kori yelled at them out of the open window. "Now what?" she asked Anya.

"Four blocks straight ahead and then another

left."

Kori stomped on the gas. "What do you suppose the speed limit is?"

"It's fifty kilometers an hour. That's about thirty MPH."

Kori glanced down at the speedometer. **90 KPH**. About fifty-five miles per hour. "This car does all right. Good acceleration. Doesn't handle too bad, either. You know, my mom's been thinking about getting herself a new car and—"

"Kori, watch out!"

Up ahead the traffic had come to a sudden standstill. Kori stomped on the brakes and the van came to a screeching halt inches from the car in front of her.

"Good brakes, too," she said. Then she turned the wheel hard and made use of the sidewalk again, laying on the horn as more pedestrians went scampering out of harm's way.

"Here," said Anya, pointing to the next cross street. "Take a left here."

Kori veered left and found herself faced with another line of cars in front of her. "Cripes, Anya, there's traffic everywhere!"

"No kidding. It's Istanbul."

"Still, there's got to be a better way."

"Okay, okay, take the next right. It will run parallel with this. But it is just an alleyway."

"Then it'll probably be less crowded."

Kori turned right at the next crossing, and then left into a narrow alley that was barely wide enough for the car but was, nevertheless, empty of other traffic.

"Three blocks on this," said Anya, "and then a right."

Kori pushed down hard on the gas pedal. Twenty yards in front of them, a man pushing a large metal garbage bin across the alley on caster wheels suddenly appeared from the rear of a restaurant. The man glanced up just in time to see Kori, letting go of the bin and diving back toward the restaurant.

"Hang on!" Kori yelled. She tried to veer around the other side of the bin but there was no room. With the man now out of the way, she decided the best thing would be to take the bin head-on. The right front of the car slammed hard against it, making a loud noise and knocking the bin back several feet and toward the side and out of the way. Kori continued, glancing quickly into the rearview mirror to see the man now standing and waving his fist after her and screaming something she couldn't hear.

"Marsha will not like this," Anya said. "I think you probably broke a headlight. At the least."

"Hey, it wasn't my fault. That guy came out of nowhere."

"Right."

"How much farther, Anya?"

"Take a right up here and then Davenport's building should be three blocks down on the right."

"How long has it been?"

"We left the consulate fifty-three minutes ago."

"It's going to be close, Anya. It's going to be awfully damn close."

"There!" said Anya, pointing up ahead. "That must be the building. That's the coordinates Cooper gave us."

Kori saw the nondescript, concrete block building ahead of them and said, "Yep, it looks like an apartment building. Certainly not the nicest one in town, though."

She pulled over in front of the building and the two agents scrambled out of the car.

"Which one?" said Anya as they ran toward the building. "Looks like two apartments on this side. Probably there are two more on the other."

"Gonna have to storm each one," said Kori.

"Closest one first, I guess."

Both agents arrived at the first efficiency apartment and Anya looked in through the open front window to see a young woman with a small boy who was down on his hands and knees playing on the floor with a toy truck.

"Not this one!" she said.

The second apartment over was bare of window coverings and Kori was able to see at a glance that the apartment was dark and empty. "Vacant," she said. "Let's go around to the other side."

The agents ran around a side alley to the back of the building where two more apartment doors presented themselves. The blinds of the first one were wide open. Beyond, Kori noticed the closed curtains of the second apartment.

"That one!" she called out to Anya.

"How do you know?" Anya asked.

"Who keeps their curtains closed on a hot day like this? These units don't have air-conditioning."

They approached the door. Kori tried the knob to no avail. "Locked," she said. "Of course."

"It's just cheap wood," Anya said, studying the door.

"Okay, then," said Kori, drawing out her Glock. "Ready? One, two, three!"

The agents threw themselves at the door simultaneously, causing it to break apart at the lock and fling itself wide open. In front of them was a tall man with a cell phone in his hand, furiously pushing the buttons. Kori leveled her gun and fired, hoping she wasn't too late, hoping the call Davenport was making to the Guardian Militia members deployed at a dozen power stations with explosives at the ready, preparing to plunge America into apocalyptic darkness, hadn't gotten through.

CHAPTER 27

Kori's shot hit the man in the hand in which he was holding the cell phone, causing him to cry out. The phone went flying against the far wall and landed on the floor. Anya ran over and picked it up. The screen revealed the phone's dial pad but no more than five digits had been dialed and the call icon had yet to be pressed.

"He didn't complete the call, Kori!" said Anya. "We made it in time."

"Down on your knees, dirtball," said Kori to the man. Holding his bloody left hand with his right, he did as Kori ordered.

"Wyatt Davenport, I presume? You're under arrest."

"Who are you?" Davenport managed to say, breathing hard and wincing from the pain pulsating in his hand.

"US intelligence agents, Scooter. Your little plan is up."

"But how? How in God's name did you find me?"

"Long story, my friend. But in the end, your wife decided she didn't want to spend the rest of her days in prison just because her husband was such a loser."

"Impossible," said Davenport. "Ann would never betray me. Never."

"Yeah, well, it just goes to show you," said Kori, "you never know who's going to betray whom these days. Take you, for instance. You're living a decent life and running your own company. You served your nation loyally. You're an all-around good citizen. A real mom-and-apple-pie kind of guy. Probably fly your flag every Fourth of July, am I right? But then one day, you decide you're going to pursue the Benedict Arnold award for infidelity. Crazy world, huh? Can you really be surprised by your wife's actions?"

"My wife loves me."

"Apparently not enough to turn her back on her own country," Kori said. Then she spotted the duffel bag. "I suppose that's the thirty pieces of silver, huh?"

Anya opened up the bag and whistled. "Wow," she said. "This is more money than **I** have ever seen. With this kind of money, a person could really get lost somewhere and never be found."

"What will happen to me?" said Davenport, now looking crushed and beaten. Kori couldn't be sure, but it looked like tears were beginning to pool in his eyes.

"Don't you know?" said Kori. "Anya, you're pretty smart when it comes to legal matters. What will happen with Mr. Davenport here?"

"Death," Anya said flatly. "Most likely by lethal injection."

"Ouch," said Kori. "You know, I've heard that sometimes they get the chemicals all wrong and you end up gasping out your last breaths for several minutes in total agony. Me, I kind of miss the good old days when they used a firing squad. Guess I'm just an old-fashioned kind of girl."

"What do you want from me?" said Davenport.

"The names and locations of your little gang of whackos," Kori replied. "And I mean like now. We know they're waiting for your call and we need to move fast to get them. If you cooperate, we'll put a good word in for you with the federal prosecutor. Maybe you'll live."

"Here," Davenport said, almost in a whisper, pulling a folded up piece of notebook paper out of his shirt pocket. "A list of names and locations."

Kori took the paper and handed it to Anya. "Take a pic and shoot it to Cooper," she said. "All local authorities need to be deployed to the scenes immediately. We don't know how long these losers will hang around waiting for this knucklehead's phone call. Someone might decide to jump the gun."

"Roger that." Anya snapped a pic of the list and texted it to Cooper with a note: **Swarm to these locations and take down these men**.

"And speaking of this group of losers, Davenport," said Kori, "how in the heck did you manage to hook up with these guys, anyway?"

"I found them online."

"Of course. A person can find anything online these days, can't they? So you're a Nazi white supremacist antigovernment type, too, huh?"

"Absolutely not. I only hooked up with them to help carry out the plan. They were a necessary part of it."

"A necessary evil, eh?"

"You could say that."

"So it was just for the money?"

"Yes," Davenport nodded. "It was just for the money."

"Cripes, I don't know what's worse," said Kori. "Say what you want about the Guardian Militia, but at least they acted on principles. Idiotic principles. Completely wrong principles. Insane principles. But principles nonetheless. You, you're just a mercenary."

"Is it so wrong to want a better life for yourself?" Davenport asked.

"When it comes to launching an attack against your country? An attack that would sow death and chaos for months, maybe as long as a year? An attack that might drag the country toward World War III? Yeah, I'd say that's wrong."

"What are you talking about?" said Davenport. "What World War III? What chaos for a year? The plan was to turn off the power for a couple of days."

"A couple of days?! Is that what you think was going to happen? Do you really think that's worth five million dollars? 'A couple of days.' Who told you that?"

"**I** told him that," came a gruff voice behind them.

Everyone wheeled toward the splintered door where a bearded man in a traditional Arabic long-sleeved, ankle-length garment stood, pointing a gun at them. "Drop your weapons, ladies," he said.

Seeing no other choice, Kori and Anya did as the man requested. "Let me guess," said Kori. "Ambassador Arman Golzar."

"Yes, and thank you for leading me to this man. And my money."

"How did you know to follow us?" asked Anya.

"I always protect my interests. I have been having Mr. Davenport here followed ever since the Faust when my chief consul gave him that duffel bag of money."

"Ah, yes, your chief consul," said Kori. "Whom you recalled to Ankara and whose throat you slit."

"How do you know about that?"

"We followed your car that day. Tell me, did you do the deed yourself or did you delegate that little task?"

"What does it matter?" Golzar said with a wry smile. "He was careless with our plans."

"You may as well know something," said Kori. "He was careless on purpose. He recognized the plan for what it was: insane. He hoped Hajar would find the letter."

"Yes, I assumed as much. I did not want to believe it. Arash Nasirian was a friend of mine. But I could not afford to take the chance."

"Lovely."

"But the plan, I assure you, was far from insane."

"Says the crazy man. Anyway, back to the question at hand. How did you learn about us?"

"My people followed Davenport here in Istanbul and first noticed you two at the Hotel Ucuz. Like, you, they lost Davenport when he ran. But they knew you two would keep looking for him, so they simply started following you. I should tell you, by the way, that your ability to find him was the only thing keeping you alive."

"Always nice to be appreciated," said Kori.

"Anyway, this morning, I decided to personally take charge of the operation and drove from Ankara to be here."

"So you planned on taking your money back the whole time?" said Anya.

Golzar frowned. "I beg your pardon, madam, but I am an honorable a man of my word. I had every intention of not only letting Mr. Davenport here keep the money, but also of giving him the balance of what I owed him, per our agreement. I followed merely in case he was unsuccessful at the task in which I had entrusted him. And I presume by your presence here that he was unsuccessful."

"Yes, but just barely," said Kori. "A few more seconds and you would have had your wish. America in darkness. But the inevitable retaliation leading to war between the US and Iran might not have been so inevitable. We're on to you, Ambassador. We know you're a rogue element. We know your plan does not have the support of your country."

"Yes, but you see, it would have eventually. I could never convince my country's leaders to back such a plan, mainly because they didn't believe we could pull it off. But once in play, they would have jumped on board."

"I wouldn't be so sure about that, Golzar," said Kori. "Cooler heads would have prevailed. But obviously, the idea of a cooler head isn't anything you're particularly acquainted with."

"We'll agree to disagree, madam. No matter. This outcome is unsatisfactory. But it is not the end, you see. It is only the beginning. We will regroup and try again and we will be successful next time."

"Who's 'we'?" asked Anya.

"I represent a group of…hmm, let me put it in Western terms so that you might understand. I represent a group of 'investors,' let us say. Except we're not invested in such things as your Western financial institutions. We're invested in a future that includes the supremacy of the people of Iran and a way of life that is not consistent with the immoral standards of your country and its evil ways."

Kori openly yawned. "Oh gosh, sorry, Ambassador. It's all very interesting. Really it is. It's just that I've heard all this before. Evil America, blah, blah, blah. You know what you need? You need a hobby. Maybe woodworking? Gardening?"

"Pottery is fun," Anya offered. "Or maybe you could take up an instrument."

"The saxophone!" said Kori.

"I am glad you're amused," Golzar said with a twisted smile. "I would like to see how amused you'll be when we finally pull off the downfall of your country. Of course, you won't be around for that, I'm afraid."

"Yeah, that's what I figured," said Kori. "You're going to do away with us like you did away with Hajar and Nasirian. Explain to me again about the 'immoral standards' of our country?"

"Down on your knees, ladies," said Golzar. "You," he said to Kori, pointing toward the floor seven or eight feet from Davenport. "Kneel down here." Kori knelt. "And you," he said to Anya, "right here." Anya knelt another seven or eight feet away.

Davenport was sobbing and then suddenly he cried out to them, "Can't you do something?! You're US agents! You must be able to get us out of this!"

"Oh, so now you want the help of the United States? That's rich," Kori chuckled. "Look, Davenport, you made a deal with the devil and now he's come to collect his due. The part that really sucks is that you've dragged us into it. We're going to die here in this cheap apartment. Thanks a bunch."

"But I didn't know the scope of the damage the attack would do. It's true! You've got to believe me! I didn't know. Golzar lied to me. Why do you think I haven't offered to complete the call? You know damn well that I could save myself right now with one phone call."

Golzar looked over at Davenport and smiled. "So it's not too late, Mr. Davenport?"

Davenport was silent for a moment, seemingly turning the options over in his mind. "Forget it," he said at last. "I'm doing nothing for you."

"Then you will die."

"Do it!" Davenport screamed.

"You're too late anyway, Golzar," said Kori. "By now, our guys are all over the substations. Too bad."

"Then there is only this left to do," Golzar said. He stepped toward Davenport, pointing his gun at Davenport's head.

"Oh, God!" sobbed Davenport.

Kori glanced over at Anya. Anya glanced back. Both wondered what the other was thinking, each hoping that the other had a plan, a way out. There was always a move. The problem was that Golzar had positioned the agents far enough away from Davenport, and from each other, that neither would be able to rush Golzar in time. Kori looked around the room, thinking maybe she could grab something and launch it at Golzar but nothing was in reach. Anya had the same thought and made the same observation. When they glanced back at each other again, they realized the truth simultaneously. Neither had a plan. Neither had a way out. This time, there was no move. Davenport was about to be murdered and they weren't far behind.

CHAPTER 28

"Drop your weapon!"

The words boomed out before the man who shouted them could be seen. An instant later, a burly man in a Turkish police uniform appeared in the doorway. Two more followed behind him, the three of them taking positions inside the apartment, all guns trained on Golzar.

Golzar cursed and laid his gun down. Davenport collapsed to the floor, his mind unable to process the events of the last few minutes. Kori and Anya each breathed a sigh of relief and stood.

"Nice to see you, fellas," said Kori. "I'm United States intelligence agent Kori Briggs. This is my associate Anya Kovalev. Your timing is impeccable."

"I am Officer Birkan of the General Directorate of Security," said the first man who had entered the apartment, the burly man with the booming voice. "These are my officers. Are you ladies all right?"

"Just fine. But how did you find us?" Kori asked in wonderment. "Or even know about us? Truthfully, I thought we were done for."

"I have been in touch with my good friend, Canadian Intelligence Agent Wallace Simon."

"Aha. So you're his contact on the police force."

"Yes. He is a good man."

"I'd say. I think we owe him a drink. You, too, Officer Birkan."

"Agent Simon informed us about these two," Birkan said, pointing at Davenport and Golzar. "We have been searching for them since this morning."

"Searching?" said Kori "I had hoped for nothing more extravagant than a simple APB."

"Well, Agent Simon imparted upon me a sense of urgency. I'm told there was a potential terrorist attack on your country hanging in the balance."

"Yes," said Anya. "A pretty ugly one at that."

"But how did you find these two?" asked Kori, nodding to Davenport and Golzar.

"We could not locate Mr. Davenport," replied Birkan, "but we were successful in spotting Ambassador Golzar. It wasn't very difficult." Then he turned toward Golzar. "Ambassador, when you are engaged in illegal activities, you really should consider using a different car than your official embassy vehicle."

"It does not matter," Golzar said. "I have diplomatic immunity. You cannot hold me against my will."

"He doesn't have to hold you," said Kori, reaching down and retrieving her Glock from where she'd tossed it. "You're now property of the US government. You're coming with us. I'll call ahead and make sure your accommodations are all set. Unless I'm mistaken, you'll have your own room in a certain supermax federal penitentiary south of Denver, Colorado. You'll find the Rockies to be beautiful this time of year."

"Nonsense. I am going nowhere but to Ankara. Officer Birkan, I insist that you release me. I have done nothing against your country. I have violated none of your laws and these American agents have no jurisdiction here."

"Well," Birkan said, "it is true that any nefarious activity you may be engaged in against a foreign country is not in our domain. But what I witnessed here today, on Turkish soil, was attempted murder. This does give me the grounds to have you arrested, diplomatic immunity notwithstanding. However, I believe my government would prefer to stay out of this sordid business altogether. We do not wish to become party to an international incident. Therefore, I think I can speak for our country when I say that we are happy to turn you over to these US agents and be on our way."

"Don't worry, Golzar," said Kori. "You'll get your day in court. Not that you deserve it. You, too, Davenport."

Davenport looked up from where he'd crumpled on the floor, a look on his face halfway between despair at being apprehended and relief at still being alive.

"Thank you, Officer Birkan," Kori continued. "I believe we can take things from here."

"**Not so fast**," came yet one more voice from the doorway. Everyone spun toward the door to see four large men with automatic weapons entering the apartment, each of them dressed similarly to Golzar and all wearing turbans.

"Guns down!" commanded one of the men, tall and dark and dangerous looking.

What next? thought Kori, laying her Glock back down on the floor. Anya dropped her weapon, too, and so did the police officers as they moved toward the far wall.

"It's getting a bit crowded in here," said Kori. "I didn't know you had so many friends, Davenport. What's the lease say about throwing parties?"

"Quiet," said Tall, Dark, and Dangerous. The room went silent. "Ambassador Golzar, I believe you know who we are and why we are here."

Golzar's grave expression provided his answer to the question.

"Well, do you mind introducing yourselves to us?" said Kori. "I'm afraid we haven't made your acquaintance."

"We are members of the Islamic Revolutionary Guard Corps, under the command of the supreme leader of Iran."

"Pleased to meet you."

Tall, Dark, and Dangerous continued, "You are the American agents, I assume?"

"We are."

"Your leadership has been in contact with ours. We know about the unfortunate terrorist plot. We have been sent here to apprehend the ambassador. Ambassador, I'm afraid your duties as representative of the Islamic Republic of Iran have come to an end. Your presence is now requested in Tehran. Immediately. The rest of your rogue group is being rounded up now."

"Oh, man, sounds like you're in trouble, Golzar," Kori said, unable to stifle a smile. "But, wait, gentlemen. His actions were aimed at the United States. By international law, he's ours. I'm afraid you have no right to take him."

Tall, Dark, and Dangerous leveled his automatic weapon at Kori, causing her to swallow hard. "This gun says otherwise," he said in a strong, even voice.

"Well," said Kori, "I have to admit you make a pretty good argument there. Anya? Any input?"

Tall, Dark, and Dangerous swung his weapon over toward Anya. "Nope," she said, then giving a sideways glance at Kori, she added, "but thanks a lot for asking. Truthfully, the finer points of international law are not my area of expertise."

Tall, Dark, and Dangerous lowered his gun and waved the others into the room where two of them seized Golzar and one grabbed Davenport, pulling him off the floor.

"Now wait just a second," said Kori. "Okay, you

can have Golzar. No problem. He's yours. Agreed. But this guy really is ours. I mean, c'mon. He's an American. He's what we call a domestic terrorist."

Once again, Tall, Dark, and Dangerous pointed his gun at Kori.

"Interesting how flexible your argument is," she said. "Seems to work in all situations. Sorry, Davenport."

A look of terror came over Davenport's face. "You can't let me go with them!" he said. "God knows what they'll do to me!"

"I wish we could help, my friend. But, as you can see, we don't have much of a choice. These guys play hardball."

In desperation, Davenport looked toward Birkan. "You can stop this, officer! We're not in Iran, we're in Turkey. This is your jurisdiction! You can't let them take me out of your country!"

"I am afraid I am in the same situation as Agents Briggs and Kovalev, Mr. Davenport. As you can see, I am in no position to argue with these gentlemen. I can only wish you luck."

"Good day," said Tall, Dark, and Dangerous as the four men strolled out of the room, Golzar and

Davenport in tow. **The condemned**. Kori would think back later and conclude that the doomed expressions on their faces were the most hopeless and pitiful she had ever seen.

CHAPTER 29

Three nights later, Kori was back in DC having dinner with her mother at Martin's Tavern in Georgetown.

The night before Kori had left Istanbul, she and Anya had celebrated closing the case with dinner and drinks at the Vogue Hotel where they had invited one of the hotel's guests to join them. Lola Jennings was thrilled to be a part of the celebration. She had decided to stick around Istanbul for another couple of days, now excited about traveling all by herself in a foreign city. She intended to do more of it. Kori and Anya called Marsha Rose, too, who was thrilled to hear of the resolution of the case and quickly forgave Kori for the broken headlight of the official consulate vehicle once she joined them at the hotel. The four women partied until closing time.

Anya said she was happy to be going home to Nikolai in Moscow, though she refused to say whether she would allow herself to be married. "Time will tell," she said, and Kori could not determine whether Anya wished for marriage, remained at least partly against it, or was completely torn about the whole thing.

Kori confessed that she'd been in communication with Canadian Intelligence officer Evan Banks and the communications hadn't always been business related. "I knew it!" said Anya. "I could tell that there was someone on your mind."

The next morning, Kori and Anya said their goodbyes at the airport—the downside of closing a case in which you work so closely with someone, where you flirt with danger together, look death in the face, and come away victorious, and even closer to one another. Once again, each said they hoped to be working together again soon, but then simultaneously added, "But not **too** soon!"

At Martin's, Kori was tearing into a New York strip while her mom was working on the crab cake platter.

"How's the book club, Mom?" Kori asked.

"Oh, it's just fine," said Joan. "Dorthea Stamper came to the last meeting and behaved herself. We didn't have a cross word between us."

"That's good to hear."

"And we've all agreed on the next book: **Where the Crawdads Sing**. I haven't read it yet, but I'm sure it will be a good one."

"Oh, yeah?" said Kori, chewing on her steak. "What makes you think so?"

"Well it's been on the **New York Times** bestseller list forever. Week after week after week. Surely you've heard of it."

Kori shook her head. "Can't say I have, Mom."

"My word," said Joan. "Don't you ever take any time to read books, dear?"

"Well, no, not really."

"Well, you should. Reading is a wonderful endeavor, Kori. It would be good for you. A nice escape from the ho-hum nature of the conveyor business, I would think. You should grab yourself a good spy thriller or suspense novel!"

"You think so?"

"Sure. That way you can enjoy a vicarious adventure without even leaving home!"

"An adventure, huh?"

"Yes! You could stand to have a little more adventure in your life, dear, even if it's just by being immersed in a fictional one. You know what they say: all work and no play…"

"You're right, Mom," Kori smiled. "An adventure without leaving home sounds like just what I need. I'll do it."

"Good for you!"

"So what else is new, Mom?"

Joan began talking about her garden and the tomatoes that were almost ready. "I'll make sure you get some," she said, before launching into an exposition about soil and moisture and proper pH levels. Kori continued enjoying her steak, all the while listening to the comforting voice of her mother, feeling, finally, like she was really home.

The following afternoon, Kori found herself at Rampart headquarters where Director Richard Eaglethorpe was conducting a final briefing on the case for his agents.

"All the Guardian Militia members are now in custody," he was saying. "Every one of them was caught red-handed. Explosives at the ready. What happens with these guys now is anybody's guess. They're either facing life in prison with no chance of parole or the death penalty. That's not our decision to make."

"Chief, what about Johnny Gardner?" Kori asked.

"The San Francisco DA made a deal with him, as you know," said Eaglethorpe. "And although he did cooperate, he didn't end up being much help. Plus, he killed Dane Reinhart. I don't know about you, but he can hang as far as I'm concerned."

"No argument here."

"I guess the DA will decide."

"And how's Mrs. Davenport doing?"

"The poor woman is shattered. After her phone call to her husband, I called a sister she has in Lansing. She's with family now. It's going to be a while before she recovers emotionally from Wyatt Davenport's lunacy."

"And, Chief," said Cooper, "speaking of Wyatt Davenport, is it true we can't extradite him here to the US?"

"Well, the State Department is working on that, employing some back-channel communications with the Iranian government. Obviously, we'd like to try Davenport here, but, frankly, I don't see it happening."

"No doubt Davenport himself would prefer to be tried here!" said Foster.

"Yes," said Eaglethorpe, "I don't imagine the Iranians will treat him any too kindly. I sense they want to make an example out of him. They don't want foreigners messing with their own diplomats."

"I don't guess Arman Golzar is going to be treated very kindly either," said Kori. "It's possible that he's already been executed. He knew it was coming. You should have seen the look on his face when those revolutionary guards came into that room."

"The Iranians are no fans of America," said Eaglethorpe, "but they don't much appreciate rogue elements getting them into wars they're not prepared for. This could have ended very, very badly. For us, for Iran, and for the world."

"Well, here's my question, Chief," said Kori. "How do we prevent something like this from happening again? Our power grid is way too vulnerable. Coop, you said it's been on your radar for a while."

"Yep," said Cooper. "It's a known weakness. It's one thing if **we** know it's a weakness, but when foreign agents recognize it as such, or domestic groups, for that matter, then we've got a dangerous, dangerous situation."

"Well, the president is putting together a task force to look into the question of power grid security," said Eaglethorpe. "I spoke to him yesterday. I expect that there will be some changes made. Perhaps the same level of security required at the nuclear plants will now be required for sub-stations."

"Let's hope so," said Kori.

"Okay, I guess that's it," said Eaglethorpe. "Agent Briggs, fine work as usual."

"Thanks, Chief."

"I'll be reaching out to Agent Kovalev to congratulate her as well. And I believe we have a couple of Canadian Intelligence officers we ought to thank, starting with Wallace Simon in Istanbul. I'm sending Agent Pratt there to button up some loose ends with the Turkish police and I'll make sure he buys Simon dinner or something. That is, unless you want to go back to Istanbul, Agent

Briggs."

"No, Chief," Kori chuckled. "Pratt is fine. 'Loose ends' isn't really my thing."

"I didn't think so. Well, that leaves your contact in Vancouver. What was his name?"

"Evan Banks, sir."

"Right. Banks. We need to pass along our appreciation in some way to him, too. Maybe I'll send a fruit basket or something."

"I don't know, Chief," said Gibson. "A case of booze might be better."

"Yeah, I wonder what he drinks," said Cooper.

"Does he golf?" Foster asked. "Maybe a gift certificate for a few rounds at his favorite course."

"Gentlemen," Kori said, "all good ideas, but I've at least met the man. Why don't you leave the thank you to me. I'm sure I can come up with something Evan Banks will appreciate."

"You don't mind handling it?" Eaglethorpe asked.

"I don't mind handling it at all," Kori said, suppressing a smile.

"Okay, then, we'll leave it up to Agent Briggs to send the appropriate thank you to Agent Banks. I'm sure you'll do a fine job, Briggs. Now, if there's nothing else, I think we can adjourn this meeting."

And then everyone stood and filed out of the

conference room, with Kori still suppressing a smile, imagining all the ways she planned to convey Rampart's appreciation to Canadian Intelligence officer Evan Banks.

– **The End** –

Did you enjoy
We'll Quit When We're Dead?

Let others know! Please consider leaving a review on Amazon, Goodreads, Barnes & Noble.com, or wherever you purchased the book.

Coming in the summer of 2022:

**Danger Level 4:
A Kori Briggs Novel**

by A.P. Rawls

Visit www.KoriBriggs.com for updates, promos, news, and merchandise.

UWS
Upper West Side Press, LLC

Made in the USA
Middletown, DE
20 April 2022